DNA Tests To Prove Paternity of Tiny Fortune Heir

Males in the Fortune clan are reluctantly rolling up their sleeves this week to give blood samples for a DNA test that should solve the mystery surrounding who fathered abandoned child Taylor Fortune. Insiders report a virtual mob of nervous tycoons outside Red Rock's criminologist office—now that's a bread line with a lotta dough!

But it's the *ladies* who are lined up and clamoring for the attention of Logan Fortune. The marriage-elusive executive's latest "acquisition" is a gal he's been spotted hugging, kissing...and *burping*.

Seems that when darling daughter Amanda Sue appeared on his doorstep, Logan promptly promoted his devoted corporate assistant to live-in mommy. Rumor has it Girl Friday Emily Applegate still fetches Logan's coffee—but now she does it in her nightie!

Don't miss next month's Fortune update exclusively in the *Tattler!*

About the Author

ARLENE JAMES

began writing romance more than twenty years
ago, when her youngest son was nine months old.
She learned to type sitting sideways so he could play
in the kneeholes of her desk. Arlene grew up on a
ranch in Oklahoma but now resides with her husband
of over twenty-three years in a lovely, historical
community south of Dallas. As her youngest child
prepares to marry, Arlene feels that her most
productive period has arrived, and she is very excited
all over again about what the future holds.

Arlene James writes for Silhouette Romance and
Silhouette Special Edition. Watch for her newest
story, *A Royal Masquerade,* part of the ROYALLY
WED series, available in March 2000 from
Silhouette Romance.

30 Dec 99

Corporate Daddy

ARLENE JAMES

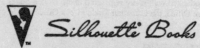

Published by Silhouette Books
America's Publisher of Contemporary Romance

Special thanks and acknowledgment are given
to Arlene James for her contribution
to The Fortunes of Texas series.

SILHOUETTE BOOKS

ISBN 0-373-65034-5

CORPORATE DADDY

Visit us at www.romance.net

Printed in U.S.A.

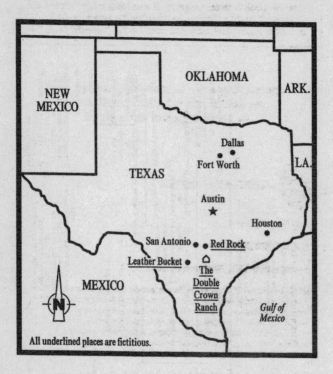

All underlined places are fictitious.

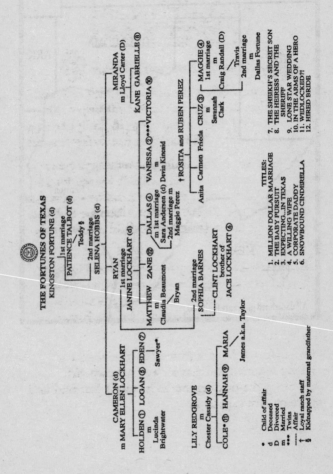

THE FORTUNES OF TEXAS

KINGSTON FORTUNE (d)

1st marriage
PATIENCE TALBOT (d)

Teddy §

2nd marriage
SELENA HOBBS (d)

CAMERON (d)
m MARY ELLEN LOCKHART

RYAN
1st marriage
JANINE LOCKHART (d)

MIRANDA
m Lloyd Carter (D)

KANE GABRIELLE ⑧

HOLDEN ① LOGAN ⑤ EDEN ⑦
m
Lucinda
Brightwater

Sawyer*

MATTHEW ZANE ⑫
m
Claudia Beaumont

Bryan

DALLAS ④
m 1st marriage
Sara Andersen (d)
2nd marriage m
Maggie Perez

VANESSA ② ***VICTORIA ⑩
m
Devin Kincaid

† ROSITA and RUBEN PEREZ

Anita Carmen Frieda CRUZ ③
m
Savannah
Clark

MAGGIE ④
1st marriage
m
Craig Randall (D)

Travis

2nd marriage
m
Dallas Fortune

2nd marriage
SOPHIA BARNES

- - - CLINT LOCKHART
brother of
JACE LOCKHART ⑥

LILY REDGROVE
m
Chester Cassidy (d)

COLE* ⑪ HANNAH ⑨ MARIA

James a.k.a. Taylor

TITLES:

1. MILLION DOLLAR MARRIAGE
2. THE BABY PURSUIT
3. EXPECTING...IN TEXAS
4. A WILLING WIFE
5. CORPORATE DADDY
6. SNOWBOUND CINDERELLA
7. THE SHEIKH'S SECRET SON
8. THE HEIRESS AND THE SHERIFF
9. LONE STAR WEDDING
10. IN THE ARMS OF A HERO
11. WEDLOCKED?!
12. HIRED BRIDE

- * Child of affair
- d Deceased
- D Divorced
- m Married
- *** Twins
- † Affair
- ----- Loyal ranch staff
- § Kidnapped by maternal grandfather

THE F⊙RTUNES OF TEXAS™

🎖 *Meet the Fortunes of Texas* 🎖

Logan Fortune: When the powerful CEO inherited his motherless daughter, he enlisted the help of his capable assistant. Would time spent in Emily's arms have Logan looking for more than just daddy lessons?

Emily Applegate: This plain-Jane secretary's heart melted when she saw Logan cuddling his newfound baby girl. Could she convince her handsome boss that there was no need to hire a nanny...because he had a potential wife and mother for his child right outside his office door?

Baby Taylor: The identity of the recovered baby is still a mystery. But rumors were running rampant among the Fortune family about his true parentage, especially since the adorable child has the Fortune crown-shaped birthmark.

Jace Lockhart: Ryan Fortune's brother-in-law recently returned to Texas for a hometown visit. And this globe-trotting journalist might just find love where he least expects it.

To MJ, the best of editors. Much thanks. DAR

One

"So she's really ours."

Mary Ellen Lockhart Fortune tucked her thick, wavy red hair behind her ears and made a silly face at her wriggling granddaughter who smiled, yawned, rubbed her eyes and flipped over onto her belly, quickly crawling toward the end of the couch. Mary Ellen and her tall, handsome son, Logan, both made a grab for the child. Logan reached her first, coming off his seat on the ottoman at his mother's knee. Holding his daughter at arm's length—much like an escaped piglet that had found the mud hole—he gingerly carried her back to the original spot and sat her next to his mother. Sixteen-month-old Amanda Sue promptly flopped and flipped, emitting a shrieking grunt in the process, as if warning him not to interfere with her plans again. Mary Ellen chuckled. Logan quivered. The battle of wills his surprise baby daughter had been waging with him these past two hours was wearing on him.

"She's a Fortune, all right," he muttered, capturing his daughter again. Amanda Sue twisted and screamed, then went limp and put back her head in a dramatic sob for release. "That temperament confirms it, as if the blue eyes, hereditary crown-shaped birthmark and the blood test didn't. Plus, her hair's almost as red as yours, a little darker, maybe."

"She looks like you and Eden," Mary Ellen said wonderingly.

"I'm not sure my sister would appreciate being lumped into the same category of looks as me," Logan said, struggling to put his daughter back on the couch, "but I did notice that Amanda Sue looks like some of Eden's baby pictures, discounting the hair, of course."

"Was her mother red haired?" Mary Ellen asked gently.

Amanda Sue stopped wriggling and looked up alertly. "Mama," she called. "Mama?"

"Poor darling," Mary Ellen crooned, gathering the child against her. Amanda Sue crammed her hand in her mouth and waited, as if listening for her mother's voice.

Logan sighed. "Her m-o-t-h-e-r was a blonde." He spelled out the word to avoid causing his bewildered daughter to ask for what she could not have, ever again.

"Her name was Bailey, wasn't it?" Mary Ellen went on. "Donna Bailey?"

Amanda Sue's ears seemed to perk up, but she made no sound. Mary Ellen eased the pacifier pinned to Amanda Sue's T-shirt into the child's mouth. The baby sucked absently.

"Yes," Logan said, wishing he could avoid the subject, knowing he couldn't.

"What was she like?" Mary Ellen wanted to know.

Logan tried to keep deep regret from sounding like bitterness. "I remember her as adventurous, full of life, independent. She was a military brat. She told me that both of her parents were lifers. So, naturally, she followed in their footsteps. She learned to fly helicopters in the army and got a small plane license after."

"So our Amanda Sue gets that fierce spirit from both ends," Mary Ellen said, petting the baby's head. Amanda Sue looked up somberly at the stranger who was her grandmother, the lilting curls springing up in the wake of Mary Ellen's touch.

"It would seem so," Logan admitted. "The way I understood it, Donna's parents died trying to set a record in a hot air balloon. I'd say the need for adventure was ingrained."

"What about Donna? How did she die?" Mary Ellen asked.

He swallowed, remembering the tall, shapely blonde with whom he'd enjoyed a few weeks of fun and games. Of all the women he'd known, Donna was the last with whom he'd expected to have made a child. He wasn't surprised, though, that she hadn't contacted him after discovering that she was pregnant. The Donna he had known was fiercely independent and proud of her ability to take on whatever life threw at her. She had followed, quite literally, in the footsteps of her parents.

"She was piloting an experimental glider," Logan explained succinctly. "It crashed."

"Poor thing." Mary Ellen sighed. Amanda Sue leaned against her, porcelain eyelids drooping over bright blue eyes. "I deeply regret the tragedy, but I can't say I'm sorry to have this little one in our lives. How did the authorities know to contact you?"

"Donna left instructions."

"Well, thank goodness for that, at least."

Logan nodded, watching his daughter slip off to sleep. She'd been fighting it tooth and nail from the moment he'd picked her up at the airport in San Antonio. The social worker who had accompanied her had predicted that the child would drop off to sleep in the car, but instead Amanda Sue had squirmed and kicked and fought the seat belt, working out of it several times. The drive down to the ranch had been a nightmare. He'd never felt so inadequate. But he had to admire her fighting spirit.

She was innocence personified, impish and cherub cheeked with ivory fair skin, curly, reddish-brown hair, and eyes that sparked pure blue fire, and in addition, she possessed the mind of a warrior. Even as he took a perverse pride in her spirit, however, he couldn't help thinking that fatherhood was going to be problematic enough without it. God knew he didn't have the slightest idea how to go on.

His own father had been a washout as both a parent and

a husband, so much so that Logan had always figured his safest bet was to avoid both states fervently. He'd thought, briefly, in the first moments of shock, about refusing custody of his unexpected daughter, but he'd quickly rejected the idea. Amanda Sue was a Fortune; she deserved to be raised as one. Thank God for his mother.

"How are we going to handle this?" he asked, suddenly wanting it all settled.

Mary Ellen studied the small hand curled around her forefinger. "What do you mean by *this?*"

"Her. Amanda Sue. How are we going to work it?"

Mary Ellen looked up then. "I don't know what you mean."

"Well, obviously she has to live here," he pointed out impatiently, waving a hand to encompass the luxurious eight-bedroom, contemporary Colonial house with its many amenities, including pool, tennis courts, decks, balconies and spacious guest quarters. Even with his brother Holden and his wife Lucinda in residence, the place had more than ample room. Still, Mary Ellen shook her head.

"She belongs with you, Logan. She's your daughter."

His daughter. The words still brought a shock of unreality with them. "I don't know anything about being a father!" he countered, and the sound of his voice jerked the baby awake. She took one look around and wailed. He bounded to his feet. "See! She'll be miserable with me!"

Mary Ellen made an exasperated sound and gathered the child into her lap, bouncing and cuddling her. "There, there, darling. He didn't mean to shout. There, there." She poked the pacifier into the cupid's bow mouth, and the piercing wail shut off instantly.

Logan pushed a hand through his wavy, dark brown hair. "I don't know how to take care of a baby," he said in a level voice that in no way conveyed the panic he was feeling.

Mary Ellen chuckled. "Logan, no first-time father—or

mother, for that matter—knows how to take care of a baby. You'll learn as you go, that's part of it."

"*My* father didn't," Logan grumbled.

Mary Ellen looked up at him with implacable blue eyes a shade paler than his own. "He did the best he could, Logan. So will you, and I'm quite sure it will be more than enough. In fact, I think you'll make a wonderful father."

"Just let her stay until we get used to one another," Logan pleaded shamelessly, but Mary Ellen was at her reasonable, logical best.

"And how will you do that with her living here at the ranch and you living fifty miles away in San Antonio?" she asked. "No, son, there's only one way to do this, and that's to dive in headfirst. Besides, I want to be a grandmother, not another parent. I've raised my family, and I did it pretty much on my own, as you well know. I want to concentrate on other things now. It's only fair. And your uncle Ryan really needs my help with the business right now. This kidnapping mess and the divorce are enough for any one man to handle on his own."

Guiltily, Logan sat down again. His own world had spun so out of control that he hadn't even thought of Ryan or Baby Bryan and his parents. "You're right. What's the latest news concerning the kidnapping?"

Mary Ellen looked at the child drifting off again in her arms. "It's the most confounding thing. Bryan disappears, the wrong baby is returned, and *he* turns out to be a Fortune, too."

Logan shook his head. "How are Matthew and Claudia holding up?"

Mary Ellen sighed. "It's hard to say. In one way, having Taylor with them is a comfort—that's what they're calling the other baby, you know, Taylor—but in another way, it's a definite problem. I mean, what if Matthew turns out to be his father? Claudia will be destroyed."

"You don't really think that's possible, do you? I mean, Matt's always been such a straight shooter."

Mary Ellen looked down meaningfully. "I'd say just about anything is possible, wouldn't you?"

Logan looked to his newfound daughter. "Obviously."

"Right now, though, I think the priority for Ryan and the whole family is getting Bryan back."

"That's understandable," Logan said, and Mary Ellen nodded, looking at her granddaughter.

"Life is so strange, isn't it?"

Strange didn't begin to describe his life right now, Logan mused, looking again at the cause. His now peacefully slumbering daughter busily sucked her pacifier for a few seconds, then pushed it out with her tongue. She smiled at something in a dream, showing tiny white teeth, and just abruptly frowned, her bottom lip pouting. She was amazing, alarmingly so, and Logan knew, deep down, that he was very lucky to have her. He only hoped that he was up to the task of raising her.

"What am I going to do with her, Mom?" he whispered.

Mary Ellen's gaze was loving and wise. "You'll figure it out, dear. I have every confidence in you."

But Logan wasn't so sure. Mary Ellen was his mother, after all. She had always believed in him, found the best in him. Even now when she had every right to blast him for his irresponsibility in conceiving a daughter out of wedlock, a daughter he had only recently learned existed, she merely smiled and trusted him to do the right thing. It was because of her that he'd worked his way to the Executive V.P. position of Fortune Tx, Ltd. He could have played on the Fortune name and the Fortune influence to get where he wanted to go, but Mary Ellen had expected him to earn his way honestly, and he had taken pride in doing so.

Business was second nature to him, though. It was part of who he was. Most of what he had achieved was the product of sheer instinct. Fatherhood, on the other hand, was like a strange planet where nothing was as he expected. Up was down and in was out in this eerie land. He had no idea of his own worth here, his own power, but he had no choice except to step out and endure whatever came, making up solutions as he went along. He took a deep breath and stepped out.

"We'll head back to San Antonio right after lunch."

Mary Ellen smiled. "You'll be fine. Both of you. Once you get her settled in and find someone to watch over her while you work, life will be rich and sweet again, just in a different way."

He hoped that she was right. He prayed to God that she was right. For his daughter's sake.

Emily Applegate, like everyone else in the building, heard the screams even before the elevator doors opened. Logan's executive assistant lifted her head, absently smoothed the heavy, sandy-brown bun on the back of her head, and listened. The cries obviously belonged to a child, a very angry, desperate child. She couldn't imagine who would have brought a child into the office, but she would shortly know. They all would. Office doors were opening. People were stepping out into the hallway.

She stayed at her desk, gold-framed reading spectacles perched on the end of her nose, and watched the stir through the glass wall of her office, thinking that Logan had picked a good day to be out on personal business. He'd left a cryptic message on her voice mail sometime last night, informing her of his change of plans. She'd been shuffling appointments and standing in at meetings all day and desperately needed about two hours to catch up on her weekly report.

Thoughts of the weekly report had been supplanted by curiosity, however, when the wails had first reached her. What caught her attention now, though, were the looks on people's faces as the wailing drew nearer. They were stunned, all of them, stunned speechless, apparently. And suddenly she knew why as Logan Fortune himself stepped into view, a squalling bundle of auburn curls and flailing arms and legs caught against his chest.

Emily stood, chin dropping, in a complete state of shock

as Logan turned, maneuvering briefcase, child and—wonder of wonders!—diaper bag to push through the glass door. He stumbled into the room, yanking free the diaper bag as the door closed against it. Inside the closed room, the sound was deafening, shrill enough to split eardrums if not shatter glass. Logan looked at her as if she was the one making it, then he juggled the child in her direction.

"For pity's sake, Applegate, take her!"

Emily scrambled forward. "Mr. Fortune, what—"

He shoved the child at her, threw her almost. Emily caught the wailing bundle and clasped her tight. Suddenly she was looking down into an astonishing pair of bright blue eyes rimmed with thick red-brown lashes and sparkling with diamond-bright tears. Emily pulled back, taking in the angelic face and tousled curls. The little one shuddered on a sob, and Emily's heart turned over.

"Well, hello there," she said softly. "What's wrong, sweetheart?"

"Ba-ba-ba-ba," the little one cried, bottom lip quivering. "Ba-ba-bobble."

Emily looked at Logan. "What's wrong with her?"

Logan lifted his chin, stretching his well-muscled six-foot frame. "She hates me, that's what's wrong with her," he grumbled, plunking the diaper bag on top of her desk.

The baby suddenly lunged for the bag, crying, "Baba-ba! Babable!"

Emily spied the top of a bottle protruding from an end section of the bag. "I think she wants a drink."

The little one shook her head wildly. "No!" She reached again, opening and closing her little hand pleadingly. "Ba-a-ba-ob-ba!"

Emily suddenly understood. For a child this age, a drink must be something taken from a sippy cup, a bottle was nourishment. "She's hungry. She wants her bottle."

Logan looked as though he'd been dragged through a keyhole backward. His strong, aristocratically sculpted features were haggard, his full mouth turned down at the corners, his dark brown hair rumpled rather than waving back sleekly from his high forehead. He wrenched open the diaper bag and started tearing through it with broad, long-fingered hands.

"It's right there on the end," Emily pointed out.

He turned the bag on its end and plucked the pink bottle from its pocket. The baby reached for it, making a sound somewhere between a relieved laugh and an accusing sob. He jerked off the nipple cover and thrust it at her.

"You should check it first," Emily advised as the child snatched it out of his hand. "The milk could be spoiled."

"Mother filled it before we left the ranch," Logan muttered, "and with the outside temperature in the fifties, it isn't likely to have spoiled yet. I just didn't know where Mother had put it."

The baby had already guided the nipple to her mouth and now put her head back, nursing strenuously. "Let's get your sweater off, little lady," Emily crooned, carefully slipping free one arm and then another while the child nursed industriously, passing the bottle back and forth from hand to hand.

Logan leaned a hip against the desk, folding his arms. "She's been screaming for the last half hour," he said. "I tried the pacifier, but she spit it at me."

"Wouldn't you spit out rubber if you wanted milk?" Emily mused, lifting her chin as the baby reached for her glasses with one hand while holding the bottle with the other.

Logan sighed resignedly. "I just don't know how to read her. She's like an alien life-form! How am I supposed to deal with that?"

Emily tossed the sweater onto the desk and shifted the little one in her arms, sweeping a well-practiced censorious glance over curious faces beyond the glass. People quickly shifted away, moving back into their offices. Emily looked at the man whose executive assistant she had been for the past two years. "Want to tell me what's going on here?"

He straightened and took a deep breath. "Emily Applegate," he said wearily, making it a formal introduction, "I'd like you to meet Amanda Sue Fortune. My daughter."

Emily nearly dropped the child on her head. "Your *what?*"

Logan nodded grimly. "Yeah, how's that for a kick in the pants?"

Emily could only stare, first at him, then at the child quickly emptying her bottle. Almost as long as she'd known him, Emily had harbored a secret crush on her philandering boss, knowing perfectly well that she had no chance with him and was better off for it. The thought, however, that someone else had borne him a child made her voice unusually raw. "Who's her mother?"

Logan winced as the child jerked the bottle from her mouth and cried, "Ma-ma-a-a!"

"Now you've done it," he grumbled, reaching for Amanda Sue.

She jerked back, clinging to Emily and crying, "Ma-mmm-mmma!"

Trying to hide his hurt at her rejection, Logan patted her back ineffectually. "It's all right, baby. She didn't mean it. It's all right. Drink your bottle. Okay? Drink your bottle." He glowered at Emily. "Watch your mouth, okay?"

"All I said was—"

"She's dead, all right? It just happened, but Amanda Sue can't possibly understand that. All she knows is that her m-a-m-a is gone and I'm here. She doesn't understand that I'm her father. She doesn't know where she is. And believe me, she's not happy about it. She's made that much perfectly clear."

Emily was still struggling with the concept of Logan Fortune as a father. Amanda Sue shifted in her arms, and a suspicious warmth spread across the front of her diaper. Emily turned her around, holding the child's small back to her chest in an effort to spare the jacket of her tan wool suit. Amanda Sue laid her head on Emily's shoulder and whimpered, then stuck the bottle nipple in her mouth and went to work on it again.

"I—I didn't know you had a daughter," Emily finally managed to say.

"Neither did I," he replied dryly, "not until the authorities contacted me after the accident."

Emily let that sink in. "My goodness."

"To put it lightly."

The implications were astounding. She shook her head. "What are you going to do?"

He straightened his tie and smoothed back his hair. "Right now, I'm going to go into my office, sit down at my desk and look over your notes on this morning's meetings. After that, well, I'll take it as comes."

She stared at him. "And Amanda Sue?"

He smiled. "She'll be with you, of course, getting settled into her new home."

"Me?"

"Who else?" he asked. "You're the only executive assistant I've got."

Emily wanted to do some screaming herself. Considering how she felt about this man, she was looking at a prescription for disaster. Her light brown eyes narrowed. "Now, wait just a minute. I've gone way above and beyond the job description for you in the past. I've lied to your many women, juggled your affairs, ordered gifts to salve wounded pride and snatched your cookies out of the fire more than once in the process, but baby-sitting your unexpected daughter is taking the term 'executive assistant' just a little too far!"

His expression turned pleading. "Come on, Em. She likes you, and she's had all she wants of me right now, and vice versa, frankly. Who else am I going to count on to help me out here?"

Emily held Amanda Sue out to him. "Obviously, you've tried your mo—"

"Don't say it!" he warned frantically.

Emily grimaced. "All right, fine. If your *you-know-what* can't help you, why not try one of your many conquests? There's got to be one willing to make points with you by baby-sitting your child."

"Have you got any idea what a can of worms that would be opening?" he retorted.

"That's not my problem," Emily said. Apparently entertained by the exchange, Amanda Sue sat atop Emily's arm and swung one little foot absently, slowly drinking her milk. Emily stubbornly stuck to her guns, despite the fact that she was weakening.

"Emily, I need someone I can trust," he argued smoothly. "This is my daughter we're talking about. I can't leave her to some scheming female more concerned with dropping a marriage noose around my neck to get at my money than Amanda Sue's welfare."

Emily sighed inwardly. Without committing herself, she asked. "How old is she?"

"Sixteen months."

With that uncanny ability of all children, Amanda Sue knew she was now the topic of conversation. She laid her head back against Emily's chest and grinned up at Emily around the bottle nipple. Emily found herself reluctantly in love. "She is a little doll."

"Don't let the looks fool you," Logan warned dryly. "That little doll has put me through sheer hell today. She can get out of a seat belt faster than—"

"A seat belt!" Emily echoed. "You had her in a seat belt, not a car seat but your standard, adult-type seat belt?"

He blinked at her. "Every car seat has its own seat belt, Emily. You know that."

She couldn't believe he was that uninformed. "Every *infant safety* seat has a belt, too, and it's designed to keep the child safely in place. Riding a child in a car without one is so dangerous that the State of Texas, and nearly every other, has made it illegal to do so. You're lucky you weren't pulled over—or worse!"

He put his hands to his hips. "See? See! That's what I'm talking about! I don't know this stuff. Why would I? I've never had to think about what kids need!"

Emily found her chair with her foot and pulled it over to sit down, Amanda Sue's weight beginning to wear on her. Amanda Sue immediately tossed her bottle aside and bucked out of Emily's grasp, sliding to the floor, where she momentarily crouched, looking around her. "Where's her stuff?" Emily asked resignedly.

"Right here," Logan said, indicating the diaper bag.

"That's it?"

"The social worker couldn't bring more on the airplane."

Emily rolled her eyes. "Well, we have a lot of shopping to do, then."

"*You* have a lot of shopping to do," he said pointedly.

"And who's going to watch the baby?"

"You'll take her with you, naturally," he said brightly, edging toward the office door. "Just take my house key from the lockbox. I'll meet you both there when I'm through here."

Emily frowned. "You're going to owe me big-time for this, Fortune."

"Absolutely," he said convincingly.

The lower drawer of Emily's desk suddenly rolled out, Amanda Sue at the handle. Recognizing nothing of interest there, she toddled around the end of the desk and out of sight, ignoring Emily as she called to her. Emily jumped up and went after her. Sensing pursuit, Amanda Sue began to run as fast as her little legs would carry her. Before Emily reached her, she'd knocked over the trash can and a potted plant. The sound of Logan's office door clicking shut came just as Emily reached Amanda Sue, who giggled as she was scooped up, then immediately howled to be let down again.

Emily laughed. "Okay, kiddo, first order of business is a dry diaper. Then we'll order you an infant safety seat. Thank God for department stores that take telephone orders. Meanwhile, we'll get acquainted. How does that sound?" For reply, Amanda Sue stuck her fist in her mouth and kicked both feet. Emily couldn't help herself. She hugged the baby tight and kissed her chubby cheek, laughing at the idea of the great Logan Fortune cowering behind his office door in fear of his toddler daughter. Poor guy. Poor kid!

The whole city was in for a shock when the news got around, but maybe, just maybe, this little bolt of greased lightning would put a kink in her clueless daddy's nocturnal activities. God knew it was time that Logan Fortune learned there was more to life than business and willing women. Much more, for those lucky enough to understand it.

Two

It was after seven o'clock when Logan let himself into the three-bedroom town house that was his private residence. As part of one of the most exclusive planned communities in San Antonio, it afforded him privacy, luxury, and a number of useful amenities such as indoor pools, gym, game rooms and sauna, all with twenty-four-hour staff. He hadn't seen Emily's sensible compact car in the drive, but it was not beyond possibility that she was here.

"Emily?"

Silence. He was unconcerned, however. Emily Applegate was nothing if not efficient and dependable. In the two years that she had been his executive assistant, his life had been sublimely simple—until now. Until Amanda Sue. Desperately, he put his young daughter out of mind, as he had done all afternoon.

Taking the mail out of his jacket pocket, he flipped on the overhead light in the entry and began to thumb through it as he moved down the cool hallway. Bill. Bill. Solicitation. Advertisement. Advertisement. Bill. He stepped into the living room and looked up, more to get his bearings than for any other reason. What he saw there, however, brought him to an immediate halt. It looked like a baby store warehouse!

Mouth ajar, he surveyed the bounty. He identified a crib, a high chair, a stroller and a playpen before turning to the rocking chair heaped with colorful fabrics in the center of the floor. His gold, butter-soft leather couch was piled with toys. Tiny articles of clothing covered the matching chair. The ottoman held stacks of books. Bottles, tubes and jars littered the end tables. Setting aside the mail, he picked up an unfamiliar object and examined it. The labeling proclaimed it the latest in digital fever thermometers.

Before he could take in the rest, the door opened at the end of the foyer and a series of bangs and grunts alerted him that even more was coming. He moved in the direction of the noise. Emily was struggling to get Amanda Sue, her diaper bag and a couple of plastic sackfulls of groceries into the foyer.

"Here, let me help," he said, taking both bags. No sooner had he set them down in the living room than she informed him that more waited in the car.

He hauled in jars and jars of toddler food, boxes of dry cereal, milk and diapers. "Where do you want it?"

Emily had collapsed onto the sofa among the toys, Amanda Sue in her lap. A long lock of sandy-brown hair had pulled loose from Emily's ubiquitous bun to lay across her shoulder and chest. He hadn't realized that her hair was so long or shiny. As he watched, Amanda Sue reached up and absently coiled the silky lock around one little hand, rubbing her eyes with the other fist even as she wriggled in an attempt to get down. Though bedraggled and exhausted, Emily, nevertheless, held on. She stared at him for a moment, sans glasses, then sighed.

"I assume you know where your own kitchen is."

"What about the diapers?"

"Upstairs with the rest of this stuff," she said, waving a hand wearily.

He wondered where upstairs he was supposed to find room for a department store but wisely kept the thought to himself. After carrying the bags into the kitchen, he stowed the milk in the refrigerator and left everything else on the counter.

When he returned to the living room, he found that Emily had kicked off her shoes and closed her eyes. The look on her face as she flexed her toes might have been pain or pleasure. He noted with unexpected interest that she wasn't wearing stockings. Her straight, knee-length skirt had hiked slightly, giving him an excellent view of her long, slender legs. Funny, but now that she wasn't groomed to within an inch of her life, she was surprisingly appealing. Rumpled suited her. Usually, it was the other way around with the women he knew. She seemed to sense his presence and opened her eyes.

"You've certainly been busy," he began, only to find himself being shushed.

"Don't wake the baby," she whispered, tucking the escaped lock of hair behind her ear and nodding down at her lap. Amanda Sue lay sprawled across her, eyes closed, bottom lip protruding in a perpetual pout. "She can't sleep long or she won't sleep tonight," Emily went on, "but if she doesn't get a short nap she's going to be too wound up to sleep at all. And God knows I could use a few minutes peace."

He lowered his voice to say, "Why don't we put her down in another room?"

Emily rolled her eyes. "We can't do that. She could fall off a regular bed or wake up and climb down, in which case the room will be wrecked before we even know it, providing she doesn't break her neck first, of course. You have to put together the crib."

Logan knew she was right. He'd never seen a kid who moved as fast or was as determined as this one. He took off his coat, stripped away his tie and rolled up his sleeves before reaching for the big, flat box containing the crib parts. "Where should I put it?"

"Upstairs, the bedroom farthest from the landing."

Grimacing, he began dragging the unwieldy box up the stairs. Putting the crib together took hours and every tool in the house, or it seemed so, anyway. When Emily came upstairs with Amanda Sue on her hip and a stack of linens tucked under one arm, she took one look at the as yet lopsided crib and the pieces still littering the floor and quipped, "Want me to call a rocket scientist?"

"Yeah, would you?" he retorted. "I'm thinking of exploring outer space."

She laughed. "It's not as daunting as it seems."

"I know. I've almost got it. Won't take a minute more."

She dumped the linens on the dresser. "I was talking about parenthood."

Unconvinced, he said nothing to that.

"I took the liberty of making us some dinner," she said.

That was good news. "Great! I'll be right down."

She nodded. "I'll start feeding the baby."

He quickly finished up, put away the tools and carried them back downstairs. Emily had set the table in the kitchen. He'd had it made to match the planked fronts of the cabinets and countertops which were accented with black wrought iron.

"It isn't much," she said, "just sandwiches and salad."

"Sounds good to me," he assured her, eyeing his baby daughter. "What on earth has she got all over her?"

"Squished carrots and beef weiners," Emily answered offhandedly.

A fat plastic spoon with a short, curved handle lay on one corner of the high chair tray. He was about to ask why Amanda Sue wasn't using it when she picked it up, banged it loudly against the tray and threw it to the floor. Emily calmly picked it up and carried it to the sink, washing it while Amanda Sue dug into the food on her plate with both hands and crammed it into her mouth.

"Why is she doing that?" Logan asked, disgusted.

"Amanda Sue prefers to feed herself," Emily explained mildly, pulling out a chair and sitting down. "It's typical behavior for children her age."

He walked around the table and took his own place, eyeing his messy daughter warily. As he devoured his meal, he marveled as Emily ate her own dinner and still managed to get some of Amanda Sue's *inside* her with the clean spoon, all without relinquishing the utensil to Amanda Sue's stubborn grasp or getting covered in mush herself. Moreover, her sandwiches were tasty and the salad crisp. Best of all, though, was Emily's iced tea.

"You'll have to show me how you make your tea," he said, sated and content.

She shook her head. "My mama wouldn't like that. It's a—"

"Ma-ma!" Amanda exclaimed, suddenly struggling to get out of her chair. "Mammma!"

"Secret," Emily finished, grimacing sheepishly. "Sorry." She worked with Amanda Sue for several minutes, offering her first the spoon and then the cup before the cries subsided. Logan sighed. How was he going to raise this little girl without her mother? There was so much he didn't know or understand.

"Kitchen or baby?" Emily asked, interrupting his thoughts.

"Huh?"

"Do you want to clean up the kitchen or the baby?"

A no-brainer. He was clearing the table before Emily could get to her feet. She stripped the baby, wiped her face and hands with her filthy shirt and helped her out of the high chair, carrying her away. A few minutes later, Logan had loaded the dishwasher—a relatively new experience for him as he usually left his dishes in the sink for the housekeeper— stowed the leftover salad in the refrigerator and tackled Amanda Sue's high chair with a roll of paper towels. When he was done, he wandered out into the living room and looked around him in dismay. Resigned, he started moving everything upstairs.

He made the last trip, then wandered down the hall to the bathroom. The door was open, and Emily's patient murmur, overlaid with sounds of splashing and squeals of glee, was clearly audible. Logan leaned a hip against the frame, his hands sliding into his pants' pockets and observed.

Emily knelt beside the tub, a towel draped across her upper body, for all the good it had done her; her skirt and sleeves were soaked. A naked Amanda Sue was strapped into an ingenuous plastic seat with suckers on the feet that fixed it to the bottom of the tub. Her wet hair plastered to her head, she was happily smacking the surface of the water with her hands and forearms, splashing walls, floor, herself and Emily.

"She really seems to like the water," he commented.

"So long as you don't wash her hair with it," Emily replied wryly.

Amanda Sue squealed and splashed at the same time, filling her mouth with water. She gagged, spat, decided it was all in fun and laughed. Logan felt a moment of concern there, but followed Emily's lead and remained calm. The kid really was having a ball, and he couldn't help laughing at her antics. After a few minutes, Amanda Sue quit splashing long enough to rub her eyes.

"Time to get out, sweetheart," Emily said, loosening the belt and sliding her hands under Amanda Sue's arms. Amanda Sue immediately started to buck and kick, screaming in protest. Emily wrapped the towel draped across her shoulder around Amanda Sue's wet body as she rose. Suddenly she thrust the wriggling child into Logan's arms and turned back to drain the tub of what little water remained.

"Whoa!" He almost dropped her, as her slippery little body twisted and bucked with surprising strength. "Hold on! Calm down!" A little fist smacked him under the chin, and his teeth clamped down on his tongue. "Ow! You little hellion!" He literally juggled her, trying to get a decent hold on the slick little body. Amanda Sue laughed and tried to throw herself upward. The next instant she was squirming and pushing and straining toward the tub again. "Do you never give up?" he asked in exasperation.

"Here." Emily thrust a tub toy into Amanda Sue's hand. It went immediately to her mouth. "The tub is empty," Emily said, as if Amanda Sue could understand every word. "It's time for bed."

Amanda Sue whimpered a moment and put on a great act of clearly feigned heartbreak.

"You little faker," Logan said. "Where'd you learn this stuff?"

"It comes naturally," Emily told him, chuckling.

He frowned as she slipped past him and down the hallway. Amanda Sue bit her tub toy and laid her head on his shoulder. Logan turned and followed Emily. "Are you saying she inherited this tendency toward theatrics from me?" he demanded.

Emily tossed him a look over her shoulder. "I'm saying that all children are natural actors. It's part of learning to communicate." She turned into Amanda Sue's bedroom, and Logan followed with the baby.

"Oh."

Emily took a piece of fabric from the dresser and shook it out, revealing a small, fitted sheet, which she began putting on the mattress in the crib. "Think you could towel-dry her hair?"

"Sure." How hard could it be, after all? He stood Amanda Sue on the end of her dresser and pulled the towel up over her head. She shoved it off so hard that she nearly toppled onto the floor. "Hey!" he cried, grabbing her at the last instant.

"Try the rocking chair," Emily said, shaking out blankets and tucking them into the bed.

He sat in the rocker, balanced Amanda Sue on his knee, and pulled the towel up over her head again. She tossed herself backward and slid down between his legs. Catching her with his legs, he trapped her there between them and rubbed the towel over her hair. She fought him with screams and shrugs. Finally he pulled her up into his lap again. She promptly tried to climb him like a tree. Emily extracted a cotton-knit nightgown from a pile of clothing and reached for the child, literally pulling her off Logan's head.

He smoothed his hair down with both hands, saying, "This kid must be part mountain goat."

Emily sent him a loaded glance. "Maybe she inherited that tendency, too."

"Just for the record," he snapped, "her mo—uh, Donna was as crazy about rock climbing as I am. That's how we met, you know. She was working for the guide, flying parties to climbs by helicopter."

"No, I didn't know," Emily said, pulling the gown's short sleeves over one of Amanda Sue's flailing arms. "Why should I? It was before my time."

"Oh. That's right, but just before." Odd that he'd just come back from a month in the Rockies with Donna as his climbing partner when he'd hired Emily. His previous assistant had set up half a dozen interviews for him, and Emily had been the very first. He'd hired her on the spot and never been so glad as now.

Emily quickly diapered Amanda Sue, who was rubbing her eyes again and beginning to lose her fight. Then she removed a tattered teddy bear from the diaper bag and handed it to the child before clipping her pacifier to her shoulder. Amanda Sue made that odd half-laugh, half-sob sound as she hugged the stuffed bear, babbling, "Sur-bay, sur-bay."

"What's she saying?" Logan asked.

"I think she's calling the bear by name."

"What would that be, Sir Bear, maybe?"

Amanda Sue shook her head violently, answering his question herself. "Sur-bay," she said, "Sur-bay." She started kissing it, making loud smacking sounds, then bit its nose.

"Sugar Bear?" Emily suggested.

Amanda Sue kicked and laughed. "Sur-bay!"

Logan shook his head. "How do you do that?" he asked Emily. "How can you understand her?"

Emily shrugged. "Practice," she said, picking up Amanda Sue and replacing the bear's nose with her pacifier. "I have several nieces and nephews."

He hadn't known that but was suddenly reluctant to admit it. She'd worked for him for two years, after all, and he hardly had any secrets from her, depending on her to help him balance both his business and social schedules—and now his domestic life. He should know more about her.

"Turn on one of those monitors," Emily said, nodding toward what looked like a pair of plastic walkie-talkies on the dresser. Logan did so. "Now turn off the light, but leave the door open." He did that, too, while she sat down in the rocking chair with Amanda Sue, bear, and pacifier.

He leaned a hip against the end of the dresser and watched as Emily engaged the baby's attention by first talking to her, then whispering to her as she rocked gently back and forth. Soon his rambunctious daughter's eyelids began to droop and she settled into the crook of Emily's arm. Minutes later, she was lolling peacefully. Rising carefully, Emily carried the sleeping child to her crib and gently tucked her in, being sure to keep the bear next to her. Turning away, she picked up the extra monitor and tiptoed from the room. Logan followed.

When they were several yards away, Emily turned on the monitor and carried it down the stairs, where she placed it near to hand on the coffee table.

"You'd better take that to bed with you," she instructed, stepping into her shoes. "She's liable to wake up several times during the night, and you'll need to reassure her. But don't worry, it's perfectly normal under the circumstances. She'll settle down before long."

He barely heard what she was saying, his attention completely focused on the fact that Emily was obviously leaving. "Where are you going?"

She sent him a surprised look. "Home, if you must know."

Sheer panic descended. "You can't go home! I need you here. Amanda Sue needs you."

Emily sighed and folded her arms, fixing him with an implacable look. "Listen, I understand that you're concerned, but you'll be fine. Just do what I did."

"B-but what if she cries?"

"Calm her down. Just remember that the key is to stay calm yourself."

"She could want something, and I wouldn't know what!" he protested.

"Yes, you will," Emily assured him. "If she wants a bottle or her bear, she'll ask for them. You'll figure out the rest by just paying attention."

"Emily, I insist that you stay!"

She gave him a look he'd seen before. It clearly said that she could find another job anytime she wanted. Unaccountably, he was hurt. This wasn't work, this was...personal. And Emily was an employee, not a friend. He bit his lip, feeling extremely foolish.

"You're right. I'm sure we'll, uh, manage."

Emily nodded crisply. "I'll be in the office early in the morning to take care of a few things I didn't get done today, for obvious reasons. I took the liberty of calling an agency and setting up a few interviews with prospective nannies, so you'll want to bring Amanda Sue into the office with you. I thought that was preferable to doing the interviews here, all things considered. But take your time in the morning. I know how hard it is to get a baby changed, fed, dressed, packed and out of the house. First appointment is at ten."

"Ten," he echoed numbly, wondering how in blue blazes he was going to get through this.

"I moved the safety seat to your car earlier while you were putting up the crib," she said. "Just be sure the restraining belt is clipped before you leave. She'll fight you, of course, but she won't win unless you let her."

He nodded, but he didn't mean it. He wouldn't tell her that the curly headed little moppet upstairs had already won the battle of wills between them a dozen times that day. He'd never been so exasperated as when driving her to and from the ranch. It was like trying to travel with a caged tiger, one smarter than him. He'd groveled all he intended to for one day, however. If Emily was determined to go, well, that was that.

When she moved toward the foyer, he almost let her go without another word, but then he thought of all she'd done for them that day and knew he couldn't. Gritting his teeth, he hurried after her. "Emily."

She paused and turned, obviously expecting more entreaties. "Yes?"

"I just wanted to thank you for everything."

She smiled wearily. "No problem. I realize you were desperate. Glad I could help."

"I still don't know what half the stuff you bought is for, but I'm sure I'll need it," he told her. "I—I just wish I could handle her as well as you do."

"You'll learn," Emily promised. "Now, if you don't mind, I just want to go home and soak in a hot tub before I fall into bed."

Logan suddenly found himself assailed by an unexpected vision that left him struggling for composure: Emily, naked and soaking in a tub of bubbles, her long hair piled loosely on top of her head. He shook himself. What was wrong with him? The Emily he'd always known was buttoned down and bunned, totally efficient, all business. He'd never wondered before what her hair looked like down or if she wore stockings or how she might pile up her hair for a bath.

"By the way," she said briskly, bringing him back to the moment, "you'd better sleep upstairs until you hire a nanny. Otherwise you're going to be running up and down all night long, and she's going to work herself into a real temper by the time you get to her. Just thought I'd better mention that. See you tomorrow."

She walked out the door and closed it behind her. Logan collapsed against the wall, groaning. He hadn't realized until that moment how much he'd been looking forward to collapsing into his own bed. No doubt about it, his first day of fatherhood had been a day of hell, and now he was reduced to the position of a guest in his own home, while fantasizing about his personal assistant! He couldn't help wondering if anything about his life would ever be the same again.

* * *

Emily heard the wails the instant she got off the elevator. Turning right, she walked swiftly past the reception/clerical area and down the long hall to the spacious corner office suite belonging to the Executive V.P. of Fortune Tx, Ltd. The wails had subsided, which hopefully bode well for her employer's developing relationship with his newly found daughter—and Emily's own day.

She pushed through the glass door into the outer office and stowed her things in the corner cabinet. The boss's door was open, allowing his irritable voice to be clearly heard. "Amanda Sue, no! Don't bend... Damn!"

Huffs of protest quickly became screams of outrage. Emily took off the jacket of her navy-blue suit and folded it over the back of her chair. Steeling herself for what she might find inside, she strolled into the inner office.

Logan Fortune sat at his desk in jeans and a rumpled T-shirt, a day-old beard darkening his lower face. He wrestled with the little body in his lap, trying desperately to clean ink-stained fingers with a wad of Baby Wipes from an open container on the desk. Papers, some in shreds, others splattered with indigo ink and still others covered with huge scribblings, were scattered across the blotter. Amanda Sue fought him tooth and nail, kicking, twisting, bucking, screaming. To his credit, Logan tried mightily to stay calm while holding her tiny wrists in one hand and dabbing and swiping at her fingertips with the other.

"Amanda Sue, please. Just let me clean your fingers. Be still just a minute, baby. If I let go you'll get ink on your pretty face. You don't want ink on your pretty face, do you? Amanda Sue, for pity's sake!"

"Rough morning?" Emily asked.

Both Logan and Amanda Sue froze. Logan's head snapped up. "Emily!" The relief in his voice was both touching and disturbing.

"Mimy!" Amanda Sue cried, struggling upright. Logan quickly took advantage of her momentary calm to finish cleaning her fingers. The pale stains that remained would eventually wear off without transferring noticeable traces to other objects. Quickly, Emily moved across the room and around the desk.

"Did she just say my name?"

"Believe me, it's not the first time," he confirmed. The instant he let go of the child's wrists, she reached for Emily, who hoisted her into her arms, heartstrings singing. The baby was dressed only in a red T-shirt, lopsided diaper and pink socks.

"At first I thought she was asking for her you-know-who," Logan said. "Then I realized she was asking for you." He pushed a hand through his hair. "I guess I don't do things as well as you do. I don't rock as well. I don't do breakfast as well. I sure don't diaper as well." He sighed and laid his head back against his chair. "We've been up since 4:00 a.m."

"And in all that time you didn't get a chance to shave—"

"Or shower," he finished for her. "Or eat or brush my teeth or anything else except cover my butt with the first thing that came to hand." He sighed and rubbed his eyes with the heels of his hands. "At least we have that much in common, my daughter and I."

Emily laughed. She couldn't help it. Amanda Sue, meanwhile, was bending herself into a pretzel trying to reach the papers on the desk.

"Someone's been drawing pictures," Emily said, dipping down so Amanda Sue could snag one. The child immediately crumpled one corner of the paper in her fist and carried it to her mouth. "Don't eat it, sweetheart. Let Emily see it." She gently pulled the paper from the baby's hand and shook it out. It contained nothing but wiggly, curving lines and one small rip. It was, nevertheless, a treasure. She handed it to Logan, while speaking to Amanda Sue. "Did you draw a picture for Daddy? How sweet. Daddy's first picture from Amanda Sue."

Logan looked at the scribblings and chuckled. "I had no

idea she even knew what to do when I pulled out the paper and pens. I was just desperate to keep her happy for a little while. But she sat right down and got busy. She even holds the pen pretty well, considering her fingers are about an inch and a half long.''

Emily smiled, wondering if he knew that he was beginning to sound like a proud papa. "You should tuck that away somewhere for safekeeping," she advised. He continued to stare at the scribbles a moment longer, then opened a drawer and dropped the paper inside. When he looked up, she knew he wasn't even going to mention the "picture" again.

"I brought as many of her things as I could grab. Would you mind dressing her? She puts up a terrific fight when I try."

Emily nodded. "Why don't you run home and change? If you hurry you can be back before the first nanny applicant arrives."

He didn't argue, just pushed back his chair and got up. Emily hid a smile when she saw that he'd put on his athletic shoes without socks and hadn't even tied the laces. "I won't be long," he said, heading for the door.

"Oh, by the way," she called, following him. He paused, but it was almost as if he was afraid she'd changed her mind about watching the baby. The poor guy had really jumped in over his head this time, but she felt sure he'd keep his lungs inflated long enough to learn to swim. "Bring the playpen with you—unless you have a better idea how to corral this one from time to time."

"Playpen," he repeated. "Right."

"And some crayons," Emily suggested. "I bought a small box yesterday. She'll break them all in short order, but they don't stain."

"Playpen and crayons."

Before he could turn away again, Emily lifted Amanda Sue's arm and wagged it in Logan's direction. "Say, 'Bye-bye, Daddy. 'Bye-bye.'"

"'Bye-bye, Daa!'' Amanda shouted, pleased to show off. Logan beamed. "'Bye-bye, Amanda Sue.''

Emily brought the baby's hand to her own mouth, kissed it and blew across it in Logan's direction. "Blow Daddy a kiss,'' she said, and Amanda Sue immediately smacked her hand over her own mouth, removed it, then pursed her mouth in a kiss and blew at Logan.

Logan laughed delightedly, so she did it again, showing her teeth in a gurgle of laughter. "'Bye-bye, Daa!''

"'Bye-bye, Amanda Sue,'' he said again, waving at her. Everyone was smiling when he pushed through the glass door into the hall, and it was precisely then that Amanda Sue actually realized her father was leaving. Her face registered shock, then dismay, and she screamed as if she'd just taken a bullet. Logan whipped around and shoved back inside, clearly worried. "What?''

"Daa!'' she screamed, reaching for him. "Daa!''

Logan looked as if he'd been poleaxed, but then his entire being softened, and he hurried toward her, holding out his arms. "Don't cry, sweetheart. Daddy won't be gone long.'' Amanda Sue went to him with a false sob of delight. Emily rolled her eyes. Logan was eating it up, however. "Don't you want to stay with Emily? She'll take good care of you till Daddy gets back.'' He rubbed her cheek with the back of one finger. "You play with Emily. I'll be right back, I promise.''

Emily reached for Amanda Sue, and the baby came right to her.

Logan stroked her cheek again. "I'll be quick as I can, princess.'' He looked at Emily with eyes so devastatingly blue in their happy brightness that they took her breath away. "I guess I did better than I thought, huh?'' He all but tiptoed to the door, despite the fact that Amanda Sue was watching him calmly now. He hurried away smiling.

Emily chuckled and hoisted Amanda Sue a little higher in her arms. "You little tyrant,'' she said laughingly. "I wonder how old you'll be before he figures out you've been playing him like a lute?'' Amanda Sue dug a finger into the scarf knotted beneath the Peter Pan collar of Emily's white cotton blouse and babbled about chins or something similar. "Well, that's all right," Emily went on thoughtfully. "Daddies ought to be vulnerable to their daughters, especially this one. God knows he's broken enough hearts of other fathers' daughters. Who'd have thought that when he finally met his match she'd be little more than two feet tall?"

Amanda Sue chuckled as if she understood every word, and then she abruptly kicked, stiffened, and tried to slide down to the floor. Emily laughed, catching her more tightly against her. "Oh, no, you don't. We're going to get you changed and ready to meet everyone. We're going to find you a nanny today. Yes, we are. A nanny for Amanda Sue."

It never occurred to her as she carried the child toward her father's office that it might not be as simple as it sounded.

Three

The woman clutched her handbag beneath one arm and patted the steel-gray helmet of her hair even though not a strand had moved out of place. It wouldn't dare, Logan decided, for fear of being plucked and banished. She looked down her lengthy nose at Amanda Sue, who sat in her father's lap, his tie once again clamped firmly between her teeth despite all his efforts to prevent it. She looked like a pink-and-white puppy with a favorite sock in its mouth. Logan had seriously tried to interest her in something else, but she was nothing if not determined, this child of his, and she looked so downright happy and adorable that he didn't have the heart to make her cry again. Some of the other candidates had laughed, but this woman's disapproval was palpable.

"I've dealt with many an unruly child," the woman said smugly, "and my methods have proven successful in nearly every case. Believe me, I know how to bring a child to heel quickly."

It had been a long, disappointing morning, and Logan was feeling the strain. Despite his own mental canine comparisons, he rolled his eyes and snapped, "Dogs are brought to heel. I hope you aren't saying you'll treat my daughter like a dog."

The woman narrowed her eyes to black slits. "Please do not put words in my mouth. I'm merely stating that a willful child requires a strong, firm hand."

Logan pinched his nose, trying to hold on to his temper. His daughter, meanwhile, was continuing to ruin a perfectly good silk tie by gnawing and slobbering on it. Emily had suggested that she was cutting teeth. But he was more concerned about the granite-jawed prison matron sitting across from him. "You do understand that my daughter has been through a terrible loss and trauma, don't you?" he asked.

The woman inclined her head. "All the more reason to provide a strictly scheduled routine. The structure will give her security and teach her self-control."

"She's sixteen months old," he pointed out. "How much self-control can she have at this age?"

"More than you might realize," the woman said complacently. "Turn her over to me, and we'll soon have a different child."

Logan wanted to smack her. How dare she imply that there was something wrong with Amanda Sue! True, she was strong-willed and much too intelligent for his own good, not to mention adventurous enough to scare the pants off him at times, but she was a Fortune. Of course she was strong-willed and intelligent and adventurous, even quicktempered. She was also beautiful and charming and perfect just as she was. He wouldn't have her changed, but he couldn't help wondering what this hyena in a middle-aged woman's guise might know that he didn't.

"Just exactly how might you accomplish this transformation?" he asked.

The woman readjusted her seat on the chair and lifted her chin. "I know the so-called experts counsel against breaking a child's spirit," she began, "but frankly my experience shows otherwise."

Now he really wanted to smack her. He set his back teeth. "Is that so?"

She seemed unaware of his censure. "I believe the old ways are the best ways," she said sagely. "My mother believed children were to be seen and not heard. She made very sure that my brother and I were well-behaved, well-groomed and well-thought-of. If we broke the rules, we were harshly dealt with, let me tell you, but privately. Publicly, she made sure we were a credit to our parents."

"Uh-huh. And what about your own children? Are they a credit to their parents?"

"Oh, I have no children of my own," she said dismissively. "I decided long ago to dedicate myself to the children of others, and one thing I realized early on is that modern parents are too emotionally attached to their children to see what it is they really need."

He couldn't quite believe he'd heard her right. Emily appeared at his elbow, saying brightly, "Okay, I think that's enough. Don't you, Mr. Fortune?"

"Quite enough," he agreed, sending her a loaded message she couldn't help interpreting correctly. She moved around the desk to the woman's side and literally seized her by the arm, pulling her to her feet.

"Thank you for coming," she said briskly, propelling the woman toward the door. "We'll be in touch with your agency."

Amanda Sue made roaring sounds around a mouthful of his tie and smacked her hands aggressively on the top of his desk, as if bidding the woman good riddance. Logan smiled. Even *she* had sense enough to know that woman didn't belong anywhere near a child. He wouldn't entrust an animal to that woman. Unfortunately, he hadn't found anyone else to whom he could comfortably give over care of his daughter, either.

A couple of the candidates were mere children themselves, just teenagers, really. Two others were in the U.S. only temporarily, one with only weeks left on her visa, and the last thing Logan wanted to do was let Amanda Sue get emotionally attached to someone guaranteed to leave her soon. One woman, while a citizen, didn't speak English well enough to properly interview. Given the circumstances, he felt Amanda Sue would be too confused to respond well. Another woman had seemed mildly impaired mentally. She was very pleasant, and he liked her a great deal, but he felt uncomfortable leaving her alone with Amanda Sue for days at a time when he was traveling. This last one was the topper on the cake, however, a real brute in support hose.

Emily steered the woman out of his office and her own, then returned, closing the door behind her. "Charles Dickens wrote books about idiots like her," she said, dropping down onto the corner of his desk. Amanda Sue started crawling up onto the desk to get to her.

Logan let her go. What could it hurt with him and Emily sitting right there? Emily seemed to agree. She reached out and took Amanda Sue's hands in hers, helping her stand from a crouch, then drawing her forward carefully. "Maybe I should call another agency," she said, fingering a curl on top of the baby's head.

"Do that," he agreed, smoothing a grossly wet, rumpled tie. "This one sure didn't send over any winners."

"Still want to schedule the interviews here?" Emily asked, and he sighed. Interviewing nannies wasn't exactly conducive to business, but he didn't want any strangers knowing where he lived. The kidnapping of his cousin's infant son Bryan had taught them all the folly of not taking every precaution. He nodded.

"Yeah. I don't want anyone I don't completely trust in my house."

"I understand," Emily said. "So tomorrow we start over. Now what?"

He looked around him, wondering if he could keep Amanda Sue here and actually get anything done, but he knew the answer to that. "Why don't you take her on home," he said finally. "I'll try to get through early here so you can get home at a decent hour. Uh, unless I can persuade you to spend the night?"

She sent him a look that said, *Please don't ask.* He ignored it.

"I could really use a good night's sleep myself," he went on, "and I have so much work to do. And you wouldn't have to cook or anything. I'll pick up something."

"I don't know. I really prefer—"

"I understand," he said, "but I'm desperate here. I haven't even checked my voice mail today."

"All right," she said, capitulating reluctantly, "but just tonight."

He nodded, deeply relieved. "Surely we'll find someone tomorrow."

If the smile she gave him wasn't quite as hopeful as it might have been, he chose not to think about it. He was covered for a few precious hours, and that was enough for the moment. Tomorrow would come soon enough, too soon probably, but he'd cross that bridge when he came to it. Meanwhile, he had a lot of work to do and a little time to do it in. But at least he wouldn't have to worry about his daughter while he was doing it, and that, he was discovering, was more important than anything else.

What a day it had been, Emily mused, wrestling Amanda Sue into her sweater. She had worked closely with Logan Fortune for two years now, but never like this. It was as if they were a couple, rather than simply a good business team, and such illusions were terribly dangerous given the way she felt about him. She'd held the attraction at bay for such a long time, but she wasn't superhuman.

She had known from the beginning of her employment with him that any personal involvement would be sheer folly. Logan was a real player in the field of romance, and Emily was anything but. Dalliance with the likes of him could only lead her to a broken heart, but here she was about to spend the night at his house. Still, what else could she do? He and Amanda Sue both were obviously exhausted, and how could she not allow him the benefit of her experience when he was trying so very hard? *One night,* she told herself, and tomorrow would be a better day for everyone.

Finally getting Amanda Sue properly attired, Emily began to gather their things, all the while balancing the child on one hip. Amanda Sue helped out by grasping handfuls of her blouse, front and back, and hanging on. It was awkward, but it beat setting her down and then trying to keep her from looting the desk while gathering everything. She was heading toward the door, laden with baby, purse and bulging diaper bag, when she called out, "We're going now."

To her surprise, Logan got up from his desk and hurried out to send them off. "Wait. Amanda Sue can't go without telling Daddy 'bye-bye." He waved at his daughter and pretended to blow a kiss, as before. His daughter, however, had other ideas. She puckered her lips and leaned so far forward that Emily had trouble holding her up. Logan laughed. "What's she doing now?"

Emily smiled. "I think she wants a real kiss."

He all but recoiled. "A real kiss?"

"It won't kill you, Fortune, and my arm's weakening."

He bent and quickly smacked Amanda Sue on the cheek, but the baby objected, wiping it away with a flat wipe of her hand and puckering up again. Logan looked to Emily for help, and it was all she could do to keep from laughing. Finally, he pursed his lips and gave Amanda Sue a dry, fleeting peck on the mouth. Satisfied, Amanda Sue grinned and settled back, her arm looping around Emily's neck. Logan colored, but the eyes with which he gazed at his daughter were very nearly worshipful.

"See you later," he said nonchalantly, but he wasn't fooling Emily. That first real kiss from his daughter had tied his heart into knots.

He turned away, but a sudden thought occurred to Emily. "Oh, wait," she said. "What about the safety seat? I can't take her in my car without it."

"You're right. Here, take my keys." He dug into his pants' pocket. "Better yet, just take my car. Otherwise, I'll have to walk down with you."

"True. If you're sure that's how you want to handle it, though, we'd better trade. Otherwise, how will you get home?"

"Good point."

She dug in her purse for her own keys and handed them

over, then thought better of it. "Uh, actually, I have to stop to get some overnight things and feed my cat, so I'd better take my apartment key."

"Right."

She pointed out the key, and he worked it off the ring, handing it over with his own.

"This thing just keeps getting more and more complicated, doesn't it?" she said, putting the keys into her bag.

Logan sighed. "To tell you the truth, I guess I'm still reeling from the news. It's like this whirlwind blew into my life and hasn't slowed down yet. I keep hoping that when it does, it'll leave behind some semblance of order, but what are the chances of that?"

"Not much, I'd warrant," she admitted sympathetically, "but it'll get better eventually."

He sighed. "At least I have you until it does," he said softly. "God help me if I didn't."

Emily felt a strange heat blossom in her chest. She quickly turned away before it could spread to her cheeks. "Better get going," she said briskly.

"Remember," he called as she pushed through the door, "dinner's on me."

She nodded and kept moving, afraid to look back for fear of what she might see in his eyes. Simple gratitude or a certain sensual warmth? The problem was, she wasn't sure which would frighten her more.

The little car chugged into the driveway and promptly died. Logan pulled the emergency brake, removed the key from the ignition switch and grabbed the bag of Tex-Mex on the passenger seat. The clutch in Emily's inexpensive car definitely needed an adjustment, as did the driver's side door, which creaked alarmingly when he opened it and maneuvered his way out.

The temperature had dropped into the upper thirties in the past few hours. Logan shivered, wondering if Amanda Sue had a heavy coat. It would be infrequently needed here in

San Antonio, but he couldn't have his little girl going around cold, not that it was apt to slow her down any.

He made a mental note to ask Emily about the coat as he trudged up the walk to his front door. Then he'd suggest she get that clutch looked at. He wouldn't have her driving his daughter around in an unsafe vehicle. In fact, he wasn't sure he wanted Amanda Sue in such a small car at all. It just didn't seem as safe as his own German luxury sedan. With that in mind, he let himself into the foyer and moved down the hall, baby giggles washing away the tiredness that had been dogging his steps all day long.

He stepped into the living room, a smile on his face, and once more froze in his steps. It wasn't unexpected clutter, this time. The room, in fact, was in pristine condition, save for the old blanket spread upon the floor and the two playing upon it.

Garbed in a footed sleeper, Amanda Sue lay on her back, one hand fisted around the open collar of Emily's blouse, which had been unbuttoned almost to mid-chest. Emily lay on her side next to Amanda Sue, propped up on one elbow. She tickled the baby's round tummy with her fingertips while Amanda Sue kicked and giggled happily and tugged on the collar of Emily's blouse, laying it open and exposing the plump swell of one firm breast. Emily's glasses had been put away and her long, sand-colored hair swung in a thick, silky fall to the floor. Her straight skirt was hiked up to the tops of her thighs, her long legs and slender, delicate feet bare.

Desire hit Logan in the gut, his gaze sweeping up those long, graceful limbs to the skirt bunched near their tops. She definitely did not wear stockings on a daily basis. All this time and he had just now noticed this enticing fact. All this time and he had just now noticed how enticing his executive assistant was.

Had he once thought her oval face was too long? Her mouth too wide? He realized now that it was nothing more than the severe manner in which she had been wearing her hair. Without her glasses he could actually see and appreciate her deeply set, golden-brown eyes and the sweep of high, prominent cheekbones. He was astonished to find that she was, in her own unique way, quite breathtakingly beautiful, and she had been sitting right under his nose for the past two years! He couldn't help wondering just how stupid it would be to seduce the best assistant he'd ever had. If he did, would she suddenly develop dollar signs in her eyes? Somehow he didn't think so.

Emily looked up just then and smiled welcomingly. "Look who's here," she said to the giggling Amanda Sue. "Daddy's home."

Quick as lightning, Amanda Sue flopped over and sat up. She clapped her hands and held up her arms. "Daa-dy!"

Logan dropped the food bag onto a corner of the dining table as he passed by and hurried toward his daughter and her fetching sitter. Going down on one knee, he scooped up Amanda Sue, and laughed delightedly at the exuberant hug and loud, smacking kiss that he got. She smelled clean and fresh, his little girl, like something new and bright and wholly Amanda Sue, and he realized suddenly that parental love was something innate and fierce. She was his little girl and he loved her. It was as simple as that. Never mind that she had turned his life upside down, that only days ago he hadn't known she even existed. She was his now, and that was all that mattered.

Abruptly, his headstrong daughter twisted around and pointed up the stairs. "Boog!" she announced.

Emily laughed. "She has the memory of an elephant, I swear. I promised her more than an hour ago that Daddy would read her a certain book for a bedtime story."

"Well, Daddy will just have to do that, then," he said enthusiastically. His empty stomach rumbled, but he dutifully rose to his feet, Amanda Sue cradled in one arm, and reached down a hand for Emily. She slipped her fingers into his palm and let him pull her to her feet. "I see she's ready for bed," he said.

"It's not always a two-person job," Emily replied lightly.

"I'm beginning to think there's nothing you can't handle," he said teasingly.

She laughed. "I'm going to remind you of that the next time I ask for a raise."

"Emily," he told her seriously, "all things considered, I'd say a raise was the very least I could do for you. Just name the amount."

She laughed again. "Nah, I don't want you saying I took advantage of you later."

"That's usually my line," he quipped.

She didn't seem to find it funny. Lifting an eyebrow, she looked away. "Is that our dinner over there?"

He nodded. "I assume you like Tex-Mex."

"Love it. Why don't I put it in the oven while you try to get a certain someone down for the night?"

"I'll give it my best shot," he said, "but if I'm not down in half an hour, call the anti-terrorist squad."

Emily chuckled, turning away. "I'm starved."

"That makes two of us," Logan said, following her as far as the foot of the stairs, where he turned and climbed upward while she went on into the dining room and kitchen. He carried Amanda Sue across the landing and down the hall, talking nonsense to her while she babbled back.

"What'd you do this afternoon, Amanda mine?"

"Mimy do sum-sum-sum." She waggled her little fingers above her head.

"Did you play with Emily, hmm?"

She nodded sharply and went on talking. "Up fruffle and pickers. Go see." She pointed to the door to her own room. Logan carried her inside and flipped on the overhead light.

It looked like something out of a fairy tale. A curving canopy had been erected above the white crib, which now sported frothy pink ruffles over and under. The rocking chair had been similarly adorned, and the window, as well. A lamp in the shape of a carousel sat atop the dresser, surrounded by baby dolls and stuffed animals. The shelves below the window had been filled with small books and colorful toys. A music box had been attached to the side of the crib. Pictures of baby animals adorned the walls. Amanda Sue pointed her little finger at each one and labeled it.

"Pupup. Kitty. Hosey. Sicgen. Pigky. Pish. Moo-cow."

Logan laughed and hugged her tight. "That's right!" He pointed and confirmed each name, correcting her pronunciation. "Puppy, kitty, horsey, chicken, piggy, fish, and a little cow."

"Moo-cow!" Amanda Sue insisted.

"All right, moo-cow. What a smart girl you are, Amanda Sue."

Bucking, she demanded to be put down. He bent and set her feet on the floor. She promptly led him on a tour of the room, pointing out every item for his approval. Finally they made their way to the rocking chair and the book that lay upon the seat. Amanda Sue snatched the book up and held it by one corner, patting the seat cushion with her free hand. "Daddy 'own."

Logan obediently sat, then gathered the child into his arms. She snuggled into the crook of his elbow and crossed one little ankle over the opposite knee, ready to be read to. He was halfway through the brightly illustrated book about—what else?—baby animals, when Emily slipped into the room. Amanda Sue beckoned her over so that Emily stood behind the chair and peered over their shoulders at the pages of the book. Amanda Sue pushed her head back, looking up at Emily. "Cav," she said, adding, "Moo-cow, cav," as she pointed to the mother cow and the baby calf.

"Good grief, she's bright," Logan said proudly.

"She certainly is." Emily moved away then, walking softly. "Mind if I turn down the light?"

"No, go ahead."

"How about a little background music?" she asked as she switched on the lamp and switched off the overhead light.

"Sure."

Suddenly the mood was entirely altered, softened, as tinkling music filled the air.

"Keep your voice low and rock gently as you read," Emily counseled in a whisper as she clipped Amanda Sue's pacifier to her shoulder and placed Sugar Bear in her lap. The child immediately popped the nipple into her mouth and got a hammerlock on the toy. Logan began to rock, carefully, quietly reading and turning the pages. Soon he realized that Amanda Sue was no longer paying attention. She had dropped off, her face turned into his chest. As he watched, she pushed the pacifier out of her mouth with her tongue and sighed. Suddenly Emily was at his shoulder, whispering into his ear. "Just get up very slowly."

He laid aside the book and slowly rose, carefully shifting his sleeping daughter as he did so. Emily floated across the room to fold back the covers on the crib. Logan followed and gently lowered Amanda Sue to the mattress. She stirred, sighed, and collapsed into deep slumber, Sugar Bear atop her chest. Logan tucked the covers around her as Emily rewound the music box. He turned on one monitor. She picked up the other and slipped from the room. Again Logan followed, gently closing the door behind him.

"She loves that room," Logan said as they moved away, keeping his voice low. "She had to show me every little thing, and she kept saying, 'Mimy do, Mimy do.' I didn't realize she was talking so much, not that I could understand much of it. She knows all the animals, though. That much, I got. Did you teach her?"

Emily shook her head. "No. You'll have to credit her mother with that and much more. Amanda Sue has been handled with great care. She's been read to on a regular basis and taught all the basics. Tonight when I brushed her teeth, she didn't protest a peep, just opened her little mouth and patiently waited for me to finish, then rinsed her mouth and gave me a big smile. She kept talking about you this evening, too. 'Daddy come? Daddy come?' I kept assuring her that you would, but I could tell she was missing you."

Logan felt a lump rise in his throat. "She's amazing, isn't she? I can't get over how bright and loving she is."

"When she's getting her way," Emily said cheekily.

He chuckled. "Too true. No one will ever run over Miss Amanda Sue, you can bet on that."

"Not that they're likely to get the chance," Emily said, looking back over her shoulder at him as she began descending the stairs.

"Meaning?"

"They'd have to go through her daddy first, now wouldn't they?"

He found that he liked the idea. A natural protectiveness seemed to come with the job. "It's so strange," he said. "She didn't exist for me just days ago, and now..." He shook his head, unable to put it into words. He didn't have to.

"I know," Emily said, reaching the bottom of the stairs. "A child changes everything."

He couldn't argue with that. They walked on into the kitchen, where she had laid out plates and flatware. Emily poured the iced tea while he got the food out of the oven and set out the containers. His stomach rumbled again as the aromas of refried beans, rice, tamales, guacamole and spicy enchiladas mingled. They sat down and dug in. The first pangs of hunger were satisfied before his mind turned to other things.

"You were quick to credit her mother earlier," he said to Emily, "but I couldn't help noticing how well you handle Amanda Sue, as well as you do everything else, in fact. You said something yesterday about nieces and nephews, but I have a nephew, and I haven't learned what you have about kids."

She smiled and put down her fork. "Maybe we should put this into perspective. You see, I'm the next to youngest of seven children, and we're pretty spread out, so I have nieces and nephews only a few years younger than me, and quite a few even younger ones. The count went to sixteen, total, this year, some of whom have children of their own.''

"Wow!" He shook his head, wondering what else he didn't know about this woman. Funny, he'd spent more time with Emily Applegate these past two years than any other person of his acquaintance, and yet he knew next to nothing about her.

She picked up her fork and cut a piece of tamale. ''That won't last long, though,'' she said.

He brought his mind back to full attention. ''What's that?''

"Sixteen.''

"Nieces and nephews, you mean.''

She nodded, chewing and swallowing her tamale. ''My little sister has just announced that she's in the family way again.''

"Your little sister?''

Emily nodded again. ''Her name's Lola. She's twenty-three and has been married four years already. We marry young in Kentucky.''

"Kentucky,'' he echoed, thoroughly irritated with himself for not knowing where she was from. Why had he never asked? ''Didn't I hire you out of Dallas?''

"That's right. After college I worked in Kingsboro, then Memphis, Tennessee, and then Dallas.'' She toyed with her guacamole, then forked up a tiny bite. ''I was the only one who couldn't wait to get out of Kentucky—well, not counting Cathy.''

"Cathy? That one of your sisters?''

Emily shook her head, a tiny smile curving her mouth. ''Cathy Wazorski,'' she said, eyes twinkling. ''She was my very best friend. We grew up plotting ways to get out of Kentucky.''

"And you found your way out through college,'' he surmised correctly.

"True. It wasn't easy, mind you. We were poor as church

mice. Mom and Dad just couldn't afford to help, so I'm still paying off the school loans, but it's worth it.''

Logan shifted uncomfortably. He knew the value of hard work. He'd *earned* his way to the top of the family company, and no one could say otherwise, but he'd never had to worry about money, certainly not as a college student. Now he wondered if Emily was not somehow a stronger or better person than he for having done it all on her own. To turn aside his thoughts he changed the subject of the conversation.

"And did Cathy make it, too?" he asked.

Emily grinned, making him feel that she'd just been waiting for him to ask. "You could say that, seeing as you probably know her as Ciara Wilde."

He dropped his fork. "You're kidding! The actress?" He fleetingly pictured the tall, shapely star with the flowing blond hair as he'd seen her in her last movie, enveloped in satin and furs, and tried to reconcile that with a picture of Emily's childhood friend from Kentucky.

"The very same," Emily confirmed proudly. "In fact, as I'm sure you've heard on the news, she's filming a movie here in San Antonio right now, and we get together as often as our schedules allow."

He shook his head. "I'm absolutely amazed."

She laughed. "Don't let the movie star persona fool you. Cathy's nothing like her public image. She's really a sweet, down-to-earth person."

He picked up his fork. "I wasn't talking about Cathy, or Ciara."

"No? What then?"

"You! What else don't I know? Not only are you the best executive assistant I've ever had, you're an expert with children, and you came by that expertise as a poor kid from a big family in Kentucky who pulled herself up by her bootstraps and now hobnobs with movie stars. Add to that your looks, and Emily Applegate is an altogether unexpected bundle of surprises.''

She frowned at him, leaning forward slightly over her plate—and unwittingly giving him an excellent view of the deep cleavage between her breasts. "What about my looks?"

As if she didn't know. "You hide them, that's what," he said. "You pretend to be this mousy, prim, pseudo librarian type, when you're really quite beautiful."

Emily gaped at him, then pointedly clamped her mouth shut and swallowed. "If that was supposed to be a compliment, then, thank you—I think. I was unaware, however, that my efforts to present a professional appearance offended you."

"I didn't say that," he protested. "I just meant that you look different without your glasses and with your hair down and…" He cleared his throat and switched course. "You just surprise me sometimes, that's all." He lifted his napkin to his mouth and changed the subject. "Let me know whenever you and your friend want to get together, and I'll see to it that you're free."

Emily bowed her head, her long, silky hair sliding across her shoulders in a multicolored cascade of biscuit brown, sand and gold. "Thank you, Mr. Fortune. I appreciate that."

He liked the way she said his name, but he suddenly decided that it was not enough just to hear her say it in casual conversation. No, indeed. Before he was through, he would hear her whisper his name with longing and shout it with ecstasy. Wise or not, he was going to find a way to have Emily Applegate in his bed.

Then he would know all her secrets.

Four

Emily mechanically stroked the brush through her long hair, lost in thought and comforted by the mindless ritual that she performed nightly. The fact that she sat on the edge of a large, sumptuous bed made of pale twisted logs and belonging to Logan Fortune accounted for both her bemusement and her tension.

What an odd evening it had been. After dinner they'd sat on the couch and discussed her thoughts on child development and exactly what he ought to be looking for in a nanny. Logan had informed her that she needed to have her clutch adjusted, then had asked her questions about her childhood and family, but to her surprise, he hadn't mentioned Cathy—or rather, Ciara Wilde—again. In fact, he'd almost seemed to be flirting with her, Emily! But no, that couldn't be so. She simply wasn't his type.

Frankly, she'd half expected him to demand an introduction to Cathy, especially since Cathy was at present right there in San Antonio, a fact that anyone who read the daily papers, listened to radio or watched a local news program on television could not escape. Emily wasn't sure what to make of his seeming lack of interest in one of the world's most beautiful women. Cathy—or Ciara, actually, though she couldn't quite think of her that way—was very much Logan's type, while she, Emily, was anything but. Perhaps Amanda Sue's advent into his life had changed him more than she realized. More likely, though, it was merely a momentary aberration.

No doubt, once they found a nanny to take over Amanda

Sue's care, Logan Fortune would revert right back to his womanizing ways. Perhaps he would even forget about his little daughter and live as though she didn't even exist. Emily couldn't quite believe that, though, not after watching him fall head over heels for the little imp these past couple of days. He hadn't even balked when she'd suggested that he ought to again sleep upstairs tonight, that his being the one to answer his daughter's cries of distress would be a bonding experience. Of course, she'd promised to take over for him if Amanda Sue again seemed intent on keeping him awake through the night, but still, he seemed anxious to forge a real relationship with his daughter.

No, she couldn't see Logan abandoning his daughter emotionally or otherwise, but neither could she see him genuinely interested in herself. She just wasn't his type, and if she were, it wouldn't mean anything because Logan Fortune was not *her* type. She wanted a man who would be happy to settle down with one woman, a man who would love and treasure her always. She couldn't settle for anything less and still maintain her self-respect.

It was a terrible pity, all things considered, because Logan was everything she wanted in a man. Unfortunately, she knew Logan too well to believe that she could hold his interest indefinitely. No, Ciara Wilde would definitely have a better shot at it. Still, she had no intention of introducing the two, none at all, if only for Cathy's sake. After all, it was common knowledge that her friend was engaged to be married to one of Hollywood's most popular hunks. Emily couldn't help feeling a little envious since her own life seemed destined to remain forever hunkless. It had been a very long time since she'd found a man whom she even wanted to meet for coffee, let alone date, any man besides Logan, that was.

With a sigh, Emily laid aside the brush, lifted the covers and slid beneath them. The soft ivory cotton of her short, man-tailored pajamas warmed against her skin almost instantly. Within moments, she was sleeping peacefully, unaware of the sultry dreams of the man in whose bed she lay.

Heart-rending sobs. Muffled words. Pounding. Emily jerked awake, aware that the door to her bedroom had been opened. Light flooded her consciousness, blinded her eyes. She blinked, clearing tiny patches of sight that revealed rugged furnishings and desert tones. She was in Logan Fortune's bedroom, and those deeply mournful sobs belonged to baby Amanda Sue. She struggled up onto her elbows, just as Logan's considerable weight caused the side of the bed to dip.

"Ma-ma! Ma-ma!"

Emily shoved hair out of her face and croaked, "What's wrong?"

"I think she dreamed about her mother," Logan said in a clearly anguished voice.

Emily sat up straight, folding her legs beneath the covers. The first thing she saw was Logan's bare chest, burnished skin molding well-defined pectorals lightly covered with crisp, dark hair that dwindled sharply into a straight line that dropped out of sight beneath the elastic waistband of his fleece pants. Only then did she see Amanda Sue, who lay in her father's lap without struggle, one arm thrown across her eyes, tears seeping from beneath it as she sobbed. This was no temper fit but deep grief. Emily leaned forward to lift the tiny arm. Amanda Sue's temper reasserted itself, and she actually took a swipe at Emily, but Emily didn't take it personally. She stroked Amanda Sue's hair, crooning softly.

"It's all right, darling. Daddy and Emily are here. It's all right."

"Ma-ma," Amanda Sue sobbed. "Ma-ma."

"I know, sweetheart. I know. I'm sorry. I'm so sorry. But Daddy is here."

A worried look on his face, Logan shifted Amanda Sue into a sitting position. "That's right. Daddy is here, and we'll take care of you, I promise. Emily and Daddy will take care of our Amanda Sue.''

Amanda Sue took a deep, shuddering breath. ''Da-dy go,'' she ordered petulantly, and Logan looked at Emily.

She could read the question in his eyes. Did Amanda Sue want him to leave her with Emily? She probably did. After losing her mother it would be perfectly normal for her to try to bond with the first available female, but it was her father with whom she needed to bond, not a temporary baby-sitter. Emily shook her head, and Logan looked down at his daughter, turning her face up with a finger pressed beneath her chin.

''Amanda Sue, Daddy isn't going anywhere. You're my little girl, and I'm going to take care of you from now on.''

Amanda Sue's snub of a nose was running, and Emily wiped it with a corner of the sheet, finding nothing else close to hand. Amanda Sue tried to take advantage of that to shift herself into Emily's arms, but Emily folded her hands in her lap. Logan went on talking to the child in a soft, gentle voice, and presently she lifted a small hand to finger the underside of her father's beard-roughened chin. He smiled down at her, dipped his head and nipped at her fingers, catching them in his mouth. She didn't giggle as she might have at another time, but she didn't pull away, either. He kissed her palm and her cheek, whispering, ''Amanda Sue is my girl. Yes, she is. Pretty Amanda Sue is Daddy's girl.''

Amanda Sue caught a huffing breath and solemnly asked, ''Wuv Da-dy?'' She seemed to be asking whether or not Daddy loved her and if she was expected to love him in return. Emily's heart turned over, but Logan went as still as a statue. Emily felt a lump in her throat. She swallowed it down and moved closer, reaching around Logan to stroke Amanda Sue's damp cheek, all too aware of the expanse of bare skin he presented.

''Daddy loves you, Amanda Sue,'' she crooned. ''You're his very own little girl.''

She gave Logan a gentle nudge in the ribs. He jerked, then cleared his throat and smiled.

"That's right, angel. Daddy does love you." He gathered her into a fierce hug, whispering, "I love you very much."

Amanda Sue's fine hair caught in her father's beard stubble as she pulled back. Fascinated, she lifted a hand to his cheek. Then abruptly she shifted her attention to Emily. Eyes bright, she grinned and declared in a playful tone, "Wuv Mimy!"

Emily felt as if she'd been kicked in the chest. Laughing to keep the threatening tears at bay, she pulled Amanda Sue out of her father's embrace and laid her on the bed so she could tickle her tummy. "And I love you, too, munchkin," she managed, telling herself as the child giggled that it was just a game. Amanda Sue would forget her once she had completely bonded with her father, a process that seemed to be proceeding apace.

The growling of Amanda Sue's stomach stopped her giggles cold. Comically, the baby lifted her head and peered down at her belly, a look of wonder on her face. Emily and Logan laughed. Emily said, "Someone's hungry."

Amanda Sue promptly flopped over and sat up, holding out a hand. "Bobble," she demanded.

Emily smiled. "All right, young lady, a bottle it is." She gathered the child into her arms and looked at Logan. "If you'll take her back upstairs and change her diaper, I'll heat the milk and fill the bottle."

"I thought she drank cold milk now."

"She does, but warm milk will help her sleep."

He lifted both brows, suddenly seeming much too close sitting there on the side of the bed. "You mean that old wive's tale about warm milk is true?"

"I do." She tickled Amanda Sue under the chin. "A warm bottle and dry diaper ought to have this little lady snoozing again in no time." She held Amanda Sue toward her father. "Go with Daddy, sweetheart, and I'll bring you a bottle. Okay?"

Amanda Sue nodded emphatically and, leaning sideways, looped an arm around her father's neck. Logan folded her against him and kissed the tip of her nose. She giggled and wrinkled her nose at the prick of his beard. Logan chuckled and stood. "Come on, then, sweetheart. We've got one end dry, now let's try the other."

"I'll be up in a minute," Emily said, watching as they left the room. Logan's broad back was straight and strong as he carried his daughter through the door. Emily swung her feet over the side of the bed and stood. Moving quickly, she padded barefoot into the kitchen, poured milk into a measuring cup and heated it in the microwave for several seconds. After testing it, she heated it a few seconds more, then poured it into a clean bottle and carried it upstairs.

Logan was still trying to get a dry diaper on Amanda Sue, who was repeatedly lifting both legs and letting them fall again. "Amanda Sue, please stop," he was pleading. "Stop kicking. Let Daddy fix your diaper."

Emily stepped to his side. The child spotted the bottle and let out a cry, reaching for it, but Emily shook her head. "Not until you let Daddy fix your diaper."

Amanda Sue promptly collapsed her legs. After a second or so, she reached for the bottle again, and Emily handed it over. Immediately, Amanda Sue lifted her legs, much to her father's irritation. Emily took the bottle back.

"That's not fair, Amanda Sue," she admonished gently but firmly. "Let Daddy finish the diaper, and I'll give you the bottle."

Amanda Sue's bottom lip protruded in a pout, but she lay still long enough for Logan to fix the diaper and snap closed the legs of her knit sleeper. Emily handed over the bottle and picked up the baby, moving to the rocking chair. "It isn't good to let them fall asleep with a bottle in their mouths," she explained. "Leads to tooth decay."

"Ah."

She sat down and helped Amanda Sue get comfortable. "Will you wind the music box and lower the lights?"

Logan nodded, then said, "Let me wash my hands."

"Good idea."

He left them for a time, then returned to do as Emily had requested. "You can go on to bed, if you want," she said, looking up at him.

He nodded, but instead of leaving the room, he began straightening the covers in the crib, then brought Amanda Sue her Sugar Bear. She grinned her thanks around the nipple in her mouth and got her customary headlock on the stuffed toy. Within minutes, the bottle was drained and Amanda Sue was rubbing her eyes. Emily looked around to find that Logan had left the room quietly. She rocked a little while longer, then gently moved Amanda Sue to her bed, tucked her in with her Sugar Bear and kissed her forehead. Amanda Sue closed her eyes and sighed deeply, well on her way to a sound sleep.

Emily slipped out into the hall and gently closed the door behind her, the empty bottle in hand. To her surprise, Logan pushed away from the wall and came to her side, whispering, "Is she asleep?"

"Almost. I think we ought to let her get herself to sleep this time," Emily replied as they moved on down the hall. "If she cries again, go back in but don't take her out of bed. Instead, reassure her in whispers and try to settle her into sleep that way, so she'll learn that she can't expect to get picked up whenever she demands."

Logan nodded, a hand on the back of his neck. "It wasn't my imagination, though, was it? She really was crying for her mother, wasn't she?"

"I think so," Emily told him. "I think she did dream about Donna and wake up missing her. It's only natural, you know, and it may happen again, but you know how to handle it now, just keep assuring her that you love her."

Logan sighed and slid an arm around her shoulders, saying, "I owe you so much. You've taught me things I couldn't have learned anywhere else. I didn't even realize how important it was to say the words until you prodded me.''

"It's always important to say the words," she said, "but you'd figure out most of this stuff on your own in time.''

Logan shook his head. "I don't know. There's still so much to think about. For instance, shouldn't she be giving up that bottle pretty soon?''

They had reached the head of the stairs, and Emily turned to face him, intentionally dislodging his arm. It was proving difficult to think clearly with that arm wrapped around her. At the same time, it felt oddly natural. She pushed her hair over her shoulder, saying, "Your instincts are better than you think. Yes, I'd say that it was time to think about giving up that bottle, but if it was me, I'd wait a few weeks, be sure she's settled in well with the new nanny and all.''

He nodded thoughtfully. "Right. She has enough to deal with just now. What about potty training, though? When do we start that?''

Emily chuckled. The middle of the night was a strange time to be discussing such subjects, but she answered him anyway as she descended the stairs. "It's too early for that, in my opinion, but it won't be long. I'd say that in a few months you ought to buy a potty chair and put it in her bathroom. Talk about it and what it's for, then later you put her in pull-ups, disposable diapers made like panties. After that, you buy some talking books, the ones with the little recorders built into them, and when you sit her on the chair, you let her entertain herself with one of those books so she'll stay there long enough to get her business done. But even then you'll have to clean her up, praise her, and reward her, remembering that she's going to have accidents from time to time, and this is all moot because the nanny is going to handle it anyway. Not that you won't have a hand in it. You're her father, after all.''

They had reached the bottom of the stairs, and Logan took her hand in his. "This is exactly what I mean, though. I wouldn't know if the nanny was going about it right or not

if you weren't here to tell me." To her heart-thumping chagrin, he lifted her hand to his lips, brushing a kiss across
her fingers between the knuckles. "I'll never be able to
thank you enough," he added in a hair-raisingly silky voice.

"D-don't be silly," she stuttered. "A-anyone w-with a
little experience could—"

"But *you* are here," he interrupted, lifting his free hand
to stroke her hair.

Emily swallowed, her heart beating a mile a minute. He
was flirting with her! She should have known that Logan
Fortune would not let a convenient flirtation pass him by.
She put on a smile, saying, "It's late. We have a busy day
tomorrow."

"Oh, right." He dropped her hand, and she turned toward
the bedroom. He fell in beside her. She quickened her pace
a bit, but he was still at her elbow when she reached the
door. Eyes widening, she turned and lifted a hand to his
chest. For a moment he seemed puzzled, but then he chuckled. "Good grief, I forgot I wasn't sleeping in my own bed."

Emily relaxed. Of course, he forgot. Why shouldn't he?
It was his bedroom, after all. Perfectly natural. So why was
her heart beating so hard it was choking her? "Everything
will settle down soon," she told him, appalled at her breath-
lessness.

A slow, lazy grin spread across his face. His gaze lowered
pointedly to her mouth. He lifted an arm and braced a hand
against the door frame, leaning close. "We could always
share," he said huskily. "It would save me the effort of
going all the way back up those stairs, effort that could be
better used in more enjoyable ways."

Stunned, Emily stared up at him, completely at a loss for
words. Before she recovered herself, he bent his head and
covered her mouth with his. All the breath left Emily's
lungs. He sucked it up greedily, widening his lips to fit them
more perfectly to hers. The room spun, up and then down
again. Her arms floated away from her sides, her hands looking for an anchor and finding it in his upper arms. She

clamped her fingers tightly to his bunched muscles, reassured somehow by the hardness beneath the smooth, warm skin.

He dropped his arms around her, his hands rubbing up and down her back as he pressed her against him. Emily was shocked, first by the thinness of pajamas that had seemed perfectly acceptable only moments earlier, then by the weightiness of her own breasts as they encountered his chest and, finally, by the hard ridge that pressed against her quivering belly.

He really was trying to seduce her—and succeeding unless she took control this very instant. Almost reflexively, she did just that, simultaneously pushing away and telling herself that it was the situation more than herself spurring his actions.

"Emily," he protested softly, and the heat in those blue eyes nearly melted her where she stood.

She slipped through the doorway, one hand seeking the edge of the door itself as her brain searched frantically for some word, some quip to put an end to the insanity. Her wits, thankfully, were in better working order than she suspected, the words slipping out almost before she thought them.

"It isn't *that* far to the other bedroom."

With that, she stepped back and shut the door in his face, collapsing against it as her knees threatened to buckle. She heard him chuckle on the other side, and after a while, he said a silky good-night and seemed to go on his way. She knew he'd sensed her waiting there, but she couldn't think about that now. It was enough to have escaped the desire that had threatened to swamp her good sense and was even now turning her legs to water.

She stumbled over to the bed and dropped down onto it. Long minutes passed before her heart rate slowed and she began to wonder how she was going to face him in the morning. She felt alive with his touch, awash with his kiss, and some part of her marveled that such a man as Logan

Fortune might actually want her, Emily Applegate. It seemed that hours passed before she could stop reliving the moment and surrender to desperate sleep.

Logan strolled into the kitchen the next morning as if that kiss the night before had never happened.

"Good morning!" he sang, all smiles.

Amanda Sue sat in the crook of his arm, her shining, auburn hair sticking out at odd angles. "Num, num, num," she said, "hunky," pointing toward the refrigerator.

Logan chuckled and smoothed her hair with his hand. "I think that means she's hungry."

"Egg," she said clearly, nodding.

Logan laughed indulgently. "If I'm not mistaken, she's just ordered the breakfast special."

"I think I can manage an egg and toast," Emily said, keeping her gaze carefully averted. She felt oddly stung by his sunny composure, which was absurd, of course.

Amanda Sue nodded, happily amending her order, "Tose un grink. Grink!"

Emily shook her head. "What's a grink, darling?"

"Grink! Grink!" She stuck out her tongue as if to show Emily that she had a bad taste in her mouth, and everything clicked. Emily took her into her own arms and moved toward the sink.

"She wants a drink." Opening a cabinet, she took down a plastic cup, filled it from the tap and lifted it to Amanda Sue's mouth. For once, the child did not fight her for possession. Instead, she gulped and gulped and gulped.

"She communicates really well, doesn't she?" Logan asked proudly.

"She certainly does." Emily smiled as she dried Amanda Sue's mouth and carried her to the high chair. He stood there a moment longer, beaming like an idiot, until Emily indicated the coffeepot on the counter. "I made some coffee."

"Oh! Excellent!" Hurrying to the cabinet, he took down a mug and filled it. "If, um, you two are all right here, I'll just take this with me and slug some of it back before I climb into the shower.''

"No problem," Emily said evenly. "I'll get Amanda Sue's breakfast."

"Great." He sipped his coffee and looked up. If anything, his smile brightened. "Good coffee. Thanks."

Something struck her as odd about the way he kept smiling, but she put it aside as he hurried from the room, concentrating instead on getting Amanda Sue into her high chair. It was then that she noticed Amanda Sue's diaper had come loose and was bunched up in one leg of her sleeper. She couldn't help laughing. Poor Logan. He wasn't quite the model father—yet.

Despite vociferous protest, Emily managed to fix Amanda Sue's diaper, then gave the child a sipper cup of juice and some dry cereal to eat with her fingers while Emily prepared her breakfast. It was a busy enterprise, constantly righting the cup with one hand and scrambling the egg with the other and somehow catching the toast as the stainless steel monstrosity on the counter literally launched it.

Yet, during it all, Emily found her mind wandering to last night's kiss and this morning's seeming indifference. Had it really affected him so little? Perhaps she ought to be glad about that, but somehow she couldn't be. She was, in fact, a little disappointed. Apparently she wasn't even worth pursuing when doing so wasn't imminently convenient. Maybe he really had attempted that lackadaisical seduction just to keep from walking back upstairs! The idea was extremely lowering, and as determinedly as she tried to tell herself that it didn't—shouldn't—matter, somehow it did. It very much did.

"No wub!"

"I have to rub your face, Amanda Sue," Emily's voice explained patiently. "Otherwise, it will stay dirty."

Amanda Sue h-h-hubbed a phony sob, but Logan could tell that she was getting her face cleaned, the little faker. No doubt about it, the kid had a strong streak of theatricality, but it still tore him to see or hear her crying. He wondered if he'd ever be strong enough to really stand up to her the way Emily did. Emily, as it turned out, was far stronger than he'd ever realized, strong enough to close the door in his face after curling his toes with that kiss last night.

He was still smarting from her easy rejection, but he'd be hanged if he'd let her know it. That kind of thing had never bothered him before, and he wasn't going to let it do so now. Like every other man in the world, he occasionally struck out, but it had never before bothered him. Why should it? The world was full of women. If one was unwilling, another would not be. He'd even learned to laugh about it, but with Emily that had been more mechanical than actual. It was different with her somehow. It smarted more. Maybe that was because she'd been right there under his nose all this time and he hadn't even realized what he had within his grasp. And maybe it was just the situation, finding himself so completely out of his depth for the first time. He couldn't deny that she was the only thing keeping his head above water just now. All he really knew, though, was that having that door closed in his face still hurt somehow, and he didn't like the feeling. He didn't like it at all.

Taking a deep, fortifying breath, he put on a smile and stepped into the kitchen. Emily had Amanda Sue sitting on the counter next to the sink and was scrubbing her down with a washcloth. As usual, Amanda Sue had smeared at least as much of her breakfast on the outside as she'd managed to get on the inside. Having cleaned her face and between her chubby fingers, Emily then rinsed the cloth and scrubbed Amanda Sue's head with it, despite the child's attempts to fight her off. Once Emily was finished, however, Amanda Sue grinned and went happily into Emily's arms.

Logan chuckled. "She beats everything going, doesn't she? Fight you one minute, hug you the next."

Emily turned, Amanda Sue perched on her hip. Her eyes never met his, as if he was entirely extraneous to the situation. "She's a strong, charming personality, all right," she agreed, tapping the child's chin. "There's no doubt she means to have her way, but she's loving, too."

"And bright," Logan said, holding out his hands.

"As a new copper penny," Emily confirmed, moving closer as Amanda Sue reached for him. "Think you can manage her for a bit while I get dressed?" Again, she didn't bother to look at him, and so he didn't bother to answer her directly.

"Not this time, young lady," Logan admonished his daughter as she lifted the pointed end of his tie toward her mouth. "Ties are for wearing, not eating. Besides, you've had your breakfast." He flipped the tie back over his shoulder as he nodded in Emily's direction. "We'll manage. In fact, after I have a bite of something, I'll see if I can get her dressed."

"In that case I'll lay out something before I get in the shower."

"Great."

She moved toward the door, and he couldn't help following with his eyes. Her long, slender legs moved gracefully, pulling taut the seat of her short, tailored pajamas. She looked adorable with that long, shiny hair swaying against the tips of her shoulder blades.

"I like your hair down," he heard himself saying.

She stopped in the doorway and turned slightly, giving him her profile. "Thanks."

He desperately wanted to hold her there, though he couldn't really imagine why. "I, um, didn't know it was so long."

"Well, I usually wear it up," she said.

"You should wear it down more often," he told her softly, pushing away Amanda Sue's hand as she reached for the tie folded over his shoulder. Amanda Sue stuck her fingers in her mouth and studied him solemnly.

Emily turned to fully face him, her golden-brown gaze

implacable. "I don't consider it a suitable style for the office."

"I don't see why not."

"That's beside the point," she retorted smartly. "*I* don't consider it appropriate."

Logan winced inwardly. She couldn't have told him more plainly that his opinion and preferences counted for less than nothing with her. Amanda Sue made another grab for his tie just then, and Logan gave his full attention to discouraging her, aware that Emily slipped from the room as he did so. He let her go. She wasn't getting away, not really, not that easily. She was keeping him at arm's length, nothing more, and not for long if he had anything to say about it. He wasn't certain why, but he couldn't let her get away with that.

All right, he had made the moves last night, but she had kissed him back. For one scorching moment she had kissed him back with the same fervor as a drowning woman clutching a life preserver. Maybe it meant nothing—and maybe it meant that she was not so cool toward him as she pretended. If the slightest chance existed that even an ember of that passion he'd tasted so briefly the night before still burned, he'd fan it to flame. One way or another, he'd make Emily Applegate burn for him. Hell, he'd burn the house down around them before he was through.

Like a little ape, Amanda Sue tried to climb over him to get to his tie. Laughing, he pulled her off his head and cradled her against his chest, making a seat of his arms. "No, you don't. Not this time. I can't have you behaving like a little savage in front of our nanny applicants again today." Or could he? Was he really certain that he wanted to hire a nanny right away?

Emily might be indifferent toward him, but she adored his daughter, and she was good for Amanda Sue. She was good for both of them. And the longer he could keep her here in his house, the more likely she was to come around to his way of thinking. He suddenly knew without a doubt that he wouldn't be meeting any acceptable nannies that day or for some time to come. They already had the one they needed at hand.

Oh, yes, this could work out very well to his personal advantage. Emily could try to keep him at a distance, but as long as Amanda Sue held a piece of her heart, she wouldn't succeed. In fact, he vowed silently, he was going to get next to Emily Applegate if it was the very last thing he ever did. She could keep right on closing that door in his face, but sometime soon he'd find a way to open it again—and his daughter would have the care she needed in the meantime. Even Emily could benefit from this arrangement. She'd been in need of some loosening up for quite some time now, and he was an old hand at removing the inhibitions of beautiful women. Yes, indeed, this could work out very well for them all.

Five

Emily dropped into the chair behind her desk, took off her glasses and put a hand to her head, where a debilitating throb had started almost an hour earlier. "I cannot believe it's this difficult to find a competent, caring, live-in nanny."

Poised on the corner of her desk, Logan folded his arms. "They seem to come in four categories. Too young, too old, non-English-speaking, and sadistic."

Emily rubbed the hollows of her temples with her fingertips, eyes closed. Why hadn't she replenished her aspirin stash? On the other hand, if she could just relax she wouldn't have given herself this tension headache to begin with. What was wrong with her, anyway? One little kiss should not have her so on edge like this.

But it wasn't just the kiss, much as she wished it was. No, it was more than that, much more. It was the new blaze in Logan's blue eyes, the unaccustomed huskiness in his voice, the brief, unexpected touches, the intimate warmth of his smile. It was this feeling of couplehood that seemed to have replaced the old teamwork. In short, it was the effort required to resist the potent, concentrated allure of Logan Fortune. She wished he'd go back to this morning's indifference. Didn't she? Once more, she pushed away such thoughts.

"So, what are you going to do?" she asked, careful not to include herself in either the decision-making or the solution.

He sighed. "Keep looking, I guess. What else? Meanwhile, though, we can't keep bringing her to the office."

We. There it was again, that pesky plural pronoun that he'd been using with such liberal ease. Emily dropped her hands and opened her eyes, ignoring the persistent ache. "At least she's napping now. She didn't so much as close her eyes last time she was here."

He chuckled and passed a hand over his crumpled tie. "Plus my neckwear's dry. We're making some headway."

"Not that we're getting any work done, mind you," she retorted.

He got up off the corner of her desk, and she assumed that he was going into his office to take care of business while he could. Instead, he walked around behind her chair and laid his warm, strong hands on her shoulders. "Let's take care of that headache," he said smoothly, "so we can talk this over and come up with a plan of action."

"It's not that bad," she lied, but his hands were already lifting to the nape of her neck. He pressed his thumbs into the hollow there.

"Lean your head back."

She resisted, shaking her head. The weight of the pain sloshed heavily inside her skull.

"Lean your head back," he repeated firmly, moving his thumbs in small circles that radiated tiny ebbs of irresistible relief.

She laid her head back. He spread his fingers, gently massaging her scalp. Despite the pinching pull at her hairline, she sighed.

"No wonder your head's pounding. This is much too tight," he said, making quick work of the pins that held her hair in place.

She made a grab for them, but they were on her desk and he was ruffling her hair with his hands before she could manage it. Instantly she felt ten pounds lighter. His fingers began to move, walking across her scalp until they found the distended veins beneath the skin, then applying pressure in small, gentle swirls.

It was exquisite. Moaning, she felt her muscles relax and

her bones begin to melt. He kept it up, occasionally readjusting his grip and the pressure he applied, until she was mindless, the headache a distant memory as clean oxygen filled her lungs and a sense of well-being pushed away her worries. When at last he stopped, she made a sound of protest, but his hands fell to her shoulders in a pat of warning.

"Emily has a headache," Logan said, and total awareness flooded her. They were not, she suddenly realized, alone any longer. She popped her eyes open. Terence Colper, public relations guru, stood on the other side of her desk, a sheaf of papers under one arm, both hands in his pants' pockets, a grin the size of Houston on his too round, too smooth face.

"Emily should get a headache more often," Colper said, grinning down at her. "You look completely different with your hair down."

Already mortified, her face flamed hot when Logan said silkily, "I told her the same thing." Mentally, she kicked him—hard—and had no doubt that her expression telegraphed it. He ignored her, smiling smugly.

Colper lifted one eyebrow, put away his grin, and cleared his throat. "I, um, have those news releases and notices you wanted to review," he said to Logan while Emily quickly twisted up her hair and stabbed the pins into place. "If you have a minute we can go into your office and have a look at them."

"Let's do it here," Logan said, reaching for the papers. "My daughter's asleep in the other room."

Colper laid the papers on the desk. "Yeah, I, um, heard about that. It was quite a shock."

"No more to you than me," Logan said wryly, spreading out the papers and bending over them.

Emily moved aside, rolling her chair out of the way. Colper slid his hands into his pockets again, eyeing her curiously. She opened a drawer and took out a blue pencil, offering it to Logan. He took it and shoved it behind one ear, murmuring thanks as he concentrated on the papers. "This is good," he said, tapping one sheet with his forefinger.

Colper rocked back on his heels, pleased. "Thanks."

Logan went on reading. Emily turned to her computer, opening a file and trying to concentrate on it. Colper shifted impatiently.

"Have a seat, Terence," Logan murmured, plucking the pencil from behind his ear.

"Aw, I'm fine," Colper said, jingling the change in his pocket.

"Suit yourself," Logan told him. "This won't take long." He crossed out a few lines with the pencil, saying, "I think we'll leave out these particulars until everyone formally signs off on the plan."

"I thought you might say that," Colper admitted. "That's why I had my people prepare a second version there."

"Ah." Logan picked up the indicated paper and read it carefully. "Better. Much better. Excellent. Let's release it next week."

"Will do." Colper gathered up the papers and neatened them.

"Want to take a peek at her before you go?" Logan asked, brushing back the sides of his coat. Emily stopped what she was doing, alerted by the now familiar note of pride in his voice, and turned, pivoting in her chair. Colper took a moment to put it together.

"Your daughter." He sounded uncertain about the prospect.

Logan smiled. "She's cute as a bug, curly auburn hair, big, blue eyes."

Colper chuckled, relaxing into his good-old-boy mode. "I wouldn't have believed it if I hadn't seen it myself. Logan Fortune, the doting father."

Logan grinned. "I can't help it. She's just so darned cute—and smart. And stubborn. Oh, man! She wants what she wants when she wants it." His tone left no doubt that he delighted in even this aspect of his daughter's personality.

Colper shook his head and backed away, pointing a teasing finger. "You stay away from me. I've heard this stuff is catching, and I don't want any part of it."

"Spoken like a truly degenerate bachelor," Logan quipped, laughing.

"Takes one to know one," Colper declared.

They both laughed, and a demanding wail followed. Colper put a hand over his mouth. "Oops."

Logan waved a hand unconcernedly. "It was time for her to get up."

Emily was on her feet. "I'll get her."

Logan held out a restraining hand. "No, I'll do it." He was on his way even as he spoke. "Emily's been invaluable. She's a real expert on kids."

Colper smiled knowingly at Emily, as if to say that she was obviously expert in lots of areas he hadn't considered before. Emily gulped and turned away, wondering what would happen to Amanda Sue after she murdered her father.

The intended victim returned then, his sleepy-eyed daughter draped across his chest. "Amanda Sue," he said, "this is Mr. Colper."

Amanda Sue looked at Colper without interest, then reached for Emily. "Mimy. Oan grink."

"I have a drink for you right here, darling," Emily said, carrying her to the water cooler. She set the child on her feet, then pulled a paper cone and filled it with water. Amanda Sue drank heartily, then made a grab for the cone, squashing it and splashing the remaining drops of water on her shirtfront. She thought it was terribly funny and chuckled gleefully. Logan chuckled with her, and she was quick to pick up on it, showing him her perfect little white teeth in appreciation before turning back abruptly to the water cooler.

"Grink," she said, reaching for the paper cone dispenser.

"Oh, no, you don't," Emily scolded gently. "You've had your drink."

Amanda Sue twisted around with a cry of dispute and wobbled her lip for effect. "Daddy, oan grink!"

Logan laughed, his hands at his hips. "What'd I tell you?" he said to Colper, such pride ringing in every syllable that Emily could almost forgive him for embarrassing her.

A grinning Terence clapped Logan on the back. "There is justice in this world, after all."

Logan made a face. "You wait, your day's coming."

"Not if I have anything to do with it."

"That's what I thought."

It was Colper's turn to make a face. "My mother always said I was meant to be a priest. Maybe she was right."

Logan rolled his eyes while Colper laughed. "Get outta here and get back to work, you bum."

Colper saluted and pushed through the door, shaking his head and smiling. Emily, meanwhile, was trying to maneuver Amanda Sue away from the water cooler. Logan stooped and clapped his hands, opening his arms. When Amanda Sue hesitated, he enticed her with a smile. Won over, Amanda Sue ran to him, holding out her own arms. He swept her up, and she shrieked with laughter. He slung her over his shoulder. "Speaking of work," he said to Emily, "it's Friday, and we haven't accomplished a thing all week. Something has to give."

"What would you suggest?"

He pretended to tip Amanda Sue over his back, holding her by the ankles, while she giggled piercingly. "This little monkey has to be my first priority," he said, "so I want you to get someone in the office to help out temporarily. That way you can stay home with her until I find help. I'll start interviewing nannies again on Monday. Meanwhile, maybe I can catch up around here."

Emily wanted to argue, but she couldn't. It was the only solution that made sense at this point. Besides, it would keep her away from him until this attraction cooled off and he turned his attention elsewhere, which she had no doubt he would do soon. So she would baby-sit his daughter at his home, daytimes, and regain her own equilibrium; however, she would *not*, under any circumstances, stay the night

again. Not that it would make any difference as far as the
office gossip mill was concerned, not after today. But what
was done was done. "I'll call down to personnel," she said
resignedly.

Logan smiled and headed toward his office with his
daughter crawling all over him as though he were a jungle
gym. "And I'll change her diaper," he said heartily.

Emily shook her head. Colper was right about one thing:
Logan Fortune was turning out to be a surprisingly doting
father. Too bad he couldn't be counted on to make as good
a husband. Pushing such thoughts aside, Emily sat down and
dialed up personnel, explaining that Mr. Fortune required a
temporary replacement for his executive assistant.

Almost the entire remainder of the afternoon was taken
up with discussing résumés and conducting quick interviews
with those deemed suitable by both the human resources
consultant and Emily. Finally, Emily settled on a young man
named Halpern Roberts. Hal was eager, presentable in a mil-
itarily clean-cut way, and smart. Plus, he showed no signs
of being either overly impressed with or easily intimidated
by the boss. Logan approved, and it was done. Emily gathered up Amanda Sue and her gear and headed out.

Her first stop was her own apartment. The place was small
and characterless, but it was conveniently close to the office
and boasted a tiny private courtyard filled to overflowing
with plants. After checking her answering machine, Emily
changed into jeans and a sweater. Amanda Sue seemed intent on exploring, even crawling under Emily's creaky old
iron bed at one point, so Emily spent a little while following
her around the place, letting her get to know it. Then she let
Amanda Sue help her water the houseplants, which meant
taking time for a quick mop-up afterward.

While Emily was swabbing the living room floor dry,
Goody, her fat yellow cat, finally put in an appearance, having decided that Amanda Sue was interesting enough to stir
herself over. The two sized up each other like a pair of
prizefighters, carefully circling and watching until finally

Amanda Sue simply sat down and patted her knee. Goody
groomed herself for a moment while Amanda Sue made
kissing sounds, then the cat casually strode over and plopped
down next to her. Emily sat down on the floor with them
and showed the child how to pet the animal, warning her
away from the ears, eyes and whiskers. Amanda Sue took
the instruction so easily that Emily would have bet she'd
been around other animals.

Goody, who was usually fairly standoffish with everyone
but Emily herself, displayed no such inclination with
Amanda Sue. Indeed, the cat seemed to accept this little
person with far more aplomb than she ever had adults.
Whereas slamming doors often sent the cat scurrying for
cover and a backfiring car once had reduced the bedroom
curtains to instant shreds, Amanda Sue's giggles and gurgles
and shrieks seemed to have no impact on the animal at all.
That long, tigerish tail maintained a lazy, rhythmic thumping
whether the baby pounded or petted, pulled or stroked.

When it came time to go, Amanda Sue seemed to assume
Goody would go with them, and Goody seemed of the same
mind, curling herself around Emily's ankles and meowing
insistently. Emily figured, *Why not?* Goody was now de-
clawed and normally well-behaved. If Logan disapproved,
she'd just take her cat and go home. Goody, who was always
eager to take a ride, hopped into the big canvas tote bag that
Emily held open and made room for the food and litter that
Emily added. Once deposited on the floorboard of the car,
Goody hopped out of the bag and wandered around, finally
settling next to Amanda Sue in the back seat. For once the
child didn't try to escape her safety restraints. Instead she
babbled to the cat as if she was a long-time companion,
feeding her bits of dry cereal from the snack pack Emily
had given her. Watching them in the rearview mirror, Emily
could only shake her head. For the first time that day, she
found herself genuinely smiling and relaxed.

Logan put his hands to his waist and surveyed what appeared to be a happy domestic scene. Apparently he'd

acquired a cat from somewhere, a big fat yellow thing that lay draped over his daughter like a delicately striped blanket, its white belly exposed to Amanda Sue's gently patting hand. Delicious aromas wafted from the kitchen, and Emily could be heard humming as she tended whatever produced the rumble in his stomach. The house looked neat and clean, despite the toys Amanda Sue had thrown out of the playpen situated in the center of the floor where the coffee table had once been. Home had never seemed so welcoming before. He walked toward the playpen.

"Who's your friend, 'Manda mine?"

Amanda Sue looked up, delight shining in her eyes. She hopped up, the cat curling away from her, and reached for him. "Up-up!" He swung her into his arms. The cat jumped out of the pen and twined around his ankles. He bent and picked it up, too, letting it drape across his hand as he lifted it to his face. The cat met him nose to nose. "Who's this?"

"Cat," Amanda Sue said.

"I can see that." Logan sat down on the couch, the cat curling into his lap as close to Amanda Sue as it could get.

"Gooey," the child informed him, poking a finger into her mouth.

"Gooey?"

"I think she's saying, 'Goody.' That's the cat's name."

Logan looked up, smiling at Emily. He found much reason to smile. She was wearing faded jeans and a soft, butter-yellow sweater that showed off her slender, shapely form. Her feet were bare. The top two buttons in the front of the sweater were open, and when she folded her arms beneath the firm mounds of her breasts, a narrow strip of creamy skin showed above the waistband of her jeans. Her long hair had been pulled back into a ponytail that swung over one shoulder. Altogether she made a very fetching picture, so much so that he had to look away to remember what they were talking about.

"Ah, Goody, that's a strange name, isn't it?"

She nodded. "It's short for Good as Gold."

He laughed and scratched the cat's ears. "Anyone else would have called her Goldie."

"Actually it's short for Good as Gold Jr. Her mother got Goldie."

"I see. So she's yours, then."

"Hope you don't mind my bringing her along, but Amanda Sue was so taken with her when we stopped by the apartment, and—"

"It's no problem," he said, scratching the animal between the ears. The cat purred and stretched and kneaded his pant legs with her paws. Amanda Sue's muffled giggle made him look her way. She squatted in the curve of his arm, the end of his tie firmly clamped between her teeth. Logan sighed, and then he laughed. If anyone had ever told him that he'd be perfectly happy to sit with a fat cat ruining the crease in pants and a kid intent on eating his tie, Emily just standing there smiling down at him, he'd have backed slowly out of the room and called the white coat brigade.

"Do I smell dinner?" he asked, still grinning ear to ear.

"You do."

"You're an angel, Emily Applegate. What's on the menu?" he asked, carefully tugging his tie from Amanda Sue's mouth. She squawked a protest and snapped her teeth at him as if intending to bite him. "Hey!"

Emily chortled. "Besides you, you mean?"

He frowned at Amanda Sue. "You wouldn't bite Daddy, would you? It's not nice to bite people." His daughter snapped her choppers together repeatedly but made no actual attempt to bite him. It seemed to be some kind of game to her. He tickled her under the chin to distract her and was surprised to find her drooling slightly. "Is something wrong with her?" he asked Emily worriedly.

"I think she's just cutting teeth."

"Really? She already seems to have all she needs."

"In front, maybe. It's time for her molars now."

"Ah."

"And we're having tortellini for dinner."

He lifted his eyebrows in an expression of approval. "Yum."

"Cheese tortellini with shrimp sauce, to be exact."

"Double yum. When do we eat?"

"As soon as you're washed up."

He stood and stripped off his coat and tie. "Will you watch Amanda Sue for a minute while I change?"

"Do you need to ask?"

He flashed her a smile as he moved toward the bedroom. She really was an angel. He wondered how long it would take him to make that halo slip. Quickly trading his business clothes for jeans and T-shirt, he stuck his feet into an old pair of loafers and headed to the bath, where he soaped and rinsed his hands.

Emily and Amanda Sue were in the kitchen, leaving Goody to curl up in a corner of the couch for a nap. He hurriedly joined them, noticing that Amanda Sue's high chair had been moved to a new spot between his and Emily's places at the table. Amanda Sue beat the tray with a spoon, demanding to be fed while Emily cut up her tortellini and steamed vegetables.

"Just a minute, baby. Almost ready."

Logan took his chair and began filling his plate. "Looks great!"

"Not so fast there, Dad," Emily said, sliding Amanda Sue's plate over to him. "I think it's time you took over this particular duty."

He opened his mouth to protest that he was starving, but then he closed it again, seeing the look in Emily's eye. She was right. Amanda Sue was his daughter. Nodding, he pried the spoon from her determined little fingers and picked up a bite of the mangled pasta.

"Not too much," Emily coached, and he shook off some of the excess before lifting the spoon to the child's mouth.

"Mmm-mmm," she said, swallowing. Before he could even reload the spoon, her mouth was open for more. He tried to manage bites of his own dinner, as Emily always seemed to do, but Amanda Sue was like a little bird with its mouth constantly open. Worse, she consistently refused the vegetables and demanded more pasta.

"Try combining them," Emily advised, calmly eating her own dinner.

When that didn't work, he took to hiding the veggie bits in mounds of pasta. Amanda Sue actually ate a few but spit out others. Finally, Emily took pity on him.

"Eat your dinner. I'll take it from here."

He practically tossed the spoon at her. While he wolfed down his own meal, he watched Emily manage Amanda Sue with new respect. She was a natural mother. Come to think of it, she was good at just about everything she put her hand to. Her business skills were certainly top-notch, and he'd learned to rely on her instincts as often as his own. She could cook, too, bless her.

And she would be good in bed.

He knew it with that sense that men of experience have about such things. He knew something else, too. It would be different with Emily. She would not be one of those women whose faces all seemed to blur together in his memory. She would always stand out. The idea made him uncomfortable somehow, but he was no less determined to have Emily Applegate. In fact, he couldn't remember ever being so determined to win a woman. He wondered how long it would be before Amanda Sue was ready for bed.

"That was delicious," he said, watching Emily carefully guiding the spoon gripped in Amanda Sue's fist toward her open mouth. The child yanked away, turning her face at the last moment, and smacked herself in the ear with the spoonful of food.

"Oh, no," Emily said, "poor baby." She took the spoon and picked up her napkin to wipe away the food. Amanda Sue let her do so long enough to grab a fistful of tortellini and cram it into her mouth, then tried to wipe off the evidence on the back of her head. Logan couldn't help laughing.

"Don't encourage her," Emily scolded, but her own mouth was wiggling. "She has to learn to eat like a lady." She filled the spoon again and put it in Amanda Sue's hand. She instantly tossed the contents over her shoulder, threw the spoon down and started trying to get out of her chair.

"Down!" she demanded.

Emily sighed and went after the floor with a napkin. "Let me get this, then you can have your bath," she said.

"I'll take care of the bath," Logan said, getting up.

She left what she was doing and popped up onto her feet, gaping at him. "Really?"

"Yep. Like you said, it's time I started taking over, so I'll bathe Miss Amanda Sue, dress her for bed, and then I'll come back down here and clean up the dishes. How's that?"

"First you'd better catch me while I faint," Emily drawled, parking her hands at her hips.

"Anytime," he said, holding out his arms. "Swoon away."

"On second thought, save your strength. Bath time may be more of a challenge than you realize."

"Coward."

"I prefer the term *prudent*."

"You *prefer* to have the last word."

"True," she said, adding smugly, "and now I have it." With that she walked out of the room.

Laughing, Logan concentrated on stripping Amanda Sue of her shirt and getting her out of the chair. When they reached the bathroom, Emily had run the water and fixed the seat in place.

"Downstairs with you," Logan ordered. "We can handle it from here. Can't we, 'Manda mine?" The baby was already trying to climb into the tub.

Almost forty minutes later, he carried his happy daughter back downstairs. The bathroom looked like a flash flood area, and he was bare-chested, his soaked T-shirt draped over the towel bar to dry. Amanda Sue, however, was clean and ready for bed in a long, cotton-knit nightgown, despite the fight she'd put up to stay in the tub. Emily was sitting with her feet up on the couch when he came down, the cat in her lap, her feet flexing back and forth. He put Amanda Sue down next to her.

"You watch her," he said, turning toward the kitchen. "I'll be back in a minute."

"Don't bother," she said, pushing the cat off her lap and pulling Amanda Sue onto it. "I took care of it."

"Thank God," he said fervently, and turned back to drop down on the couch at her feet. She laughed and started to pull them up, but he stopped her, his hands fastened firmly around her ankles. "You deserve a good foot rub for that," he said, remembering the feel of her scalp beneath his fingertips and the way she'd moaned as he'd massaged her headache away. He wanted to hear those moans again—and more.

"My feet are fine," she insisted, but he pulled them down into his lap, anyway.

"They aren't tired? Don't hurt at all?" he asked, smoothing his hands over their tops.

"Not much," she mumbled.

"Wearing dress shoes every day must be a real pain," he said, starting with the left foot. He dug his thumbs into the arch and rubbed them outward in smooth, even strokes.

"You wear dress shoes every day," she pointed out, her breath catching a little as he massaged her instep.

"But they don't have high heels."

"Aah." Her eyelids fluttered, and she murmured, "Good point."

He lengthened his strokes to include the ball of her foot.

"Oh, my."

"Feel good?"

"Heavenly." She sighed and closed her eyes, smiling.

He moved to the right foot. Long before he finished she was as loose as a rag doll and purring as surely as the cat, a fact not lost on Amanda Sue, who immediately demanded such attention for herself. Literally scooting down Emily's body, she lay back atop Emily's legs and lifted a little foot for her father's attention. He and Emily both got a good laugh out of that, but it was nothing compared to the attack of outright glee that Amanda Sue demonstrated when Logan tickled the soles of her feet.

Emily sat up and got in on the act, kissing Amanda Sue everywhere that Logan tickled, knees, ribs, chin, behind the ear and so on. Then Amanda Sue decided to turn the tables and tickle Daddy, beginning with the bend of his elbow. He pretended to laugh, much to her delight, and then it was Emily's turn to play her part.

Emily balked.

Amanda Sue poked her sharp little fingernail into the tender inside of Logan's elbow and commanded Emily, "Tiss!"

Logan looked a challenge at Emily, who flushed, but then bent and quickly brushed a dry kiss over the spot. Amanda Sue went for the underside of his chin then, and panic flashed in Emily's golden eyes. Quickly, she turned on the cat. "What about Goody? Are Goody's paws ticklish, do you think?"

Amanda Sue promptly plopped over and tried to tickle the bottoms of Goody's paws. Logan stared a steady rebuke at Emily over the top of the child's head, but Emily would not even meet his eyes. He knew that she got the message, though. It wasn't going to be that easy. What was flowing between them would eventually back up and flood them both. He could wait.

When the cat grew tired of the game, it simply got up and went away, leaving behind a yawning Amanda Sue.

"It's somebody's bedtime," Logan said pointedly, expecting Emily to once more talk him through the process of getting his stubborn daughter to sleep. When Emily rose, he scooped up Amanda Sue and headed for the stairs.

"I'll see you Monday morning," Emily said, halting him in his tracks.

"What?"

"I have to go," she said, stepping into her shoes.

"Go?" He frowned, knowing he sounded like a perfect idiot.

"Logan, I'm going home," she said firmly. "It's the weekend. I want to sleep in my own bed, clean my house, relax. You're fine here on your own with Amanda Sue. You know what you're doing now."

"With the normal stuff," he protested, wrenching out of Amanda Sue's way as she reached for his nose. "What if something unusual happens?"

Emily gave him a look that clearly said he wasn't pulling anything on her tonight. "If something comes up that you really can't handle, just call me."

Bitterly disappointed, he cast around in his mind for some argument to sway her. Unfortunately, he found none. All that was left for him was graceful capitulation. "Okay. You're right. She's my responsibility, after all. You go on home. We'll be fine."

She turned away without another word and started looking for her cat, which had disappeared. "Goody! Come on, Goody. Let's go for a ride. Goody, Goody, Goody."

Amanda Sue put her head back and shouted, "Gooey!"

"Did she go upstairs?" Emily asked.

Logan shook his head. "Don't think so."

Emily looked around a few minutes more, but came up empty. "I'll check the laundry room. I put out a temporary litter box in there."

"If she's not there I'll help you look for her."

He put Amanda Sue into the playpen and tossed all the toys back inside with her, then followed Emily into the kitchen. She went to the laundry room door and looked inside. "There you are."

"Find her?" He went after her, arriving just as she turned back. They bumped, chest to chest. "Whoops!" His arms automatically came around her. For just an instant, they stood together, caught by a single thought, a shared memory of lips melding and desires flaring out of control.

"Emily," he whispered, aware of a faintly pleading tone.

She swallowed, her gaze dropping to his mouth, and he felt a flash of triumph. But then she jerked back, skittering away as though he'd suddenly grown fangs.

"I, uh, left the t-tote bag in the corner," she stuttered.

He tamped down his disappointment and irritation. "I'll get it."

He slipped past her and retrieved the bag, while she took care of the laundry room. She reemerged with the cat in her arms, explaining, "I bagged and disposed of the litter I'd put in there."

He nodded and handed her the tote bag. She placed the cat inside, grasped the handles and carried it toward the living room. Keeping his face carefully expressionless, he followed at a distance. She kissed Amanda Sue goodbye, stepped into her shoes, and all but ran toward the entry hall with the bag in tow. He strode after her.

"Emily?"

She stopped but didn't turn to face him.

He let her sweat a moment, then he said casually, "Have a good weekend."

Her shoulders sagged momentarily, then straightened rigidly. "Thanks. You, too." She flashed a weak smile over her shoulder and made her escape.

Logan leaned against the wall and folded his arms across his chest. She'd run, all right, as fast as her long legs would carry her, but the day was coming when she wouldn't—and they both knew it.

Six

Emily groaned when the telephone rang. It was the middle of the night, and she hadn't slept a wink. Now what? She sat up, pushed her hair out of her face and reached for the lamp on the bedside table. Snatching up the phone in mid-ring, she snapped, "What?"

"Emily?"

She closed her eyes at the sound of his voice. No doubt that was Amanda Sue screaming in the background. "What's wrong?"

"All I can figure is that she's sick!" he exclaimed. "She won't take a bottle, and she keeps kind of gagging."

"Did you take her temperature?"

"I tried, but—"

"Just put the sensor in her ear. It only takes a moment to—"

"I tell you, I've tried!" he shouted. "She won't let me!"

Emily tamped down her impatience. "Listen, you're bigger than her. How—"

"Have you ever tried to put that thing into something as small as a baby's ear when she's kicking and screaming and twisting like a cyclone?" Emily sighed, and he rushed on. "You said she might be teething, so I read that book you bought, and it says she can have a fever and an ear infection and an upset stomach from that. So I tried to give her an aspirin, but—"

"No!" Emily interrupted anxiously. "Never give a child under twelve aspirin, Logan. You have to use acetaminophen. It says that clearly in the book."

"Well, how would I know that?" he bawled. "The book's under the dresser where she kicked it!"

Emily rolled her eyes. Obviously, she was going to have to go over there. "Just sit down in the rocking chair with her," she advised, flipping back the covers. "I'm on my way."

"Hurry!" he barked, and hung up the phone.

Emily raced for the closet. Less than a minute later she was grabbing a coat off the rack by the door and heading out to the car. On normal weekdays, one could expect the streets to be empty at this time, but in San Antonio the weekend was already in full swing by the cocktail hour on Friday evening, and this Friday evening/Saturday morning was no exception. Emily navigated the traffic as quickly as possible, ever mindful that encountering a drunken driver was entirely likely. Finally, she reached the gate to Logan's secure community. The guard waved her by without a pause; obviously Logan had called to inform him of her imminent arrival. She parked the car and hopped out, rushing up the walk in her house slippers and hastily donned jeans, T-shirt and coat. She hadn't even taken time to put on underclothes! When a shirtless, attractively disheveled Logan yanked open the door, she suddenly wished she'd taken a little more care with her appearance.

"Thank God!" he exclaimed, grabbing her by the arm and hauling her inside.

"Where is she?"

"In her bed, bawling her heart out."

He hadn't exaggerated. Amanda Sue lay facedown, sobbing as though her heart was, indeed, broken into bits. Emily tossed aside her coat and drew close. Reaching out a hand, she softly stroked the shiny hair, at the same time crooning, "Amanda Sue?"

The child jerked up to a sitting position, tears streaming down her face and reached out, crying, "Mimy!"

Emily gathered her close. She felt warm but sweaty, not

feverish. Just to be sure, Emily put a hand to her forehead. Amanda Sue jerked away. "Gooey?" she asked. "Gooey!"

Logan sighed audibly, and Emily sent him a look. "Not that again," he groaned.

"What again?"

He shuffled his feet uncomfortably. "She was doing that earlier, asking for the…c-a-t."

Amanda Sue shifted in Emily's arms and reached over her shoulder toward the door. "Gooey!" she insisted. "Gooey!"

"When was this?" Emily asked.

"Just after you left."

"I see."

"The thing was," he went on uneasily, "she got upset, you know, when I told her that *it* was gone, and she started crying, so I distracted her."

Emily nodded and jiggled Amanda Sue. "Go on," she said over the child's urgently escalating calls.

"Well, eventually she fell asleep," he said, and a red flag instantly rose in Emily's mind.

"You mean that eventually you put her down, don't you?"

Logan scratched the back of his neck. "Uh, not exactly."

"So how did she go to sleep, then?"

"She fell asleep."

Emily lifted an eyebrow to let him know that this explanation was not nearly complete enough. He grimaced and went on.

"She fell asleep on the floor," he said, rushing now. "We were playing. In point of fact, I'd been chasing her, and she just eventually, you know, sat down. And then she kind of laid down, and the next thing I knew her eyes fluttered closed and she was asleep."

Emily tried very hard to keep the censure out of her tone—and failed miserably. "So then what did you do?"

He gulped. "Well, I just, you know, let her sleep. I had some reading to do, and I thought once she was good and asleep, I'd just carry her to bed. Only, the time kind of got away from me. She'd been lying there a couple of hours, I guess, before I realized how late it was getting. Then when I picked her up—well, I'm not very good at this stuff yet, you know."

"She woke up," Emily surmised. Amanda Sue had subsided somewhat and was watching them both now, her hand in her mouth, her breath coming in little gasps.

He nodded. "Yeah, and she was kind of cranky."

"Naturally."

He gave her a dark look. "You said yourself that she has the memory of an elephant," he pointed out. "She started asking for the *you know*. And I just tried to ignore it, but she got more and more upset, and I started to worry, so I got out the book, and—"

"I think I've got the picture," Emily said crisply, turning down the lights and moving toward the rocking chair. "I want a warm, wet washcloth."

He left the room immediately. Emily sat down in the rocking chair with Amanda Sue, who immediately started to buck. Emily let her squirm, speaking in a low, calming tone. "It's all right, darling. I know you're tired and angry, but we can fix that. Be still now. Let Emily hold you. That's right, darling. I love it when you sit in my lap and let me hold you. You're a beautiful, charming little girl, and your daddy's very lucky to have you. Just a minute now, and we'll wash your face all clean again."

Logan finally returned with the warm cloth. Amanda Sue fought it at first, but she was very tired, and the warmth was soothing. When her face was clean and her tears dried, Emily began to rock. "Hand me Sugar Bear," she said softly to Logan.

Amanda Sue made a desperately needy sound when the bear was produced and immediately got it in a headlock.

"Should I heat another bottle?" Logan whispered, but Emily shook her head. She would explain later that with clogged sinuses it would be difficult, if not harmful, for the child to nurse. Amanda Sue put her hand in her mouth and heaved a deep, ragged breath. Emily began to softly sing. Amanda Sue almost dropped off several times, then would jerk herself awake and look around, but finally her eyes closed and didn't open again. Emily rose and laid the child in her bed. Amanda Sue stirred, but Emily continued to softly sing and patted her back until she settled again. Finally, she picked up her coat, signaled Logan to follow and they quietly left the room. She waited until they were downstairs to tell him what a jerk he was.

"Will you kindly try to remember that Amanda Sue is merely a small person and not the alien life-form you make her out to be."

"That alien life-form stuff was a joke," he said, frowning.

"Well, chasing a child around the house until she literally collapses is not! For pity's sake, you're supposed to calm a child at bedtime not hype her up."

"I didn't know!" he protested. "I was just trying to distract her."

"Next time try reading her a book!"

"What are you yelling at me for? I didn't do it on purpose." he complained. "You know I'm new at this. I'm doing my best."

Emily stepped back. He was right. She had to give him the benefit of the doubt on this. He would never intentionally upset his own daughter in an attempt to get her, Emily, back over here. In fact, he'd probably forgotten all about that silly flirtation. "I'm sorry. It's late, and I'm tired."

He hung his head, heaving a deep sigh. "I'm the one who should be apologizing, calling you out at night like this. I just didn't know what else to do."

Emily nodded. She could be gracious and take part of the blame here. "I never dreamed she'd get so fixated on my cat. Maybe you ought to get her a cat of her own."

"Now that's an idea," he said, brightening. "Hey, why don't we do that tomorrow? You can help us pick it out. What do you think, a pet shop or the pound? I usually lean toward the pound, frankly, but maybe Amanda Sue's first kitty ought to be something special, a purebred, maybe. What do you think?''

Emily smiled, imagining Amanda Sue with a fluffy white ball of fur or maybe a sleek Siamese. It would have to be a cat good with children. They couldn't just take the first pretty thing they found. Emily envisioned a happy shopping trip, Amanda Sue's exclamations of delight, the sweet little feline faces clamoring for attention, Logan proudly shelling out the cash required to keep his little princess happy. It would be such fun, just the three of them and a world full of kittens. The three of them. Just like a family. Suddenly reality snapped into place, and Emily literally recoiled. Logan cocked his head.

"Well, what do you think?" he pressed.

Emily squared her shoulders. "I think pet shopping falls far, far beyond the duties of an executive assistant," she stated flatly.

His face fell. "I wasn't thinking of it like that, actually. I just thought it might be fun."

"I'm sure it will be, but you don't need my help."

"You don't want to go?" It was half question, half statement, and it begged a reply.

Emily cleared her throat. If she said no, it would be an outright lie, so instead she calmly told him that she already had plans for the weekend.

"Ah. Of course. Well, maybe I'll just get her a stuffed kitty, and you can bring Goody over when you come next," he said mutedly.

"On Monday," Emily clarified. "When I come on Monday."

Logan gulped as if just then realizing that he'd have the whole weekend to get through. "Right. Monday. Well, you enjoy your weekend," he said, ushering her toward the entry hall. "Don't worry that I'll be calling you again, either," he went on. "I completely forgot that I can call Mom out at the ranch. She couldn't just drive over, of course, but she can talk me through whatever I need to know. You just, um…'' They were at the door, and he reached around her to open it, saying, "That is, good night, Emily. Again."

She felt lower than a rat jumping ship. "Good night," she said, throwing on her coat.

"Oh, wait." He laid a hand on her shoulder just as she started to turn. "I know I keep saying this, but it's because you keep bailing me out. Thank you."

He smiled down at her, and after an moment his gaze dropped to her mouth. Suddenly she was intensely aware of her surroundings, of the dark, cool foyer, the bright, cooler night, the soft pull and slide of her own clothing against her bare skin. The thought occurred that if he kissed her now, really kissed her, as before, he'd know she wasn't wearing a bra. Might he touch her then? Would his hand rise of its own volition to cup her breast? She could almost feel it, the weight and heat of his hand, the muscled mass of his body. She tilted her face up, breath bated, mouth dry as cotton. His head lowered—and he pressed a kiss in the center of her forehead.

Emily experienced a moment of confusion followed swiftly by sharp disappointment. The next thing she knew she was standing on the doorstep, Logan watching from the partly opened door. He smiled, and she smiled. Forcefully. Then there was nothing left to do but turn and walk to her car, get inside and start the engine. Logan waved one last time and closed the door.

Emily frowned as she put the transmission into gear. What was wrong with her? She was shaking like a leaf, and it wasn't the cold. More importantly, what was this yawning emptiness inside her, this feeling of deficiency? Hadn't she been whole and reasonably satisfied with herself and her life just…when? Yesterday? The day before? She tried to think as she drove away from the luxurious town house. Everything had been fine right up until… He had kissed her. He had kissed her, and everything had changed. She had the awful feeling that nothing would ever be the same again.

* * *

Logan collapsed onto the sofa and lifted a hand to the back of his neck, rotating his head in an effort to relax the muscles. Exhaustion pulled at him. It was two o'clock in the afternoon, and his energy and strength were absolutely depleted. He used to think that he was in such good physical condition. He'd spend his free afternoons swimming or playing racquetball or volleyball—not to mention climbing mountains or skiing, tennis, golf, the occasional pickup basketball game, rafting or galloping around the ranch on horseback playing cowboy. If anyone had told him that one strong-willed toddler would prove his ultimate challenge, he'd have laughed them out of Texas. Yet, here he was, savoring this moment of quiet inactivity with Amanda Sue tucked up safely in her bed for her afternoon nap, hoping and praying she'd stay down for at least an hour—and looking forward to the moment when she lifted her curly auburn head and demanded he attend her.

Chuckling, he laid his head back and closed his eyes. How did these young mothers do it? Never again would he take the average mom for granted. His house was a wreck. His kid was a miniature whirlwind, tearing through things before he could even open his mouth, let alone get to her. So far she'd scattered his CD collection through three rooms, emptied his closet of all his shoes—some of which he despaired of ever finding again—destroyed a number of magazines, plastered his kitchen with cereal and tuna salad—which was definitely *not* one of her favorite foods—and turned his house into one giant toy box. He knew that he ought to get up and set everything straight, but he simply did not have the energy. Twisting around, he put up his feet and prepared to catch a snooze himself, so naturally the doorbell rang.

Muttering, he leaped up and hurried to put a stop to it before Amanda Sue woke screaming. He yanked open the door, prepared to scowl—and smiled instead.

"Emily!"

"Hi. How's it going?"

He couldn't help giving her the once-over. She looked delectable in a body-hugging, dark wine-red turtleneck sweater and matching leggings. Her long hair, held back by a wide white elasticized headband, swung against her shoulders in a soft, brown-gold fall. Her feet were covered, in deference to the cold weather, no doubt, in tasseled loafers and white socks with the tops folded around her slender ankles to form fat, neat cuffs. The corduroy car coat thrown over her shoulders reminded him that the nip in the air now permeating the entry hall was coming from outside.

"Come in!" he said, hopping back out of her way. She hesitated for maybe one second before stepping over his threshold and closing the door behind her. He led the way into the living room, wincing as he saw it again. "Uh, this isn't as bad as it looks."

She stepped up next to him, and he felt rather than heard her indrawn breath. "Oh, my," she said.

He bowed his head, scratching the back of his neck. "Okay, so it is as bad as it looks, but she's asleep right now, so I can..." He couldn't say it any more than he could do it. Walking over to the couch, he dropped down onto it with a heartfelt sigh. "I feel like I've been dragged behind a horse through a pasture of cactus and a herd of cows."

She had the gall to laugh while standing there bursting with healthy energy and looking as though she'd just walked off the page of a magazine. Why had he never before realized how stunningly beautiful she was? For the first time in his life he actually felt uncomfortably ill groomed. He needed a shower and a shave and clothes that didn't look ready for the ragbag. Self-consciously he raked his fingers through his hair, thinking that he probably needed a haircut, not to mention a comb.

"Put your feet up for a few minutes," she said. "I'll make us some coffee."

He wanted to say that she didn't have to do that, but instead he said what he felt. "That sounds great."

Tossing aside her coat and small handbag, she headed for

the kitchen. He fought the urge to run for the shower. Lying back on the couch, his head pillowed on the arm, he closed his eyes and tried to think how to turn this unexpected visit into a romantic encounter. The next thing he knew something delicious and compelling tickled his nostrils, rousing him. "Hmm?"

"Maybe I should let you sleep."

He came fully awake and sat up, rubbing his eyes with the heels of his hands. "Man, that smells wonderful."

"Here, then," she said, pushing the mug into his hands. He cupped the warmth and let the rising steam bathe his face with the delectable aroma of coffee and the siren call of caffeine. Finally, he sipped.

"Good."

She sat down in the chair across the room from him. "So, tell me about your morning."

He shook his head. "Two terms come to mind. *Greased lightning* and *putting out fires.*"

She chuckled again. "Well, I don't see any smoke damage, so I'd say you did pretty well."

"That's what you think," he retorted. "My housekeeper's going to take one look at this place and quit. I might as well start interviewing maids along with nannies."

"We'll take a swipe at it together in a few minutes. Then, afterward we'll discuss the concept of setting limits."

He was grateful as all get out, but he couldn't help saying, "I thought you had plans."

"Got through early," she said dismissively.

He knew he shouldn't probe, but he couldn't seem to stop himself. "Did you get to spend some time with Ciara Wilde?"

"No, actually I got to spend some time at the laundry and paying bills."

"Oh. Well, in that case I'm glad you got through early."

"I thought you might be," she said wryly. She sipped her coffee, then added, "I can't stay too long. I have groceries in the car."

"I'll bring them in," he said, getting to his feet.

She waved him back down, capitulating easily. "They'll be okay for now. Why don't you take a minute to freshen up? You'll feel better."

This time he did race to the bathroom, where he quickly brushed his teeth, combed his hair and got out the electric razor. It didn't do a great job, but it was better than nothing, and he didn't have time for a manual shave. He took the time to change his shirt, opting for a soft, blue plaid flannel in hopes that she would think he'd chosen it for its warmth instead of its eye-enhancing color. The jeans would do, he decided, and went out. She was in the kitchen, so he picked up his coffee mug and followed her in there.

She was down on her knees with a wet paper towel, scrubbing food off his floor.

"Here let me do that," he said, knowing he should have done it sooner.

"What is this?" she asked in a tone of disgust.

"Something my daughter does not relish," he said, getting down there with her. "Tuna salad."

"Ah. What a pity I didn't bring Goody. Tuna is one of the few things she'll eat besides her dry feed."

"Another good reason to get a cat," he quipped, and she actually smiled at him.

"You'd do better with a mop at this point."

"Right. What do you think, pound or pet shop?"

She laughed. "Try the laundry room."

"Good idea! I knew I kept you around for some reason." He got up and went to the laundry room for the mop, which he carried to the sink and dampened beneath the spigot.

"Better wipe down that cabinet front first and let me clean her chair."

"Yes, ma'am."

He used the sponge, rinsing it out carefully when he was done, then helped her wipe down the high chair with an antibacterial cleaner. When they were done, she refilled both their coffee mugs and tiptoed to the table while he swabbed the floor. He joined her a few moments later, and they sipped coffee, discussing how to toddler-proof his house and teach his daughter to keep her hands off his things without resorting to spankings or hand slaps and a one-word vocabulary of no. When the floor was dry, they went to the living room to straighten up there. She found one of his dress shoes beneath the chair and his cowboy boots beneath the stairwell. He marveled at this last. How on earth had little Amanda Sue gotten those heavy boots under the stairwell without him noticing? What else had she done that he remained unaware of? His skin crawled with the thought.

"Those plugs you bought for the electrical outlets are in a drawer in the kitchen," he said. "I'll go get them."

He not only got them, he used them, plugging every electrical outlet within four feet of the floor. While he did that, she picked up the toys and remaining shoes scattered through the living and bed rooms. Then she tossed out the torn magazines while he put the CDs back in order and moved the storage rack into a corner behind a table. Some minor shuffling made sure that Amanda Sue couldn't get to his magazines again, and while he was at it, he put a special childproof catch on the doors of the entertainment center. He was almost through with that when the monitor on the coffee table crackled and a little voice said sleepily, "Daddy?"

A thrill shot up his spine. He glanced at Emily, whose smile seemed to say he'd done well for some reason. As she made herself comfortable on the couch, he galloped up the stairs. Amanda Sue was yelling at the top of her lungs by the time he got there.

"Dad-dy! Up!"

"I'm here, sweetheart."

She plopped down on her butt and smiled at him, then toppled backward and spread her legs. He didn't have to be told in words that she was ready for a dry diaper. Laughing, he changed her, cleaned his hands with an antibacterial wipe and wrestled her shoes on her while she repeatedly demanded a "grink."

"Emily's here," he told her as he hurried toward the stairs with her in his arms.

"Mimy," she cried at the top of the stairs. To his surprise she didn't immediately go into Emily's arms, however. Instead she clung to him, pointed to the kitchen and said, "Grink."

"We'll be right back," he said, hurrying away. With Amanda Sue on his hip, he got the juice from the refrigerator and took down a clean cup and lid. He sat her on the counter, trapped her there with his body and filled the cup. She was reaching for it before he got the lid snapped on, but he managed. When he handed her the cup, she murmured something that sounded very much like, "Kank 'ou." Mechanically he said, "You're welcome."

"Looks like you've got it all under control," Emily said from the doorway. He turned, one hand automatically reaching for Amanda Sue, being sure she stayed put.

"You can say that after the way this house looked when you came in here?"

"Get used to it." Emily smiled.

"You mean, it's always this hard?"

"Yep, but people keep having children."

He looked at Amanda Sue, and the real wonder of parenthood finally hit him. It was simply that even knowing how hard it was, he'd do it all over again. He shook his head. "Do you suppose it's biological?"

Emily seemed to know exactly what he was talking about. "I don't know whether it's biological, emotional, or something no one's even thought of yet," she said, "but I've seen it time after time, and I know this, too. It doesn't always happen. I know people who shouldn't have been parents, who shouldn't be *allowed* to be parents. And then I know those who will never realize their full potential as parents for one reason or another. But you're one of those meant to be a daddy. Don't doubt that about yourself."

He couldn't speak for a moment. She'd hit the most vulnerable spot in his psyche. Finally he got control of himself. "I've been so afraid I'd be like my father," he said, "but maybe there's more of my mother in me than I realized."

"Mama," Amanda Sue said hopefully, sitting down her cup with a crack.

Logan jerked around. "Oh, darlin', I'm sorry. I didn't mean to say that." He pulled her into his arms. "Mama isn't here, honey. I wish she was for your sake, but she's not. She would be if she could, but Mama can't come, Amanda Sue, so Daddy is going to take care of you from now on. My poor angel. I love you, 'Manda mine."

Amanda Sue laid her head on his shoulder and hugged him back calmly.

Logan felt triumphant that he was able to soothe his daughter, and when he looked once more at Emily, he knew it wasn't wishful thinking—and he knew exactly who he had to thank for it. There were four remarkable females responsible for these changes in him. His mom was first, of course, because of her parenting and her trust in his inherent decency, and then there was Donna, who had given him the treasure that was Amanda Sue. Of course, Amanda Sue herself was the catalyst, the lynchpin, the very center of his suddenly centered universe. But it was Emily who carefully schooled and trained him.

Emily stood in the breach when instinct failed and changes overwhelmed him. Emily made him believe that he could be the father he wanted to be, the father Amanda Sue deserved. It was Emily who made him want things he'd never wanted before, made him value things he'd never even thought about before. Yes, if Amanda Sue was the center, then it was Emily who made it glow with hope and an inexplicable sort of satisfaction.

He was suddenly a little afraid, afraid that he wouldn't be able to get her. That he wouldn't be able to keep her around as long as he needed her. What, after all, did he know about keeping a woman around? All he'd ever known was walking away. How often had he done that, without even a second thought? He'd walked away from Amanda Sue's mother without even wondering if he might have made a baby with her. All these years he'd assumed that every woman who caught his eye would stay with the least encouragement from him, if not for him, then for the Fortune millions.

But he'd always known, on some level, that Emily was the exception. From the beginning she had responded to his flirtatious overtures with pithy put-downs and a capable, no-nonsense efficiency that had made her indispensable. He wondered if his pride hadn't made him see her as mildly attractive rather than the astounding woman who now made his heart pound with longing. He wondered if he'd met his match in Emily Applegate.

Would she be the woman he couldn't get? Or the woman he was meant to have?

Seven

Emily couldn't believe she was doing this. Whatever possessed her to agree to go swimming in the dead of winter or what passed for it in this part of Texas? More to the point, what had possessed her to agree to spend Sunday with Logan Fortune? Oh, the indoor pool in Logan's complex was properly heated—along with the indoor tennis, racquetball, basketball and volleyball courts, not to mention the weight rooms, running track and, of course, the sauna—but that wasn't the point. She should be keeping her distance from Logan, but she hadn't even managed to stay away for the weekend.

Still, he had a point about not being able to work out with Amanda Sue around, and the little imp did love water. So here Emily sat, suited out in last summer's bright yellow-gold, halter-top, V-neck, red-trimmed, one-piece bathing costume, wet to the skin, her hair dripping down her back, self-consciously trying not to notice how sexy Logan looked reclining next to her poolside in nothing more than boxer-style swim trunks. The man was built like a brick wall, firm, hard, and sturdy, but no brick wall had ever made her want to press herself against it in breathless anticipation. No brick wall had ever made her skin tingle and her heart pound by just brushing against her under water. Amanda Sue yanked on her hair, reminding Emily why she was here, and then launched herself over the arm of Emily's chair at her father.

"Hey, sugarplum!" Logan caught her against his chest, smiling his welcome and tucking her towel around her wet romper to keep her warm. "Did Daddy's girl enjoy her first swim?'' He glanced at Emily. ''At least, I assume it was her first swim.''

''I think that's a safe assumption,'' Emily said, ''at least as far as a real swimming pool goes. She might have splashed around in a kiddie pool before this, but she didn't seem at all familiar with her surroundings when we first took her in.''

''Yeah, I noticed that. She seemed a little intimidated at first, almost afraid.''

''Well, she's not afraid anymore,'' Emily said, chuckling.

Logan tickled Amanda Sue's tummy through her wet romper. She slapped her hands against the spot and giggled. ''Not this girl,'' Logan teased. ''This girl's part fish.'' He made a fish face, sucking in his cheeks and puckering his mouth. Amanda Sue leaned forward and kissed him. Both Emily and he laughed. Amanda Sue looked around her to see what was so funny, then laughed with them.

''What a little doll!''

Emily looked up to find a leggy blonde in a white bikini smiling down at them, or rather, at Logan. She wasn't the first of Logan's neighbors to gush over Amanda Sue. The child was a virtual woman magnet, and when Amanda Sue and Daddy took center stage, Emily found herself relegated to the background. She resigned herself to another period of invisibility.

''Hi, Lorinda,'' Logan said brightly. ''This is my daughter, Amanda Sue.''

''My goodness, she's a dream! Just look at that hair!''

''Yeah, she takes after her granny that way.''

''And she has your eyes.''

''That's what they tell me.''

A petite brunette name Mercedes with ink-black hair and the classical features of her Mexican ancestors joined them, and the gushing began all over again.

''I didn't know you had a daughter!''

''Yep, she's sixteen months old.''

''What a beauty!''

"You'll get no argument from me on that."

"Oh, a proud papa," Lorinda cooed. "How sweet."

"Will she let me hold her?" Mercedes asked.

"Sure," Logan said, only to have Amanda Sue flop over onto her belly and throw her arms around his neck, hiding her face in the hollow of his shoulder. Logan chuckled. "Make a liar out of your old man, will you?" He beamed up at the brunette. "Guess she's having an attack of shyness."

"Oh, that's all right," the blonde cooed, petting the back of Amanda Sue's head.

The child made a sound of protest that sounded remarkably like the bleat of a sheep, shrugged Lorinda away and reached for Emily, who caught her up and pulled her onto her lap, whispering, "Amanda Sue? What's wrong? You're not shy. You're not a shy girl."

"Oh, you must be her mom," Lorinda said, the words edged with ice despite the white smile that accompanied them. No one else had been brash enough to come right out and ask, but Emily had felt the weight of their speculation. She had hoped, for Amanda Sue's sake, that everyone would remain quietly, politely curious. She should have known better.

With her attention focused on Amanda Sue, Emily tried not to tense. The child had gone perfectly still at the mention of her mother, her eyes searching steadily across the limits of her vision. Emily waited calmly for the usual heart-wrenching demand, but Amanda Sue seemed to know that it was pointless. She put her hand in her mouth and slumped back against Emily's chest.

"Amanda Sue's mother was killed recently in a plane crash," Logan said quietly. Then he smiled and reached for Emily's hand, saying, "Emily, here, is my good right arm, the Ace Number One Executive Assistant of all time—and then some." He touched noses with Amanda Sue, his face close to Emily's breast, and added, "Don't know what we'd do without her, do we, 'Manda mine?"

He shook his head in emphasis, and Amanda Sue copied the movement, which was why, Emily felt sure, that she felt a spurt of delight. The women crowded around Logan, offering condolences and thinly veiled consolation. Emily felt her chest expand with a burning surge of jealousy. She thought for a moment that it might choke her, but then Logan threaded his fingers through hers and lifted their entwined hands onto the arm of her deck chair, and she felt a guilty flash of smug satisfaction.

Amanda Sue sat up just then and pointed at the pool, wheedling, "Whimmin, Daddy."

"You ready to go swimming again, darlin'?" he asked, then glanced at Emily while the other women twittered about how cute it was that his daughter could ask for what she wanted. "What do you think?"

"Another fifteen minutes," she said, ignoring those women, "then a nap."

Amanda Sue shook her head. "Nap no!"

"Nap, yes," Logan said, getting to his feet and hauling her up into his arms. "But swimmin' first."

"Whimmin," she said, nodding emphatically. She held her hand out to Emily, opening and closing her fingers. "Mon, Mimy. Whimmin."

The women laughed again, but they were moving away as Emily got to her feet. "Nice to meet you," one of them said, and Emily realized belatedly that she was the one being addressed. She managed a smile and a nod as Logan grabbed her hand and towed her toward the shallow end of the pool, Amanda Sue on his hip.

Amanda Sue looked down and watched the water move up her father's legs toward her as he descended the steps. When the water reached the tops of his legs, Logan sat down, and Emily sat down opposite him. In an already familiar game, Amanda Sue pushed away from her father and began paddling and kicking furiously in an upright position. She sank like a stone, and Emily shared with Logan a moment of silent panic, but just as he reached for her, Amanda

Sue propelled herself upward and broke the surface of the water again, grinning with delight. Logan reached, instead, for Emily's hands. Stretching out their arms, they made a platform for her. Amanda Sue settled on top of their arms, then leaned over carefully onto her side, rolled onto her back and lay there, waiting for them to remove their support. She floated between them like a cork, still and solemn as she concentrated all her tiny being on staying afloat.

"I can't believe she does this," Logan said. "She's as fearless as a water sprite. Scares me to death."

Emily smiled sympathetically. "When they're utterly intrepid like this, you can't help wondering what they'll attempt when you're not around."

"Exactly. What I have to wonder is if you ever learn to really let go of them?"

She laughed. "Obviously. Otherwise, you'd be at the ranch right now, and I'd be in Kentucky."

"Oh, good argument for fostering independence."

"I'd rather be here, too," she quipped thoughtlessly.

The smile he gave her was warm enough to melt glass. Just then Amanda Sue put her feet down and sank again. She bounced off the bottom of the pool and reached for her father, blinking water out of her eyes and sputtering husky laughter.

"Whoa!" Logan caught her before she sank again and pulled her against his chest. "Had enough floating?"

"Woo ack!"

"Okay, you can swim on Daddy's back."

He swirled her around in the water by the hands and pulled her up onto his back, placing her arms around his neck. Amanda Sue held on that way while he moved slowly into deeper water. Emily moved behind them, helping Amanda Sue kick her legs from the hips, her hands around Amanda Sue's knees. Logan headed back to shallower water, avoiding other swimmers. Growing bolder, Amanda Sue loosened her hold on him until she maintained contact only by gripping the hair on the top of his head.

By the time they reached the steps across the end of the pool, a number of older children had gathered there. Amanda Sue was clearly intrigued. Logan sat her on the second step, and the children welcomed her into their company. Within minutes a splashing contest had erupted, and Amanda Sue was in the thick of it, holding her own with flailing arms and legs while her protective daddy held her in place with both hands around her middle. When one little boy about four or five years of age popped up out of the water suddenly at her side, Amanda Sue shrieked with laughter. Soon they were all doing it, and even when the game grew old Amanda Sue continued to feign shocked delight. Finally, she'd had enough and reached for Emily.

One tiny hand caught in the V-neck of Emily's well-worn suit and tugged, exposing the full mound of one breast almost to the nipple before Emily could pull her closer. Embarrassment scorched Emily from the chest upward. She sank down to sit on the bottom of the pool, Amanda Sue cradled to her chest while she hoped that no one had noticed. None of the children giggled; no one else hooted or snickered. Emily began to breathe a sigh of relief, only to look right up into Logan Fortune's blue, blue eyes. Her heart stopped at the look of raw hunger on his face. For a long moment, his gaze held hers. Then he turned and plunged into a long gliding stroke that carried him quickly the length of the pool.

He was on his sixth lap when Amanda Sue grew restive. "Daddy, Daddy!" she called, but Emily doubted that he could hear her over the sounds of his own strokes. She began to whisper to the child about what a strong, powerful swimmer her daddy was, pointing out how his arms cleaved the water, head turning side to side, legs scissoring beneath the water. Amanda Sue studied him as if she actually understood all that Emily was saying, but every time he drew near the shallow corner where they sat, she called to him again. Finally, he stood and waded toward them, water sheeting off his body and flattening the dark hair dusting his chest. He was breathing heavily, but he had a smile for his daughter.

"Time to go, sweetheart. Daddy's ready for a nap."

"Nap no," Amanda Sue said, reaching for him. "Grink. Num-num."

"Okay, drinks and yum-yums first," he said, wading toward the steps, "then nap."

Emily followed behind them, feeling oddly forgotten and superfluous. Logan carried his daughter into the open shower with him, then stripped away her sodden romper, diapered her and dressed her in the dry clothing he'd brought with them, while Emily rinsed off the chlorine all alone, wrapped a towel around her head and pulled her jeans on over her wet suit. He brought Amanda Sue to her so he could go into the locker room and change. He returned wearing jeans and a sweatshirt, his wet suit rolled into a towel. Emily had dried and fluffed Amanda Sue's hair with a towel, then thrown on a terry-cloth jacket that belted at the waist. They stepped into shoes and headed out.

By the time they got back to the house, Emily's teeth were chattering. Logan ordered her into the bedroom to get changed and dry her hair while he fixed Amanda Sue a snack. She found the hair-dryer right where he said it would be, but it was a low voltage, handheld comb-type, and by the time her long, thick hair was dry enough to endure, some considerable time had passed. She quickly stripped off her suit in his bathroom, then dragged on underwear, damp jeans and a big, roomy, moss-green sweater. When she opened the door and stepped out into the bedroom, Logan was there, waiting.

Suddenly her heart was pounding, her chest too tight to breathe. He leaned a hip against the corner of the dresser and folded his arms determinedly. She fought the urge to gulp and struggled to keep her tone light and casual. "Where's Amanda Sue?"

"Sleeping."

She nodded. "Sorry I took so long. It's all this hair." He

said nothing to that, so she busied herself stowing her wet suit and towel in the bag, making small talk to cover the electricity arcing through the air. "I knew she was exhausted, poor thing, but she really seemed to enjoy the pool. We probably shouldn't have kept her in so long. I'm pretty tired myself, so I know you must be." She gathered her things and moved toward the door, smiling lamely. He stepped in front of her. She looked up, both dismayed and thrilled to see the look on his face.

"Say my name," he demanded huskily, taking the bag from her hands and tossing it away.

She blinked up at him. "What?"

"Say my name," he repeated, holding her gaze with his. "You rarely call me by name." His hand rose and hovered around her shoulder, brushing gently at her hair. "I want to hear it." He cupped her face with his palm, urging, "Say my name."

She didn't know how to refuse. She closed her eyes and whispered, "Logan."

"Again," he insisted, sliding his hand around to the nape of her neck, threading his fingers through her hair. She knew what he wanted, and it was more than she could give him. She opened her eyes, intent on honesty and good sense.

"Logan, I—"

He kissed her, his hand bringing her face to meet his. Good sense retreated as sensation charged in, and she found herself kissing him back. His free hand covered her breast, the very breast that Amanda Sue had so innocently exposed, and Emily knew that she'd been waiting for it, needing it. When he pulled back and his hands fell to the bottom of her sweater, she knew she couldn't allow him to do what he was doing, but somehow her arms rose as he pulled the sweater up. Then he was tossing it away.

"Logan, I can't—" she began, but his mouth came to hers once again, his hands sliding over bare skin as they circled her torso. She didn't even realize that he'd unfastened her bra until he shoved it away. She tried once more

to resist, gasping, "Logan, wait." But then his hands cupped
and lifted her breasts, and lightning shot through her, throwing her head back and stopping her heart.

"Beautiful," he said in a choked voice. "Sweet heaven,
I want you!"

He backed her against the bed and toppled her over. Pulling his T-shirt over his head, he followed her down, bracing
his upper body weight on his elbows.

"I want to make love to you, Em. Let me make love to
you."

She could feel herself melting, opening, surrendering.
Frightened, she lifted both hands to his chest, holding him
off. "I can't."

"I need you, Em," he told her, holding her with his eyes
as surely as his body. "I always have, but now more than
ever."

"I can't," she said, breathlessly desperate. "You're my
boss."

He pushed her hands away and lowered his head, rolling
it gently side to side, nuzzling her breasts, scorching her with
his breath. "We're a team," he said, "a good one, the best."

"You're my...boss," she repeated. *And you'll never love
me.*

"I want to be more," he whispered, his mouth bathing
the peak of one breast with moist heat. She was drowning,
sinking. Frantically, she dug her hands into the mattress,
shoving herself backward, dragging her body against his. He
crawled after her, over her. She scrambled backward and
right off the side of the bed. He let her go, collapsing onto
his side with a huff of disappointment. She got her feet under
her and careened away, bouncing off the wall and the corner
of the bed, her hands covering her breasts. Logan rolled onto
his back, the heels of his hands pressed into the hollows of
his eyes.

She saw her sweater hanging off the edge of the dresser
and lunged toward it, yanking it on even as she dipped down
to scoop up her bra and cram it into her rear pocket. He

came up into a sitting position then, and she leaped back. He looked away, a muscle working in the hollow of his jaw. "That's just great. I want to make love to you, and you recoil like I'm going to beat you."

"I'm sorry," she said, stepping closer again. "I didn't mean it like that."

"Oh, that's better," he drawled cryptically. "You just can't stand for me to touch you."

"I didn't mean it like that, either," she said softly.

He looked at her then, accusing her with his eyes, a thin veneer of anger doing little to disguise the bitter frustration beneath. She had to lace her fingers together to keep from reaching out to him. "You know I want you to touch me."

He shifted and reached out. "Then what—"

She stepped back, trying not to skitter. "Just because we both want it doesn't mean that it's right," she explained quickly. "You're my employer, Logan, and that's a real problem for me. My career is important to me. I've worked hard, and I'm proud of what I've accomplished."

"You can't think this is about sleeping your way to the top," he said scathingly.

"Not at this moment," she said, "but later, when I'm ready to move up, would you be able to turn me down if I wasn't right for the position?"

"That won't happen. I haven't found anything you can't do and do well."

"Maybe. You can't know what's coming, though, neither of us can. And it's more than just the job."

He frowned, but he folded his hands in a sign of patience. "What then?"

"I'm not comfortable with casual affairs."

"You find something *casual* about this?" he demanded.

She ignored that. "We're not really suited for one another, Logan. Without Amanda Sue, we'd never have gotten to this place."

He couldn't deny that, and he didn't try. "Amanda Sue may have brought us together like this, but—"

"It's the situation, Logan," she argued. "Can't you see that? You never looked twice at me until I came into your home and Amanda Sue opened a place in your heart you'd never have willingly opened yourself."

Again, he couldn't argue. He sat silently for a moment, then quietly asked, "What if I told you that I was afraid to look too closely at you, Em? That I think I always knew deep down that this would happen if I did?"

She smiled wanly. "I'd say that you're as good as your reputation."

He bowed his head. After a moment he got up. "I'm not sure I can put the genie back in the bottle," he said, "but I'll try if that's what you want."

Emily swallowed relief. "Thank you," she whispered. He picked up her bag and handed it to her, careful that their hands didn't touch.

"Will I see you in the morning?" he asked.

"Of course."

He nodded and stepped aside, his gaze averted. Emily slipped from the room and grabbed her coat up off the living room chair. She was hurrying down the walk toward her car when the disappointment caught up with her, but even as the tears clouded her vision, she knew she'd done the right thing. She couldn't doubt it. But, oh, how she wished it could be different! If only he could love her as she loved him, but she had more sense than to believe that. For two years now she'd watched him wander from one affair to another. She knew who and what he was. Amanda couldn't have changed him that much.

But even as the denial grew within her, she felt the truth echoing in her heart. If only he could love her as she loved him. If only. If only.

She was at the town house by seven Monday morning. Logan was dressed for the office, a bath towel draped across his chest and clothespinned at his shoulders.

"I'm feeding Amanda Sue her breakfast," he explained with a wry grin.

She followed him into the house, wagging the heavy bag in which her lazy cat reclined contentedly. She put the bag down in the living room, then accompanied Logan to the kitchen. When they walked in Amanda Sue opened her mouth like a nestling spying the mother bird's approach. Laughing, Logan sat down and forked up a syrupy piece of toaster waffle, which explained the elaborate protective measures for his clothing.

"She slept through dinner last night," he explained. "I thought it was best not to wake her. Obviously we overtired her in the pool yesterday. So she was up with the birdies this morning, demanding the early worm." Amanda Sue was practically gulping the mushy waffle bites. Logan carefully spaced them to keep her from choking and offered her sips of milk at intervals. When she began to slow down, he began to speak again. "I want to discuss something with you. Unless you object, I want to use our own personnel department to screen the nanny applicants. They'll have to outsource the applications, of course, but I think they'll be able to weed out the obvious losers for us. It may take some time for them to come up with some prospects, however. I hope that's all right."

"It's fine by me," she said, helping herself to coffee from the pot he'd made.

Amanda Sue was through, so he removed the towel, got up and carried it to the sink, where he wet one corner before carrying it back to Amanda Sue's chair. Apparently she'd been so hungry that she hadn't fought him for possession of the eating utensils and food that morning, because he had only to wipe her face and hands to have her cleaned up.

"One more thing," he said, pulling his daughter out of her chair and setting her on her feet. "My housekeeper will be in this morning. I've explained the situation, so she's expecting you. I just wanted to be sure you were expecting her."

"That's fine."

Amanda Sue dropped down and crawled under the table.

"Her name's Consuelo," Logan said, folding the towel, "but she prefers Connie."

"Connie, right."

Goody finally put in an appearance, slipping into the room on silent cat paws and heading straight for Amanda Sue beneath the table. The child let out a yelp of delight, and Emily went down on her haunches to observe the meeting. Goody circled Amanda Sue, rubbing against her shoulders and chest, before plopping down across her legs with a sweep of her tail. Amanda Sue patted the cat's side and wrapped an arm around its neck. Goody purred and pretended not to be enraptured. Emily shook her head in wonder.

"A mutual admiration society," Logan observed, stooping to peer beneath the table.

"Absolutely. I've never seen Goody take to anyone like this, not even me."

"Well, that's my Amanda Sue for you," Logan said proudly. He reached out for her. "Come on, sweetheart. Daddy has to go."

"Go," Amanda Sue said, crawling out from under both the cat and the table.

Logan swept her up into a fierce hug. "Umm. I love you, 'Manda mine, but I have to go to work. Emily's here to spend the day with you."

"Go," Amanda Sue said, reaching toward the door. "Mon Mimy."

"Not this time, baby," Logan said. "Daddy has to get some real work done for a change. You stay here and play with Emily."

Emily stepped up and offered her arms. "Goody wants to play. Let's go play with Goody."

Amanda Sue leaned into Emily's arms, acquiescing calmly. "Gooey! Pway. Mon."

Logan kissed his daughter's cheek and turned away. Two

steps later, he turned back, but this time his regard was all
for Emily. With a sigh, he retraced his steps, bowed his head
and kissed her on the forehead. "I may be your boss," he
said, "but I'm also your friend. I'd be the worst sort of
ingrate not to feel that much. You may not want more from
me, and that's fine, but you'll just have to deal with at least
this much."

She smiled, deeply touched. "Have a good day," she
whispered.

Nodding, he skimmed a hand over the braid hanging between her shoulder blades and took his leave with a wave
to his daughter. "See you later, angel. Both of you."

The day passed quickly. When Logan walked in the door
at twenty minutes past five, Emily walked out ten minutes
later, minus her magically disappearing cat. "You'll just be
bringing her back tomorrow," Logan pointed out. "She
might as well stay." He didn't say that Emily might as well
stay, too, but the thought was there, unacknowledged, between them.

Tuesday followed much the same pattern as Monday. On
Wednesday she took Amanda Sue into the office to meet a
prospective nanny. Hal had a notepad full of questions for
Emily, and she felt gratified to find that she was not as easily
replaced as it had seemed. The nanny said that she preferred
to work with newborn infants but would consider Amanda
Sue if nothing else came up in the immediate future. Logan
told her that wouldn't be necessary, and Emily fully agreed.
Three more applicants were interviewed during those next
two days. One of them was, frankly, perfect, but Emily
couldn't bring herself to argue when Logan passed up the
young, pretty, Swiss-educated woman on the grounds that
she might eventually decide to return to Europe. Emily hated
to admit, even to herself, that she couldn't bear the thought
of Logan actually living with such an attractive female. Simply put, she would be jealous of any woman who possessed
any chance of fixing Logan's interest, which was more than

enough reason to refuse Logan's invitation to accompany him and Amanda Sue to the ranch for the weekend.

"Mom's called nearly every day," he said, telling Emily nothing she didn't already know. "Now she says she's given us long enough to make the adjustment and it's time to introduce her granddaughter to the rest of the family. I can't argue with that."

"I agree," Emily said from the armchair in his living room. "It's time the rest of the Fortunes knew what a treasure they've got, but I really can't go."

"May I ask why?" Logan pressed gently, watching Amanda Sue pretend to be a cat and Goody pretend not to notice.

"I'm hoping to get together with Cathy," she said.

He nodded. "Is that the only reason?"

"No."

Sighing, he folded his hands. "Well, have a good weekend, anyway."

"You, too," she said, getting up to go.

He plucked Amanda Sue off the floor and followed Emily to the door. "Tell Emily 'bye," he instructed sweetly. Amanda Sue hugged Emily's neck and kissed her.

"'Bye-bye, sweetheart. See you Monday."

"We'll miss you," Logan said just before she went out the door. She tried not to look back—and failed.

I'll miss you, too, her heart whispered. *I already do.*

Eight

"Eden." Logan threw his free arm around his younger sister's neck and hugged her, knocking his hat askew. "Haven't seen you lately. How are you?"

She laughed, and the sound of it was so infectious that Logan laughed, too. "Well and busy," Eden said. "I've so wanted to meet my niece, but Mom asked all of us to give you some time alone with her." She pulled back when Amanda Sue shoved at her. "Possessive already, sweetheart?" She grinned at Logan. "You always did have a way with the opposite sex, didn't you, brother dear? And your little girl seems to have fallen victim like all the rest."

"Well, not *all* the rest," Logan muttered, thinking of Emily, but then he smiled and stepped through the open doorway of his mother's large Colonial-style home. Eden shut the door. Obviously she had been watching for him, anxious to be the first to make the acquaintance of her niece. He didn't disappoint her. Tugging his hat into place, he said, "Amanda Sue, this is your aunt Eden." Amanda Sue put her hand in her mouth and stared, wide-eyed, at the dark-haired Eden.

"Logan, she's gorgeous."

"What'd you expect?" he teased. "She's got Mom's hair, but it's getting darker."

"And those eyes!" Eden gushed. "I expect she's a real charmer, too."

Logan chuckled. "Extremely charming—as cyclones go." Eden laughed and clapped her hands delightedly.

"You've had Daddy on his toes, have you, sweetheart?" she said to her niece, and Amanda Sue grinned, taking advantage of the moment to reach for her father's hat.

"Ah-ah-ah." Logan leaned back out of reach, pushing away her hand. "You can't have Daddy's hat." As expected, Amanda Sue shrieked and threw herself backward, sobbing in protest. He was ready for her and simply held on, waiting it out with an apologetic shrug for his sister. Amanda Sue had used every weapon in her arsenal since he'd first put on the blasted hat, but he was determined not to give in on this. A cowboy's hat was sacred, dammit, and even if her daddy wasn't the working variety, she'd be spending her life around the real thing, so she had to learn. Besides, some lessons were uncompromising by their very nature.

"Poor baby!" Eden crooned, and to Logan's disgust Amanda Sue launched herself into her aunt's arms, the very ones she'd pushed away only moments earlier. "Daddy just doesn't understand that no woman can resist a cowboy hat," Eden commiserated. "No Fortune woman, anyway, and you're definitely that."

"Mimy," Amanda Sue whined. "Oan Mimy Gooey."

"What's she asking for?" Eden said.

"Emily. Emily Applegate and her cat."

"Emily, your assistant?" Eden asked, obviously surprised.

"And Amanda Sue's temporary baby-sitter," he said, removing his hat and jacket and stowing them in the foyer closet along with the small diaper tote.

Eden lifted her slender eyebrows. "How did that happen?"

"Did you ever interview nannies for Sawyer?" he asked cryptically.

"Ah. It isn't easy, is it?"

Logan shook his head, really looking at his sister for a change. At twenty-seven and five-feet-and-seven-inches, she was a willowy beauty. Her long dark hair was looped into a soft roll on the back of her head, accentuating her high cheekbones and aristocratic features. Her expressive blue eyes rivaled Amanda Sue's for color and sparkle. Logan marveled, understanding for the first time what she'd been through, what she'd accomplished, as a single mother to her young son with only the help of a housekeeper/nanny. "Have I told you lately just how much I admire you?" he asked softly.

Eden studied him, gently embracing her niece, who had become interested in the byplay since the hat had been put away. "I've never seen you like this," his sister finally said.

He spread his hands. "I've never been like this."

Amanda Sue took it as an invitation and swayed toward him. Smiling, he pulled her against his chest. She patted his cheeks with both hands and said pleadingly, "Oan hat."

He put his nose to hers and said, "No."

She stuck out her bottom lip, and he kissed it. She wiped the kiss away with an angry swipe. He kissed her again. She swiped again. He rained kisses all over her face, and she succumbed to giggles.

"Oh, this is too wonderful," his mother said from behind him. He turned to embrace her, grinning ear to ear.

"Mother."

She looped a hand behind his head and pulled him down for a kiss, then turned her attention to her granddaughter. "Hello, my beauty. Grandmother's so glad to see you."

Amanda Sue seemed to remember her. Confident that she was adored, Amanda Sue even puckered up for a proper kiss but clung securely to her father's neck.

"Let's take her in to meet the others," Mary Ellen said. "Then I want some one-on-one with both of you, if that's not a contradiction in terms."

Logan chuckled and proudly carried his daughter into the family room, flanked by his mother and sister. He'd expected his brother and sister, but the room was crowded with other Fortunes, too. Both his cousin Matthew and his wife Claudia were there, along with the mystery child they'd named Taylor. Their own infant son Bryan had been kidnapped on the day of his christening, and Taylor had been returned to them in his stead. Bryan's whereabouts remained as much a mystery as to whom Taylor belonged. They knew he was a Fortune, because of his hereditary crown-shaped birthmark and rare blood type, but so far no Fortune had claimed him. For the first time, Logan was fully aware of how Matthew and Claudia must be suffering, and he was touched that they had taken the time and trouble to welcome his daughter.

His cousin Dallas and new wife Maggie were there, too, looking radiantly happy as they watched their five-year-old son Travis tumbling on the carpet with Eden's dark, handsome little Sawyer who was the same age. His cousin Vanessa and her new husband Devin, the FBI agent assigned to helping the local sheriff, Wyatt Grayhawk, find baby Bryan, were also in attendance. Knowing how concerned Vanessa was about her nephew, how concerned they all were, Logan was astounded at the size of the gathering.

His brother Holden and sister-in-law Lucinda were the first to step forward. "Wow!" Holden said. "She looks just like Mom!"

Lucinda, with her smooth bedside manner, already had Amanda Sue reaching for her. She was more used to delivering babies than treating them, but she took no time at all to announce that Amanda Sue was beautiful, healthy, and well cared for. When Vanessa tried to coax Amanda Sue away from her, though, the child reached for her daddy again. Holden laughed and exclaimed, "She actually likes him!"

Logan couldn't help smiling. "Of course she does! In fact, she loves me. Don't you, sweet girl? Amanda Sue loves Daddy, doesn't she?"

She nodded dutifully, placed both hands on either side of his face, gave him a loud messy kiss and crooned, "Daddy hat?"

Eden snickered, and Logan rolled his eyes. "Emily says

she has a memory like an elephant," he complained, explaining the hat situation.

"Sounds like Vanessa," Devin commented dryly.

"Stubborn and beautiful," Vanessa's brother Dallas supplied.

"Willful and intelligent," Vanessa's other brother Matthew chimed in.

"Sounds like Eden to me," Holden cracked.

"She's a Fortune, all right," Logan declared, chuckling. "No doubt about it."

Everyone laughed, and Amanda Sue joined in, though it was obvious to all that she didn't have the slightest idea what was going on. Her giggles brought all eyes back to her, however, and she seemed to enjoy the attention. She played to her audience, smiling at each with an attack of the cutes that had her batting her eyelashes and gyrating her shoulders. The five-year-old boys giggled at her antics, and it was only then that Amanda Sue seemed to notice them. She looked at her daddy, eyebrows raised as if to ask why he hadn't told her there were other children present, bucked and demanded, "Down!"

Logan set her feet on the floor, and she took off at her usual run, bowling right into the boys with her arms spread wide. They made appropriate noises and went down. She threw a leg over Travis, who was by far the largest, and climbed onto his back as though he were a horse. Sawyer thought that was terribly funny. Travis got up on all fours and rocked back and forth, snorting like a bull. Amanda Sue held on to his shirt with both hands and invited Sawyer aboard. "Mon," she said. "Mon."

"That is a very secure child," Lucinda observed.

"Donna deserves a lot of credit," Logan said, "and Emily, too." Then he had to explain about each woman, and conversation progressed from there.

Play got a little too rough at one point, and Amanda Sue bumped her head. Logan immediately came off the couch, where he was sitting with Eden and Mary Ellen, and knelt beside his daughter. She clambered up into his arms, complaining loudly about the affront. He kissed her bump, told her to play more carefully and asked if she needed a diaper change. She pretended not to hear him, ensuring that she did. "I'll do it," Eden said, but Amanda Sue shook her head wildly and struggled to get away.

"No! No ditee! No ditee!"

"Just hand me a clean diaper and the wipes, will you, Eden?" Logan said. Catching Amanda Sue with the long reach of his arm and gently laying her down, he quickly opened her corduroy jumper and stripped away the soiled diaper. Amanda Sue struggled constantly, but the diaper appeared quickly, and Logan had her cleaned up and changed in short order. "There," he said, rolling the soiled diaper into a plastic wrap and wiping his hands clean, while Amanda Sue scrambled up and launched herself at the boys again.

Logan got to his feet, and it was then that he noticed the absolute silence. He looked around him at the rapt faces. "What?"

Everyone burst into laughter. "You're better at that than I am!" Matthew exclaimed.

"I never would have believed it," Holden said, clapping Logan on the shoulder as if proud of him.

It was Mary Ellen who put the cap on the moment, however. "I knew you'd be a wonderful father," she said, embracing him.

Logan couldn't help grinning. "You knew more than I did, then," he said truthfully. "Emily says I've come a long way, though, and what she doesn't know about kids hasn't been learned yet. She's taught me lots."

"I have to meet this Emily," Eden mused thoughtfully.

"What are you talking about?" Logan said. "You've met her."

"Well, of course, I've *met* her, but I'd like to have a conversation with her. You know, a visit."

"I'm sure she'd like that," Logan said. "She'd probably

appreciate the adult company since she's at the house during the days with Amanda Sue while I work. We got a temp to take her place in the office."

"Oan grink."

"Okay, sweetheart." He swept her up into his arms and looked to his mother. "What've you got for a little girl to drink, Granny?"

Mary Ellen traded a significant look with Eden, but then she smiled. "Why don't we go see?"

He followed his mother toward the kitchen, Amanda Sue held close to his chest. He didn't hear the comments and speculation voiced by the others in his absence. If he had, he might have realized just how much he'd changed since Amanda Sue's arrival in his life. He might even have realized that he had finally lost his heart—to someone besides his little girl.

It was Mary Ellen who suggested that Logan and Eden pay a visit to their uncle Ryan at the main house on Sunday and introduce him to Amanda Sue, since he'd missed the family gathering. Ryan had much on his mind, she pointed out, and needed all the support he could get. Logan was only too eager to continue showing off his little daughter, and Eden was always ready to lend her support when anyone in the family needed it. They drove the two miles over to the big, sprawling hacienda, enjoying the rolling fields of mesquite and cactus interspersed with hardy grasses and the occasional tree.

"Isn't it funny," Eden said, "that no matter where we go or what we do, this place is still home?"

Logan nodded. "I've been thinking I'd like to live out here summers so Amanda Sue could experience growing up here."

"It'd be a long commute," Eden said.

"True, but I think it'd be worth it."

"What does Emily say?"

"Haven't mentioned it to her yet. I think she'd agree, though."

Eden smiled in that secretive way she'd developed of late. "What?"

She just shook her head.

He thought to himself that Eden was acting oddly, but then he fell to wondering what Emily would really say about his idea of living summers on the ranch. Should he think about building his own house, or would it be better for Amanda Sue to live in the house with his mother and his brother's growing family? He loved the idea of Amanda Sue running through the same house in which he'd grown up, but maybe it would be best to build his own place. Maybe he'd ask Uncle Ryan about it after everything settled down. He was in no hurry, after all.

The house came into view, and it really was a magnificent sight, wholly at one with its surroundings and seeming as old as the land itself. They parked in front of the door and got out.

As expected, Rosita Perez, the housekeeper, let them into the house. Logan threw his free arm wide, Amanda Sue snuggled against his side with the other.

"Rosita, my love!"

Rosita poked a plump finger into his ribs. "Ha! Don't think you can charm me, Logan Fortune. I've known you for a scamp since before you could walk, and I can still burn your backside when you need it."

He grinned, but then he said, "Well, better get out the paddle, then, Rosita. I'm afraid I've brought proof of my perfidy this time."

"I'm betting she'll forgive you for this one," Eden said with grateful knowledge. Rosita stepped forward, reached up and wrapped both arms around Eden's shoulders. Eden had to bend forward to accommodate the plump housekeeper's short stature.

"How are you, my Eden? We don't see you enough."

Eden kissed her cheek. "Thank you, Rosita. I'm well and busy."

Rosita looked into her eyes, nodded and stepped back, lifting a hand to smooth the wide, white streak in her neatly braided and wrapped, ink-black hair. Once more she turned her attention to Logan and, this time, his daughter. Folding her hands at her waist, Rosita tilted her head, studying Amanda Sue, who had her hand in her mouth as usual.

Rosita nodded sagely. "She has the Fortune will. She needs a strong but loving hand to guide, but never contain, her. She is fortunate, I think, in her father—even if he is a scamp." She smiled then and reached up to embrace both. Logan had to bend far forward to accommodate her, and as he did so, Amanda Sue reached out and lightly touched the white streak in Rosita's hair.

"A precious child!" Rosita gushed. "Just what your uncle needs right now. Come, all of you. He will be glad to see you."

They followed her through the cool, antique-filled interior of the old house, crossing floors of tile and plank and, finally, carpet. Rosita pushed open the heavily carved door of the so-called library and led them inside. "More company, Mr. Ryan. Wait until you see the little *señorita!*"

Ryan was sitting on one corner of the massive old desk standing dead center of the big room. Couches and chairs were strewn about in comfortable groupings, one of which featured a television set. The walls were lined with shelves of books, leaving room only for a massive fireplace and various doors, a pair of which opened onto the courtyard.

On the leather sofa facing the desk sat none other than Lily Redgrove Cassidy, wearing a long, slender denim skirt, matching vest, embroidered long-sleeved blouse, and red, hand-tooled leather boots, her long, dark hair lying atop one shoulder in a thick braid. At fifty-something, her dark, voluptuous beauty had merely matured and ripened, leaving Logan in no quandary at all as to what drew and held his uncle's interest. She stood even before Ryan did and moved forward gracefully, beckoning to someone Logan hadn't seen until that moment. Hannah, Lily's oldest daughter, rose from a deeply cushioned armchair and smiled.

Clad in neat, pleated khakis, a classic silk shirt and a brown corduroy jacket, Hannah would never seem more than plain in her mother's presence, which Logan found a darn shame. He knew her to be a good soul, a kind and loving woman with a quiet beauty that was too often overshadowed as it emanated from inside and cared little for outward expression. In that way, she was much like her mother, much more so, he suspected, than her younger sister Maria.

"Hannah!" Eden said. "How nice to find you here—and your mother, too, of course."

Hannah hurried to Eden's side, but Lily was headed straight for Amanda Sue, saying, "Oh, Ryan, she's gorgeous! That auburn hair, and those eyes!"

"Good grief, she looks like you, Eden!" Ryan exclaimed, chuckling. "Except for that hair, which is Mary Ellen and Logan combined, I think." He clapped Logan on the shoulder and shook his hand while Lily coaxed Amanda Sue into her arms.

"How old is she?" Lily wanted to know.

"Going on seventeen months," Logan answered proudly.

"She's walking, then," Lily said.

"Running, more like," Eden answered.

"She's fast, all right," Logan confirmed, "and according to Rosita she's got the Fortune will."

"What Logan means to say," Eden teased, "is that she's as stubborn as he is—and as charming and bright."

"Brighter," he said.

"And more charming," Hannah teased, giggling as Amanda Sue touched a fingertip to Lily's mouth and announced, "Mouf."

Lily smiled and kissed her fingertip. An old hand now at showing off, Amanda Sue next touched Lily's delicate patrician nose. "Noze." Very carefully she touched Lily's eyelid and other facial parts. "Eye. Ghin. Sheek. Foorhed. Eer."

Finally she touched wisps of hair framing Lily's face and said, "Preey herr."

"Bright, charming, *and* she's got good taste," Ryan said to general laughter. He smiled down at Lily, who was making kissing sounds into Amanda Sue's hand. "Let's all sit down and have a chat." Ryan suggested.

Rosita said, "I'll bring coffee and sugar cookies. Would the baby like milk?"

"That would be great, Rosita," Logan confirmed, moving with the others toward the largest grouping of furniture. "Just be sure it's a plastic cup, and bring lots of napkins."

When they were all seated, Amanda Sue crawled over into Ryan's lap. A moment later she moved on to Eden, then Hannah, and finally her daddy, where she stayed until Rosita returned with "num-nums." She filled Logan's lap with cookie crumbs, spilled milk on his jeans and insisted on blowing on his coffee before every sip, while the adults touched on various topics: Amanda Sue's mother, the kidnapping and how Ryan had been pressing the authorities for action, the ranch, Hannah's bridal shop in San Antonio, Eden's son Sawyer and her consulting business and, finally, the remaining members of Lily's family, her oldest son Cole and youngest daughter Maria.

"Cole is well," Lily said proudly. "His practice keeps him much too busy, but I still wish he'd find a nice girl and settle down. Maria, now..." Lily shook her head sadly and sent a speaking glance at Hannah. "I never really know what's going on with my younger daughter or how she is. Maria prefers to keep her distance."

Hannah sighed. "Maybe I should talk to her."

"I think that's a good idea," Rosita said, never shy about speaking her piece. "You should drive down to Leather Bucket now while you're this close, and take Logan and Eden with you."

"Yes, do that!" Lily prodded. "Ryan and I will entertain the baby."

"Sure, we'd be glad to," Ryan said.

"Oh, I don't know," Logan mumbled. "Amanda Sue doesn't usually like me to leave her with anyone but Emily."

Eden rolled her eyes. "Honestly! There are doting fathers, and then there are doting fathers. You always did take everything to the extreme."

"It's just that she's had her world turned upside down once already, and she's a little insecure about me disappearing on her."

"Emily who?" Ryan wanted to know, and Logan was obliged to explain that his talented, efficient executive assistant just also happened to be the world's leading expert on child care.

As if to bolster his assertions, Amanda Sue tapped him on the chest and said seriously, "Oan Mimy."

"We'll see Emily tomorrow," he promised.

Amanda Sue pointed toward the door through which they'd entered and said, "Go!"

"All right," he said, getting up. "Come on, girls. We'll take my car and drive down to Leather Bucket."

"I guess that's that," Rosita said briskly. "The little *señorita* knows her mind, eh?"

Laughing, everyone got up and headed out. They said goodbyes at the door, and Amanda Sue dutifully dispensed kisses to Ryan, Lily and Rosita, but her attention was on the car. Hannah got into the back with Amanda Sue, while Eden rode up front with Logan. They were leaving the drive when Logan asked, "Was it just me, or did Rosita seem anxious for Ryan and Lily to be left alone?"

Hannah smiled. "I keep telling her not to worry. Mama isn't going to change her mind at this stage. Confidentially, we're already planning the wedding."

Logan craned his neck around at that. "No kidding? That's great!"

"I hope it works out for them," Eden said quietly.

"So do I," Hannah added soberly. "Sophia has been giving Mama fits, and I can tell Ryan's losing patience with her.''

"That divorce has already dragged on too long," Logan commented. "Someone should do something about Sophia."

"I would welcome suggestions," Hannah said darkly. "I just don't understand why she's doing this. She doesn't love Ryan."

"She loves his money, though," Eden muttered wryly, and Logan couldn't help thinking that her acerbic judgment about summed up his uncle's spoiled, immature second wife. The whole family knew he'd made a mistake marrying her, but after having been widowed after his first wife Janine died, Ryan had been especially vulnerable. It was beginning to look, though, as if Lily Redgrove Cassidy would turn out to be the love of Ryan's life. They both deserved this happiness. After being separated from one another for over thirty years, it was high time that their old romance was rekindled. Logan wished them well.

The rest of the drive was given over to small talk about shared experiences, children and business. Logan knew he went on too much about his daughter, but he couldn't seem to help it. He was unaware, however, how often he mentioned Emily. He did realize that he missed her, though, even now with the chatter going back and forth so fast that he could hardly keep up with it.

They stopped in the small town of Leather Bucket for soft drinks. Amanda Sue had fallen asleep in her car seat, so Logan stayed behind in the car while Eden and Hannah went into the convenience store. Finally, Hannah directed them to the run-down trailer park where Maria was living. This time, Eden insisted on staying behind with her sleeping niece. Reluctantly, Logan got out of the car and opened Hannah's door for her.

"Don't be upset if Maria is rude," Hannah whispered as they climbed the dusty sloping yard. "She's got some kind of hang-up where you Fortunes are concerned. I think Mama hoped that having you and Eden drop in for a visit might convince her to lighten up.''

"No problem," Logan said. "I've learned to be too stupid to insult when it suits me."

Hannah shot him a look of pure gratitude. He noticed that she squared her shoulders and took a deep breath before running up the rusty iron steps to the door of the trailer. He stepped up beside her just as she tapped on the door and thrust it open, calling out, "Maria! It's—'' The last word trailed away as Hannah took in the scene inside the trailer's shabby little living room. Logan ducked his head and followed her inside.

The floor was strewn with baby toys. A bag of disposable diapers had been torn open and left to spill out onto the couch. A rumpled crib stood against the double window next to a small television set. Most shocking of all, Maria stood defensively at the end of a narrow hallway, a child in her arms. She was dressed in blue jeans, a dark T-shirt, running shoes, and a frilled black apron, her dark hair caught at the nape with a rubber band. The handles of both a purse and a bulging diaper bag were slung over one shoulder. Clearly, she was not happy to see them.

"What do you think you're doing?"

"Dropping in on my sister," Hannah said firmly. "Who's baby is that?"

Frowning, Maria shrugged and pulled up the hood on the lightweight bunting the child wore. "He belongs to a neighbor. I've been baby-sitting for extra cash, but if she doesn't pick him up soon I'll be late for work. It's almost time for the dinner rush."

"You're a waitress, I take it," Logan said with a smile, hoping to lighten the mood.

"That's right," Maria retorted. "Anything wrong with that?"

Logan shook his head. "It's hard work."

"A Fortune wouldn't know about that, I guess," she said cattily. Hannah caught her breath, but Logan forestalled a scolding with a hand clamped lightly on her forearm. Maria seemed disappointed that she hadn't elicited an outburst from someone. She cocked one hip and said in a marginally more friendly tone, "I haven't seen you in ages. Logan, isn't it?"

"That's right."

"Figures. I hear Holden's married now, so the little woman probably wouldn't be letting him out of her sight yet, not if she's smart, anyway. The question is, what are you doing here with her?" She nodded at Hannah.

"My daughter's in the car with my sister, Eden," Logan said calmly. "We met Hannah and your mother at Uncle Ryan's and thought we'd give her a ride when she said she'd like to check on you."

"*Check* on me?" Maria tossed her head and lifted a cryptic eyebrow. "Why am I not surprised? You just can't accept the fact that I'm perfectly capable of living my own life, can you, Hannah?"

"We only want to know that you're okay," Hannah said, but Maria scoffed at that.

While the sisters bickered, Logan couldn't help comparing Maria with both her mother and her sister. She had Lily's dark good looks, but she was a little too thin for his taste, and she completely lacked her sister's warmth. She was, in fact, as cold and hard as ice. It was difficult to imagine her as an adequate baby-sitter. He glanced sympathetically at the infant in her arms, seeing only the impression of a plump face and waving fist. He certainly wouldn't want to leave his Amanda Sue with the likes of Maria Cassidy, but he supposed that some parents had little choice. Still, she was sure no Emily. But then, who was?

Maria cut the visit short by insisting that she had to go. "If his mom won't come get him, I'll just have to take him to her," she said.

"Let me help you," Hannah offered, reaching for the child as Maria drew near, but Maria jerked back sharply.

"No! H-he doesn't like strangers. I won't have him screaming all the way down to Sandy's."

He didn't seem particularly skittish to Logan, but it wasn't any of his business. He did notice that the child seemed well cared for, and his opinion of Maria improved incrementally.

"Let me carry the diaper bag, at least," Hannah said, but Maria spurned even that offer.

Stepping past Logan, she slipped out and down the steps, calling over her shoulder, "Just close the door behind you."

Logan motioned for Hannah to go first and followed, pulling the door closed. "I'm going after her," Hannah said, and he nodded.

"Take your time. I'll wait in the car."

He got in behind the wheel. Eden said, "I didn't know Maria had a child."

"Apparently he belongs to one of the neighbors." He checked Amanda Sue, who was drooling all over her sweater in her sleep. "You think she's cutting teeth? Emily says she could be."

Eden smiled. "I like this version of you, Logan. You're a good father. Has *Emily* told you that?"

"As a matter of fact, she has."

"Emily seems to have taken quite a major role in your life lately," Eden said.

Hoping to squelch Eden's speculation, Logan looked into the rearview mirror, watching Hannah try to talk to her stubborn sister as they trudged down the rough street. "You have to understand," he said. "I don't think I could do it like you have, Eden. Emily's great help. She's made me a far better father than I would be on my own. And Amanda Sue deserves the very best I can give her."

Eden reached across the seat and took his hand. "She has it."

"I mean to see that she always does," he told her. "Here comes Hannah."

He started the car and backed it up, stopping when he reached Hannah, who got in and swept her hair back with one hand, sighing. "I just don't know what's happening with my sister. It's like she's mad at the world. I doubt she'll be baby-sitting that little one anymore after the way she talked to his mother. I could tell the woman was shocked to hear that she was making Maria late."

"I wouldn't worry about it," Logan said. "She's probably keeping more than one. She certainly has the makings of an adequate nursery."

"Maybe so," Hannah said. "I asked her if she wasn't afraid of losing what money the woman owed her, but she didn't seem concerned."

"Maybe she gets paid in advance," Eden said. "Lots of sitters do."

Hannah nodded, but Logan could tell she was puzzling over something else as he turned the car around and headed out of the trailer park. He noticed, too, that Maria, who was supposedly in such an all-fired hurry, stood defensively by her old car until they were all the way at the end of the street.

"How old would you think the mother of such a young child would be?" Hannah asked as he turned the car out into the intersection.

Eden shrugged. "Early twenties to late thirties, usually, but we all know that these days a new mother can be a teenager or a middle-aged matron."

Hannah nodded, but the next instant she was shaking her head. "That woman's too old," she whispered.

Something nudged Logan to speak up. "What woman?"

But Hannah waved a hand and laughed at herself. "Never mind. It's not important. Maria may not be the loving daughter and sister we've always wanted her to be, but there's nothing new in that. At least I can tell Mama that she's all right."

Logan smiled, but he couldn't help thinking that he'd be brokenhearted and probably fit to be tied if Amanda Sue turned out like Maria Cassidy. But he wouldn't let that happen. He wasn't quite sure how he'd prevent it, but somehow he would. He wondered what Emily would have to say about it, and suddenly he missed her with a pang of such longing that he made up his mind to leave for San Antonio as soon as possible. He'd intended to put it off until nightfall, hoping Amanda Sue would sleep through the drive, but he knew now that he wasn't going to wait a minute longer than necessary to say a polite farewell. Suddenly beyond endurance, he depressed the accelerator a little further and imagined that Emily waited for him, arms open.

Nine

Emily sat dejectedly on the bed in the waning twilight. Goody sprawled next to her, meticulously cleaning her paws, but Emily could not find the energy to raise her hand and stroke the tigerish fur. This was ridiculous. She'd always loved lazy weekends, lounging around with her cat, a good book and a cup of coffee or hot cocoa, snug in her little apartment despite the cold rain pouring down outside. She hoped the rain wouldn't cause problems for Logan and Amanda Sue on their drive up from the ranch, but then, that was precisely the problem. She just couldn't get those two our of her mind, couldn't seem to get interested in anything else.

She looked at the clock on the bedside table. Four minutes of five. Oh, would this weekend never end? If only Cathy hadn't been too busy to come over. She'd sensed during their two brief telephone conversations that Cathy needed the break in her busy schedule even more than she, Emily, needed distraction from the monotony of a solitary weekend.

Monotony. Who was she kidding? She was missing Logan and Amanda Sue as if they were her arms and legs. She felt incapacitated by their absence, however temporary, and she knew with awful certainty that it was just a taste of her life to come. How was it that the future had seemed so safe, so acceptable, so normal, only a few weeks ago?

When the telephone rang, she very nearly didn't pick it up, but then she thought about cold rain falling on slick roads and unexpected panic had her grabbing for the receiver before the answering machine could switch on.

"Hello?"

"Em? Is that you? Are you okay?"

Logan. Relief swept through her, and another emotion that scared her half to death welled up, pushing a lump into her throat. She closed her eyes and tried to sound relaxed. "I'm fine. How are you?"

"Tired," he said, "and hungry. We just got in."

"You're home." She couldn't prevent the relief from creeping into her voice.

"Safe and sound." She heard insistent little-girl babble in the background. Then, "Hold on a sec. Amanda Sue wants to talk to you. Say 'hi' to Emily," he coached, sounding far away.

"Hi-i-i, Mimy."

Emily smiled, tears building behind her eyelids. "Hello, darling. How was your weekend at the ranch?"

"Traz n Awya run-run n gibby-ub Guhmama gimme num-num un eed iggle tummy."

"She's patting her tummy, whatever that means," Logan supplied. "I think she's telling you about her cousins Travis and Sawyer."

"Yeah," Amanda Sue confirmed, "Traz n Awya."

She went off on another tangent, babbling away as if totally confident every word was understood. "Guhmama" came up several times.

"I think she's talking about her grandmother now," Logan interpreted. "She's nodding."

Finally Amanda Sue's babble came to an end with, "Mon, Mimy. Mon bing Gooey hom."

Logan chuckled. "She's telling you to come on home and bring Goody with you."

Emily smiled, wanting nothing more than to do just that, but she had no justification for such unwise action, none at all. She swallowed against the lump in her throat. "I'll see you tomorrow morning, darling. You have a nice dinner and get some rest."

"Which darling would that be?" Logan said directly into

her ear. "The short one has had her say and abandoned the post in favor of making my bed a shambles by building a 'house' with my pillows, a little trick taught her by her rowdy cousins."

Emily laughed. "Sounds as if she had a very eventful weekend."

"We both did," he said. Then, softly, he added, "We missed you."

Heat expanded the lump in her throat so that she couldn't speak for a long moment. "H-how is your mom?"

"Oh, Mom is great. She loves being a grandmother again, but she's worried about my uncle Ryan." He filled her in briefly on Ryan's difficulties. The kidnapping she knew about, the divorce and possible remarriage were news—to which she wasn't at all sure she was entitled. "We had a strange visit with Maria Cassidy," he went on. "That's Lily's youngest daughter. She seems to hate Fortunes on principle, which is odd since she used to work at the big house. It made me feel sorry for Lily and Hannah—she's the older daughter. It made me glad that my sister Eden isn't like Maria. Hannah's nice enough. My sister wants to come and see you, by the way."

"Me?" Emily was shocked.

"I told her to drop by the house anytime. That's all right, isn't it?"

She wanted to say no. She didn't know why, but she very much feared meeting Logan's family socially, getting to really know them, like them. What if she and Eden didn't appreciate one another? What if they did? She took a deep breath and said the only thing she could. "Sure."

"Okay, then. So, how was your weekend?"

Miserable, she thought. "Fine," she said. "I love staying in and snuggling down when the weather's miserable like this."

He sighed. "I guess that means I can't talk you into coming over tonight."

She bit her lip. "I don't think that's wise. My old car—"

"You're right," he said. "I don't want you out in that thing. We could always come and get you."

"You shouldn't be taking Amanda Sue back out in this weather," she said briskly. "I'll see you in the morning."

"But not for long," he complained. "I'll be in the office all day."

"I thought that was the point," she said, smiling because he wanted to spend time with her, then frowning because she wanted to spend time with him.

"Daddy," Amanda Sue demanded loudly in the background. "Hungy num-nums."

"I guess I'd better rustle up some dinner," he said reluctantly. "You're sure you won't—"

"I'm glad you're home safely," she interrupted. "Kiss Amanda Sue for me. I'll see you in the morning."

"Come early," he urged after a moment of silence.

"Early enough to make breakfast," she promised.

"Didn't you miss me at all?" he asked softly, and she wondered how he managed to get that tone of vulnerability just right. She knew that it was a well-rehearsed technique, and still it was all she could do not to tell him exactly what he seemed to want to hear.

"Good night, Logan," she said, and if her voice was all husky and thick with feelings she shouldn't feel, well, she just couldn't help it. She hung up the phone and lay back beside Goody. "He didn't really miss me," she whispered. "No, not really." He couldn't have, because she couldn't bear it if it was true. She just couldn't.

The week proved rather uneventful for Emily, probably because it was so crushing for Logan. Just when it seemed that he might get caught up at work, a pair of bombs detonated—a deal undone at the last moment and an unexpected, short-term financial crisis brought on by a nervous stock market and rumors about his uncle Ryan's impending divorce. He had no time to interview prospective nannies, and Emily didn't press him about it, not even when he called several times a day to vent his frustration and discuss the situation at the office.

Strangely, though she usually enjoyed the intense moments of decision-making and crisis-defusing, Emily found that she did not particularly miss the office. She appreciated that Logan called her and asked her opinion or just ranted and raved in her ear, but that was enough for her—for the time being. She loved being home with Amanda Sue. Staying one step ahead of the world's fastest, brightest toddler was more than merely challenging.

She was pleased that Logan called to talk to Amanda Sue during the day and that he walked through the door in the evening with his arms open. Seeing Amanda Sue run to her daddy at the end of the day, giggling and so delighted to have him home, made Emily think that it was worth anything to be there to witness it. The difficulties of his day always seemed to have disappeared somewhere along the way, and he would sweep his little daughter up to hug and kiss her, tossing her over his shoulder to ride piggyback into the bedroom so he could change clothes. They'd romp and play while Emily got dinner on the table. Then, somehow, she and Logan would manage to eat and carry on a sensible conversation while feeding Amanda Sue, even though she would occasionally bang on her chair tray and demand, "Me, Daddy! Me!"

"I see you, 'Manda mine," he would say. "You have tomatoes in your hair, and you're rude, but you're still beautiful, and I love you. Now hush up."

Life felt altogether too good that week, until Emily came down the stairs on Friday after putting Amanda Sue down for her morning nap and found Logan standing in the living room when he ought to be at work. "What's wrong?" she said, suddenly certain that it was something terrible.

He stepped forward sluggishly. "I have to go to New York this evening."

She wasn't sure when the ax would fall, when the bad

news would hit. Leaning back against the counter, she asked calmly, "How long will you be gone?"

"At least through Monday," he said in a funereal voice. Suddenly he stepped forward and engulfed her in a fierce embrace. "Oh, God, Em," he said, "I don't want to go!"

She put her arms around him, half afraid, half…amused. "What's the problem, Logan? Anything I can help you with?"

He jerked back. "Yes! Come with me!"

"What?"

"You and Amanda Sue—come with me."

"It isn't business?"

"Of course it's business, but I want you with me. I want you both with me."

She put her hands to her hips and rolled her eyes. "You want to fly your daughter from San Antonio to New York and back again in a matter of a few days, just so she can sit in a hotel room? Are you nuts? She'll be ripping the paper off the walls by the end of the second day—and I'll be helping her!"

He frowned then. "You don't have to sit around the hotel. New York's full of museums and galleries and—"

"Oh, right! Let's turn Amanda Sue loose in the museums of New York! Wouldn't you like them still standing when she's old enough to actually benefit from them?"

His frowned deepened. "She's not that bad."

"She's a toddler, Logan. She doesn't have any business going with you to New York!"

Sighing, he pinched the bridge of his nose. "You're right. It's just…I don't want to be away from you, either of you!"

"Oh, please. I can understand you not wanting to leave your daughter, but it's the weekend. I wouldn't be here, anyway."

"Don't you get it?" he said angrily. "I missed you like crazy last weekend. You! And I had no intention of doing it again. I've been looking forward all week to having at least one day with you, one whole day, and now there will be no weekend at all, just one long, miserable week with a hole in the middle!''

He meant it. He was *that* intent on seducing her. Shaken, Emily tried to think what to say, what to do. She opened her mouth, but nothing came out. Abruptly, Logan turned and swept out of the room. For several moments she just stood there, trying to decide what to do next. It was as if her body decided for her. She knew even as she stepped away from the counter that she was going after him and that she didn't have any business doing it, but that didn't seem to matter.

He had dropped his suit jacket on the floor and was throwing clothes into a suitcase on the bed when she came into his room. ''Shouldn't you fold those?'' she asked timidly.

He stopped what he was doing, hung his head, and finally sat down on the edge of the bed, legs splayed before him. ''I shouldn't have shouted at you,'' he said apologetically. Loosening his tie, he stripped it off. ''It's just so frustrating!''

She came farther into the room and picked up his jacket, which she hung on the bedpost. ''I know.'' She retrieved his tie from the pillow where he'd tossed it, folded it neatly and laid it on the table beside the bed. ''All parents feel some frustration, especially single parents. You can't help being torn between work and your child.''

He was shaking his head. ''This is not about Amanda Sue, dammit!'' Suddenly he came up off the bed in a single, fluid motion. Fastening his hands around her elbows, he shook her gently. ''This is about *you!* You and me.'' Dismayed, she turned her head away, but he cupped her chin and made her look at him. ''Tell me that you're not attracted to me. Make me believe it!''

She opened her mouth, but one glance into his fiercely burning blue eyes told her that lying was hopeless, so instead she pulled a deep breath and attempted to marshal her thoughts. ''Logan,'' she began carefully, ''we've discussed this before, and—''

He yanked her against him and covered her mouth with his. Frozen in shock, she could do nothing more than stand there, wrapped against him by the confining strength of his arms, but then he widened his stance, urged her closer still, and slanted his mouth across hers in a plea so poignant she could not leash her reaction. Her body softened, even as her mind screamed silently that she must remain firm. Groaning, he dropped his hands to her bottom and pulled her against the hardness pulsing from his groin. His kiss moved across her cheek to her ear, where he breathed hot words that shivered down her spine.

"Em, oh, Em, I need you so!"

She shuddered, her knees weakening, and grabbed at his shoulders. "Logan." She couldn't think what else to say. His mouth came back to hers, hotly possessive, urgently persuasive. Lost, she pushed her arms up around his neck, and in reward he stabbed his tongue into her mouth, reaching deeply as his hands swarmed over her back.

Something opened inside her, softened and swelled. Suddenly her breasts were tender, the nipples pushing against his chest. His mouth broke away from hers and came to rest again just below her ear. He bit her, and it was not a dainty nip with the edges of his teeth, but a hot, wet, openmouthed, almost vampiric but utterly painless fixing of his teeth in her flesh. She nearly collapsed, shuddering as sensations too numerous and keen to identify rolled through her in convulsive waves. He licked his way to her earlobe with the tip of his tongue, and fixed his teeth there, at the same time shoving up the bottom of her sweater with both hands until he reached the band of her bra and released it.

Frantic to feel his mouth on hers again, she made no protest when he pulled the sweater over her head and brushed away the bra. His hands on her bare back made her skin prickle. Or was it the prickle of his beard against her palms that made her seize his mouth with hers? She objected with a moan when he shoved her away and down onto the bed. He followed on his knees, settling astride her, and a wave of his arm knocked the suitcase off the bed, while with his other hand he tore at the buttons on his shirt, breaking one and ripping away another. With a growl of frustration, he gave it up, yanking the shirt over his head, turning the sleeves inside out as he pulled his hands free one at a time.

Chest heaving, he leaned over her, his weight levered onto one arm. She knew that he was looking at her, staring at her breasts, but somehow she couldn't be embarrassed. Impatiently, she threw a hand around his neck and pulled him down atop her, gasping when bare skin met bare skin. Her nipples felt hard as rocks, the hair on his chest coarse and silky at the same time. He was heavy, solid, warm and firm. Reaching down, he pulled one of her knees up, making a place for himself between her legs, and shifting his weight onto one forearm.

"You're beautiful," he told her, his gaze never leaving hers. "I mean it, Em. You're incredibly beautiful, and not just here and here." He smoothed a hand over her face and down to cup one breast. "You're beautiful inside and out. I think I always knew it and it frightened me for some reason. Maybe I sensed on some level that if I acknowledged it, I'd start to fall in love in with you."

"Don't!" she whispered. "Don't say what you can't mean."

"I won't," he promised her, tugging at her nipple with his fingertips. Then he bowed his head and sucked the nipple into his mouth.

She nearly came up off the bed. He slid his hand down between her legs, cupping her there through her jeans. Rolling his hips against hers, he used his body weight and the erect length of his hardness to press and move his hand against her while his mouth tugged at her breast. Lightning knocked her eyes back in her head. He shifted, grinding his hips and his hand against her and angling his upper body away so he could show the other breast equal attention, but this time he licked and nibbled and kissed until she thought she would go insane. Undulating beneath him, she pulled up both knees and dug her heels into the bed, desperately needing greater contact. He gave it to her.

Sliding his mouth up to her throat, he shifted until his body fully covered hers and, taking his hand away, rocked against her. His hardness against the seam of her jeans sent a flash of heat upward. His chest dragged against her swollen breasts, sending that same heat flash down again to explode low in her belly. He licked and nibbled a path to her mouth, surging against her repeatedly.

"Come for me," he commanded.

Kissing her, he speared his tongue into her mouth and quickened the tempo of his hips, stroking hard against her, his arms sliding beneath her shoulders. It was not enough, and at the very same time it was too much. She clasped her arms about his neck and ground her mouth against his, helpless to resist the building tidal wave of climax. Tears pricked her eyes. Her nipples tightened almost painfully. When the great wave crashed over her, she wrapped her legs around him, as well, riding the crest for an instant, then tumbling and rolling beneath it. She didn't remember breaking the kiss, but was vaguely aware of her strength fading into limp mindlessness.

She didn't know how long he simply held her, his cheek pressed to hers, but eventually he lifted his head and said thickly, "I wish I had time to really make love to you. I want to be inside you the next time you do that."

She opened her eyes, trying to think why that shouldn't be, and he kissed her quickly. "I have to get the baby," he said, and rolled away. In that very same instant, Emily realized that Amanda Sue was screaming the house down, shrieking at the top of her lungs. The baby had awakened from her nap and obviously had been demanding attention for some time now—and she hadn't even heard her!

Dazed by this fact, Emily pushed up onto her arms, and the reality of the whole situation hit her with killing clarity. She was half-naked, moist with the remnants of a shattering sexual climax given to her by one of the world's most knowledgeable lovers, while the child in her care screamed with frustration. All her fine convictions, all her reasonable determinations had been swept aside by the potent touch of a man who could never really be hers. Shame bowed her head and brought tears to her eyes. Quickly, she scrambled up and began searching for her bra and sweater. The bra had been kicked under the bed. The sweater was stuffed down between the end of the mattress and the footboard. She yanked them on, trembling from head to toe. The rubber band holding back her hair had slipped to the end of her ponytail, but she had no time to fix it.

"Are you decent?" Logan asked cheerfully, coming into the room. He had turned Amanda Sue's face into the hollow of his shoulder and carried a clean diaper, with which he shielded her view.

No, she thought. *I guess not.* But then she pushed the guilt away and lifted her chin. "Is she all right?"

Amanda Sue sniffled and said around her fingers, "Oan num-nums."

"Of course, sweetheart," Emily said, her voice trembling. "I'll get lunch on the table." Avoiding eye contact with Logan, she slunk toward the door. He tossed aside the diaper and reached for her, but she pulled back at the last instant and slipped free. She needed time to compose herself, time to figure out how to handle this.

She had decided nothing by the time Logan, now wearing a T-shirt and jeans, carried Amanda Sue into the kitchen and put her into her high chair. He came to Emily and slid an arm around her waist while she cut into small pieces the sandwich she'd made for Amanda Sue earlier. "Emily," he said, kissing the side of her neck, "I want you to know how much—"

"I can't talk about this now, Logan," she interrupted, stopping what she was doing. "Please."

He looped his other arm around her chest and kissed the top of her ear. "All right," he agreed after a moment. "If that's the way you want it."

"Thank you."

He turned her to face him. "Don't thank me," he said, "because the deciding factor here is time. Just so you know, when I get back from New York, I don't intend to let you out of my sight again until we've settled some things between us."

Settled. She knew what that meant, and she knew that it could end only one way for her. She wondered if she had the courage to face it, the strength to walk away when the time came, for it would surely come. It was inevitable. It was what lay between then and now that she could not envision. She couldn't even think about it, not yet. Amanda Sue banged on her tray, demanding her "num-nums," and giving Emily an excuse to turn away again.

"Let's eat lunch," she said, "then you can spend some time with your daughter before you have to go."

"My daughter and you," he said, reaching around her for the nearest plate.

She closed her eyes as he moved away, wondering if he could possibly understand what he was doing to her, asking of her. Of course he couldn't. They were miles apart on the idea of affairs. While romantic love for him was a transitory condition, it could never be so for her. If she allowed herself to make love with him, it would be because she was in love with him and always would be. He would break her heart. He was doing it already. She had to find a way to protect herself from the inevitable.

God help her.

Steeling herself, she moved to the table and tried to behave as if she had not just come one step away from giving herself totally to her notoriously fickle boss. It was easier than she expected, thanks to Logan himself, but then he'd had a great deal of experience at this sort of thing, while she had virtually none. Amanda Sue helped, too, demanding her usual generous share of attention. Emily gave herself some space by insisting that she clean up while Logan spend time with his daughter. Afterward, she volunteered to neatly pack for him the things he had laid out on his bed and tried to keep the baby from flinging around.

It was a strange experience, folding Logan's intimate articles of clothing, organizing his toiletries, making sure his suit and tie were spotless, a very wifely sort of thing. She allowed herself to imagine, for a moment, what it would be like to be married to Logan Fortune, to share this big bed with him nightly, to wake beside him every morning, to bear his child. But would she be enough for him? Could he ever remain faithful to just one woman? She couldn't allow herself to believe it. She dared not believe it.

When she returned to the living room, he was giving Amanda Sue a "horsey" ride on his back. Emily sat down in the armchair to watch them. Logan ambled over on all fours, Amanda Sue holding tight to his hair with both hands, and "dumped" Amanda Sue off over his head, wrestling her around to his lap as he sat on the floor next to Emily's legs, his back to the chair. He played the name-the-body-part game with Amanda Sue, with much tickling and giggling and smooching going on. When they'd run out of Amanda Sue's body parts, he lifted Emily's foot and asked, "What's this?"

"Poot!" she announced confidently.

"Amanda Sue's foot?" he asked.

"Yeah," she confirmed, giggling at the obvious mistake.

"Well, this must be Amanda Sue's ankle, then," he said, kissing the part in question. Again his daughter insisted that it was. "And this must be Amanda Sue's leg," he went on, sliding his hands up Emily's leg. When he reached Emily's thighs, he pulled her off the chair onto the floor next to him, much to Amanda Sue's amusement. Amanda Sue laughed when he kissed Emily's belly, claiming it to be hers. When he kissed Emily's shoulders and neck, arms and hands, elbows and knees, it was at Amanda Sue's instigation. Finally Amanda Sue pointed to Emily's mouth, and Emily knew that she should put a stop to the game, but before she could do so, Logan was kissing her quite thoroughly, so thoroughly that Amanda Sue grew impatient and finally dug a finger between their mouths to separate them.

Logan snatched her up and tossed her over his head, pretending to scold her for pretending that Emily was her. Emily tried to move back into the chair, but he caught her hand with his and anchored her to his side. When Amanda Sue calmed down from her "scolding," he sat her in his lap and explained that he had to take a little trip by himself but that Emily would take care of her until he got back.

"Yeah, Mimly un Mana," Amanda Sue said, as if this was nothing new to her. Logan looked at Emily with raised eyebrows.

"I think her pronunciation is improving. She actually got the 'L' in Emily that time."

"Well, she's a very bright little girl," Emily said, fighting this feeling of belonging, of connection, of *family,* that so often enveloped her when the three of them were together like this.

"Yes, she is," Logan agreed, his forehead pressed to the little girl's. Then he glanced at the clock over the mantel and sighed. "I have to get on the move." He reluctantly passed the baby into Emily's arms and got to his feet. "I've ordered a cab so you can keep my car. The keys are on my dresser. I want you to drive it instead of that old heap of yours. Promise me you will."

She couldn't argue that it wouldn't be safer for Amanda Sue, so she agreed.

"I assume you'll be staying here nights," he said, "but it's okay if you decide to take Amanda Sue to your place. I'll call here first, but if I don't reach you, I'll call there. Remind me to buy you a cell phone of your own when I get back. Meanwhile, you can reach me through mine anytime you want."

Emily said, "We'll be fine."

He nodded and turned toward the bedroom. In a few minutes he returned to the living room carrying his briefcase, suitcase and a heavy trench-style overcoat. He deposited them in the entry hall by the door and returned to the living room, where Emily had gotten up and moved to the couch, Amanda Sue with her. He sat down next to them and gathered both into his arms.

"Is it just me or is her hair getting darker?" he asked Emily, stroking Amanda Sue's curly head.

"You know, it may be," she said. "This is about the time it starts turning. Yes, I think you're right. It's not as brassy bright as it was, more brown."

"My mom will be heartbroken," he said, chuckling.

"Not for long," Emily said. "Amanda Sue's a strong personality, one of a kind. It's appropriate that her appearance reflect that."

"You're absolutely right," he agreed, kissing his daughter on the top of her head. "I love you, 'Manda Mine."

"Wuv oo," she echoed almost thoughtlessly, sliding off Emily's knee and going after Goody, who had put in an appearance after disappearing for a time.

Logan chuckled and shook his head. Leaning back, he pulled Emily tighter into his embrace. "God, I wish I didn't have to leave you," he said against her temple, "but at least I have you to come home to."

She closed her eyes, the emotions of joy and doubt and fear mingling in simultaneous bursts within her. Her throat was clogged with them, her lungs restricted, her heart shocked. A horn sounded in the distance. Logan sighed.

"That must be my cab," he said.

Emily sat up. Logan got to his feet. Once more he picked up his daughter and kissed her.

"'Bye-bye, Daddy," she said unconcernedly, bending down to reach for Goody. With a laugh, he let her down again. "Walk me to the door?" he asked Emily.

Nodding, she got up and followed him. The car horn blew again just as they got there, so Logan opened the door and waved at the driver. Then he turned back to Emily, his hands resting lightly at her waist. "I'm going to miss you," he said. Smiling wanly, he added, "You've no idea how much I miss you every moment you're not with me now."

She gulped, wanting to believe that, not daring to. He bent his head and kissed her tenderly, pulling away again only when they were both breathless.

"I'll call tonight."

She nodded and pulled open the door again as he gathered up his baggage. One more look and he stepped out onto the doorstep. Suddenly she couldn't let him go without giving him something, some bit of what was in her heart. "Logan," she said, and he immediately turned back. "I'll miss you, too."

The smile that grew across his mouth also grew across her own. He stepped forward and kissed her hard on the mouth as the taxi driver blew its horn one more time. Then he was running down the sidewalk, coat flying out behind him. She stayed in the doorway until the taxi drove away. Only then did she fully face the fact that she was already in way over her head with Logan Fortune. She was crazy to try to make herself believe that she could hold herself back from him. Simply put, she was in love with him, so how did she keep herself out of his bed? Even if she could manage that feat, how did she keep herself from hoping for more from him than she knew he was capable of giving? Neither prospect looked good at the moment, but she knew that she would be less than she wanted and needed to be if she didn't at least try.

Ten

Despite her cavalier attitude at his leave-taking, Amanda Sue missed her daddy more than Emily had expected. She monopolized every telephone conversation with him and continually asked for him whenever Emily wouldn't give her what she wanted and at bedtime. It was no overstatement to say that both Amanda Sue and Emily were fairly sick of one another's uninterrupted company by Monday afternoon, when Logan called to say he'd have to stay another day or two. So it was with genuine welcome that Emily later opened the door to Eden Fortune and her darling son.

Eden stuck out her hand, a smile on her face. "I know we've met before, but I want you to know that I expect you to call me Eden."

"Logan told me you'd be stopping by, Eden," Emily said, returning her smile and her handshake. "And this must be Sawyer." She bent down to shake his hand, too, noting his ink-dark hair and big black eyes. Shyly, he hid his face against his mother's leg, but not before smiling at Emily. "Amanda Sue will be so happy to see you, Sawyer," Emily told him. "She talks about you all the time."

He looked at her with surprise rounding his eyes and mouth. "She talks?"

Eden laughed, and Emily smiled, nodding. "Oh, yes. You probably can't understand her, but she's definitely talking. Believe me, she always knows what she's saying even if we don't."

"Yes, I'd say that's a child who definitely knows her own mind," Eden commented with a grin.

"That she does," Emily said with a chuckle. "Come on in and see her."

Amanda Sue was in the living room with Goody, lying on her tummy whispering to the cat as if it understood every word. When Emily walked in with their company, saying, "Amanda Sue, look who's here," she jerked her head up, calling, "Daddy!" An instant later, she popped up and ran at Emily with her arms open wide, as if frightened to find someone other than her father standing there.

"Amanda Sue," Emily said, "don't you remember Aunt Eden and your cousin Sawyer?"

Amanda Sue looked them over and nodded her head. Abruptly she kicked to get down again, and Emily let her slide down to the floor. She poked Sawyer in the cheek with her fingertip, then said, "Mon, Awya. See Gooey."

"Goody is the cat," Emily explained, but Sawyer was already allowing himself to be led away.

Eden shook her head. "I swear, that child's mind works at lightning speed."

"Not to mention her legs," Emily added, grinning.

Eden chuckled. "Keeps you running, does she?"

"I don't mind," Emily said, ready to play gracious hostess. "Can I get you something to drink?"

"Oh, no, not just now, thanks. What I really want is just to sit down and talk with you."

Emily smiled and lifted a hand in invitation. "Let's have a seat on the couch then."

Eden nodded and walked across the room, seating herself smoothly. She wore a forest-green, wool, A-line skirt, fringed loafers, a navy sweater set trimmed in green-and-red plaid and opaque navy stockings. It was casual wear, but she still managed to look as though she'd just stepped off the pages of a fashion magazine, her dark hair swept forward over one shoulder. Emily felt slightly dowdy in her faded jeans and black turtleneck, her hair rolled up on the sides and held in place with combs, her old running shoes on her feet.

"My brother talks about you nonstop," Eden said, her words knocking Emily back in her seat.

"Oh, I...that is, he...uh..."

Eden laughed. "According to him, you're the world's leading authority on child care, the most efficient assistant who ever lived, the smartest, prettiest, sexiest, most engaging—"

"Please!" Emily said, her face burning with embarrassment.

Eden subsided, studying her. "I just had to get to know this paragon of virtue who finally seems to have captured my brother's heart."

Emily shook her head, even as hope fought for life inside her. "I'm just the baby-sitter, and temporary at that."

Eden cocked her head in a movement so reminiscent of Logan that Emily felt a spurt of intense longing for him. "Are you saying that you don't care for my brother?"

"No! I... That is, we're—"

"Never mind," Eden said, leaning forward to pat her hand. Her smile seemed to say that she'd already heard everything on the matter that was required. "Tell me about you, now. Logan says you're from a big family."

Emily let herself be pulled into this new topic of conversation and began to relax as it became obvious how easy Eden was to talk to. She seemed genuinely interested in Emily's life story and freely shared tales of Logan as a child. Later, she told her own story, revealing that she'd never married Sawyer's father. "I was a fool to believe him when he said he loved me," she confessed, "but I can't say that I regret anything I did. I have my son, after all."

Emily nodded, understanding how she could feel that way. "I know what you mean," she said thoughtlessly. "I have to keep reminding myself that Logan is not the sort to settle down, no matter how much I might want him to be."

"Oh, I don't know about that," Eden said, smiling thoughtfully, and only then did Emily remember that she was talking to his sister!

"I'm sorry, I didn't mean that to sound critical."

"Not at all," Eden said. "If I were in your position, I'd feel the same way. But I know my brother, and I think you may be underestimating him in this. Amanda Sue has changed him, but I think that deep down he's always craved a family of his own. He just hasn't trusted himself to be a better father and husband than our father was."

"Whoa," Emily said, "we're getting far afield here. Logan and I are in no way discussing marriage."

Eden opened her mouth as if to argue the point, then seemed to think better of it and closed it again. After a moment she smiled and asked, "What are you and Amanda Sue doing for dinner?"

"I was thinking of ordering in actually," Emily admitted. "Care to join us?"

"Pizza is Sawyer's new favorite food," Eden said suggestively.

Emily laughed. "Pizza it is."

It was over dinner that Emily mentioned Ciara Wilde. Eden's eyes grew large, and she sucked in a quick breath, motioning with a slice of pizza that she had something to say as soon as she swallowed. "You know, I'd get a real kick out of meeting her—uh, if it wouldn't be too much trouble. I mean, she might not want to meet me, or you might not want me horning in on an old friendship. I'd understand, of course. No big deal."

Emily laughed because it sounded like a big deal to Eden. "No problem," she said. "I'll mention it to Cathy—I can't help thinking of her as Cathy—and see how she feels about it, but I'm sure she'll be glad to meet you. She's really very sweet—and very beautiful."

Eden wrinkled her nose. "I was half hoping she'd look less stunning in person."

Emily shook her head. "Nope. More. It's positively ego-bruising, but she's so dear you'll soon forget all about that, not that you have anything to worry about. You could be a movie star yourself."

"I wish!" Eden exclaimed.

They giggled about that, like little girls, and much else. By evening's end, they were fast friends.

"I'm so glad I stopped by," Eden said, ready to take her leave with a sleepy Sawyer in her arms.

"Oh, me, too," Emily said, readjusting Amanda Sue's weight on her hip. "Amanda Sue and I are grateful for the company, and I know Logan will be glad she got to play with her cousin again."

"Yes, I want them to become close. Thanks for everything, Emily, for taking care of my niece and my brother and for a lovely day."

"Don't be silly. I hope to see you again soon."

"You will. I promise." Eden leaned in and kissed Amanda Sue's cheek. "Goodbye, darling."

"Say 'bye-bye to Aunt Eden," Emily coached her.

"'Bye," Amanda Sue complied, waving her hand, her eyelids at half-mast. She'd exhausted herself by playing busily with sweet, affable Sawyer that day. "'Bye, Awya."

"'Bye," he mumbled against his mom's shoulder. Then he suddenly lifted his head. "Hey, she does talk!"

Emily and Eden laughed, for that wasn't the first time that day Amanda Sue had communicated her thoughts to Sawyer, just the first time he'd realized it.

"Good night, Em," Eden said, opening the door. "You tell my brother that I said he's a lucky slob."

Emily told him just that when he called later. Logan only chuckled and said that he'd known Eden and she would get along. Emily gave him a detailed account of the visit, omitting only their discussion about her feelings for him. Logan recounted his own day, which had been dismally unproductive, and wished aloud that he was home.

"Well, don't worry about us," she said. "We're fine. Sawyer wore Amanda Sue out, though, so she went to sleep early."

"That's okay," he told her. "It's nice to get to spend

some time on the phone with you. Tell me, how did Amanda Sue like her first pizza?''

Emily told him how his daughter had plastered a pepperoni slice on her cheek after she'd found it too spicy to eat, much to Sawyer's amusement, and how she'd eaten the other toppings off the crust without ever allowing the crust into her mouth. They chatted on for some time, and before she knew it, they'd been on the phone for two whole hours! Logan only laughed, saying, "I can afford to pay my phone bill.''

"But I wanted to take a long, hot bath before bed," she complained. "I've hardly had time for a quick shower lately.''

Logan groaned. "Are you trying to kill me? It's bad enough that I can't stop thinking about your beautiful breasts and delectable mouth, now I'll be thinking about you floating naked in bubbles all night!''

Emily was too shocked to reply. Logan took advantage of her silence to tell her exactly what he'd do to her if he were there to share that bath. By the time she could stammer some excuse and get him off the phone, she was trembling head to toe—and she didn't go anywhere near the bathtub that night. But that didn't stop her from thinking about all those wicked things he'd said. And it didn't keep her from dreaming about them, either.

It was going on 3:00 a.m. when Logan let himself into the house, seven hours earlier than expected and worth every moment of the sleep he'd missed by not waiting for the morning flight he'd originally booked. He was so glad to be home that he wanted to shout, despite the exhaustion nagging at his bones.

The house was quiet, utterly silent. He paused in the hallway and let the peace soak in, but then he had to chuckle. It wasn't the peace and quiet that he'd missed. It was the chaos of a willful urchin who had his heart wrapped around her little finger and another surprisingly willful female who made him ache to have her, all of her, in every possible way—and only her. He felt a little euphoric about that. If he'd needed proof of his feelings—and in all honesty he had—he'd gotten it that weekend in New York.

An old playmate had turned up unexpectedly. She'd invited him to join her for dinner, and since she was already seated and his name was way down on the list of those waiting for tables, he'd done so gladly. They had talked animatedly, mostly about Amanda Sue, but when she had asked him to accompany her back to her apartment for an after-dinner drink and "games," he hadn't felt the least compunction to go. For a moment he couldn't quite figure out why. The woman hadn't changed appreciably. She was still a beautiful, sexy, no-strings-attached player, just the sort he'd always preferred—until now. That's when it hit him. He was committed to Emily, really committed. He didn't want any woman but her. Now if only he could convince Em. He knew that his reputation worked against him in this, but he suspected, hoped, that her heart was already engaged to some extent.

He needed to see her, but he felt compelled to check on Amanda Sue first. Dropping his baggage and coat in the living room, he bounded up the stairs, suddenly energized but aware of the need for silence. The door to his daughter's room was ajar. He pushed it open and slipped into the dimly lit interior. A sudden hiss brought him up short as he moved toward the bed.

"Well," he whispered, finding the cause in the arched-back cat at Amanda Sue's feet, "I see we have our very own attack cat. Looking out for my baby girl, are you?"

Goody relaxed, hackles folding back into smooth, tiger-striped fur. The cat walked over to the bedside rail and put its paws up on the top edge. Logan put out a tentative hand, and a sleek head rubbed against it, a purr rumbling up from the bed. Logan turned his attention to his little daughter. It always amazed him that a human tornado could sleep so soundly, so still. She looked like everything good in the world, lying there on her stomach, her cherub face turned toward him, one little hand tucked up under her chin. He reminded himself to have pictures made of her soon. More than once these past days he'd started to pull out his wallet, only to remember that he carried no photos of his darling daughter.

Goody stalked back and forth at the end of the bed, waiting impatiently for Logan to look his fill and go. Logan smiled at the cat. "She's worth protecting, isn't she? She's worth the world, my Amanda Sue. Okay, *our* Amanda Sue. But who's protecting Emily now, hmm? Tell me that?"

Maybe it was a job for which he could apply. He blew a kiss at his daughter and went out of the room, leaving the door carefully ajar. Walking past the bathroom, he went to the guest room door. Here the door was ajar, as well. Carefully pushing it open, he poked his head inside and saw Emily lying dead-center of the full-size bed. She rolled onto her back as he watched and sighed deeply through her nose, one hand coming up to rest on her stomach. Her long hair was trapped beneath her, and he itched to free it, spread it out upon the pillow and comb it with his fingers, feel it against his skin. He stepped out of his shoes and tiptoed inside.

It was warmer upstairs than down, and the covers had drifted down around her waist, revealing those mannish pajamas she seemed to favor. He'd have to buy her a proper nightgown, something in silk and lace that plunged in front and was slit to the waist on the sides. Better yet, he'd like to keep her so warm that she gave up sleeping in clothing altogether. He was feeling rather warm himself at the moment. Smiling, he peeled off his sweater and undershirt, released and tugged free his belt and dropped everything in a heap on the floor, his socks going on top. He took the time to fold his slacks and drape them over the chair by the door. Naked except for a pair of silk boxers, he eased beside Emily on the bed and propped himself up on one elbow. She took a deep breath, her chest expanding beneath the cotton shirt.

Carefully, he slipped the big buttons free of their holes and slid his hand inside. She moaned and edged toward him.

Leaning down, he brushed his mouth across hers, inhaling the perfume of her, the clean, womanly aroma of Emily. "I'm home, Em," he whispered. "I missed you."

"Miss you," she mumbled. Then her lips quirked beneath his, and she pulled back into her pillow. "Logan?"

"Yes." He moved his hand up to cup her breast. "I couldn't wait to make love to you."

She pushed a hand over her face, asking faintly, "Did I dream you?"

He chuckled silently. "I don't know. Did you? It would only be fair. I've been dreaming about you."

"What time is it?" she asked more cogently.

"Around three in the morning."

She looked at him in surprise, her eyes gleaming in the moonlight that spilled through the window. "You aren't supposed to be here until ten."

He smiled and tightened his hand. "I told you, I couldn't wait." He didn't give her a chance to say anything else, just bowed his head and kissed her deeply. Her arms drifted up lazily and settled around his shoulders. Easing his weight down, he shifted until he lay partly atop her, upper body braced on one forearm. He kissed the corner of her mouth, then licked his way inside, drinking of her nectar.

Spreading her pajama shirt wide, he slid his hand downward beneath the covers until he encountered the soft elastic waistband of her pants. "Em," he whispered against her mouth, "Emily, my Emily." He laid his forehead against hers. She was warm and pliant everywhere he touched. He wanted her on fire for him. "Let me in," he pleaded. "Please let me in."

She caught a gasping breath that sounded almost like a sob. "I don't think I can keep you out!"

Elated, he rose above her on his knees and shoved down his boxers, stripping them off before sweeping back the covers and inserting his fingers beneath the waistband of her cotton pajamas. He gently eased them down, spreading kisses in their wake and smiling against her skin at the small gasps and trembling sighs he elicited. Remembering how she had come apart in his arms the last time he'd had her beneath him, he longed to bring her to climax again, but he had promised himself that he would be inside her the next time, that she would be tied to him in that much at least.

Dropping her pajama bottoms on the floor, he kissed the arch of her foot and nibbled an appetizing ankle before covering her body with his. The feel of all that skin was exquisite. Emily put her head back and cried out softly as he rubbed his chest against hers, his hips finding the cradle of hers, their legs tangling. He sank his teeth into the delicate flesh beneath her chin, and she undulated beneath him like a wave upon a crystal blue ocean.

"Let me in, sweetheart," he repeated against her mouth. "Let me in." She turned her face away, but he nuzzled her ear, kissing and tasting. After a moment she opened her legs. He settled between them, her silken nakedness screwing his eyes shut in breathless ecstasy. Clamping down on the sensation, he gritted his teeth and brought himself back to the moment, aware for the first time that she had gone rigid. Bracing his upper body weight on his elbows, he used his hands to coax her face back to his.

"I need you, Em," he whispered, and her bottom lip trembled. He kissed it, nibbled it, licked the sensitive flesh inside until her arms came around him again. He kissed her fully, making it last a long, long time, sliding his tongue in and out, biting gently, sucking, licking. When she began to writhe sinuously beneath him, he slid a hand down to one knee and pulled it upward, intending to ease down between her legs so that he could push upward again and finally join them. It was exactly then that Amanda Sue screamed.

"Aaaaaah! Da-a-a-dy-y-y-y!"

At once exasperated and concerned, Logan turned his head in the direction of the door, the sobs and wails tearing at him even as he wanted to ignore them.

"Daddy! Da-ha-ha-dyyy!"

"I'll go," Emily muttered, as if waking from a drugged sleep and pushing against him.

Logan bit back a sigh. "No, I'll do it." He kissed her quickly and pushed back off the bed. He let his gaze sweep over her sleek body as he yanked on his slacks. "You're beautiful," he said. "Perfect. I won't be long." Then he turned away and was out the door. "I'm coming, Amanda Sue."

At the sound of his voice her cries took on an eager tone, and he knew with a pang of delight that his little girl had, indeed, missed him. Despite his frustration, he couldn't help smiling as wide as the moon as she came into his arms, sobbing out his name. Goody quickly disappeared now that reinforcements had arrived. "Coward," Logan teased, his irritation having disappeared in the wealth of the moment. What did he have to be irritated about when his soft, warm little girl clung to him with undisguised affection and the love of his life waited for him to return to her bed?

He changed a very wet diaper and then spent some time talking to his daughter, telling her how much he'd missed her and how glad he was to be home. "I love you, angel, love you so much." It struck him how often he used those words now and how seldom he had used them in the past.

"Oan bobble," she demanded, putting him firmly in his place. He chuckled. Had Emily been giving her a bottle again? He thought they'd just about broken the habit before he'd left. Maybe his absence had been more traumatic than he'd realized.

"Let's see what Emily has to say about that."

He carried Amanda Sue to the guest room, knocked on the door frame and stepped inside, "Honey, she wants—" He stopped, staring at an empty bed. Turning around, he looked to the bathroom. The door stood open, the room dark. A feeling of unease gripped him. "Emily?" he called, hurrying toward the stairs. He had taken three of the steps when he heard the front door close. The hollow, muted sound was a knife in the chest. "Emily?" he said again, but he knew that he was talking to an empty house. He stood there on the staircase, one hand on the banister, the other holding his daughter to his chest, and felt his heart cracking in two.

It was after ten later that morning before she showed up again. Logan sat in one corner of the sofa, angry, hurt and exhausted, while Amanda Sue played in his lap with a set of interconnecting plastic rings he'd brought her from New York, the cat spread out beside them. He had left the bottle of expensive perfume he'd bought for Emily on the dresser in its cellophane-sealed box, wondering if she would ever wear it. He'd come very near to pouring it down the toilet.

She tucked her keys into her pocketbook and dropped it onto the chair seat. "I thought you might want to sleep late," she said, her gaze failing to meet his.

"How kind," he drawled sarcastically. "Of course, that's assuming that I actually managed *to* sleep."

She winced slightly at that, but made no direct comment. "Have you had breakfast? Want some coffee?"

"Yes and no."

She nodded and cast a longing glance toward the kitchen, but he was beyond pity.

"Well, aren't you going to say how Amanda Sue and I needed some time alone together after my absence?" He waited but she didn't say anything. "Maybe there was a fire somewhere that demanded your immediate attention?" he prodded. When she didn't reply to that, he quirked a brow into an angry arch. "Oh, I know. Ciara Wilde forgot her lines and telegraphed you a mental message for help."

Taking a deep breath, she faced him finally. "You took me by surprise," she explained tonelessly. "When I had a moment to think rationally, I realized what a mistake we were making."

"A mistake," he echoed. "Because I'm your boss. The job is *that* important to you?"

"Yours isn't?" she shot back.

"No."

She scoffed, her expression clearly skeptical. "You're telling me you'd give up your job with the family company for a night of sex!"

He wanted to throw something, hit something. Fortunately Amanda Sue was sitting in his lap. Hands coiled into fists, he strove for some semblance of calm. "I never said that. You know perfectly well I never said that. What I want from you is—"

"It's a bad idea, Logan!" she interrupted sharply. "And it isn't going to happen again." She folded her arms protectively, her gaze trained on the floor at her feet. He stared at her for a long time. She was as closed to him as ever, perhaps more so. She didn't care about him. It was a job to her, nothing more.

"All right," he said finally, struggling to keep the hurt out of his voice. He gathered his daughter into his arms and got to his feet. "In that case, you're late for work, and because you're late, so am I. I suggest you watch Amanda Sue while I get dressed."

Emily nodded without looking at him. He set Amanda Sue on her feet. Emily crouched down and held open her arms. Amanda Sue ran to her, and he turned away. For the first time in his life, he knew what it meant to really lose, and he wondered how he could possibly endure it.

When the telephone rang, she knew that she had been waiting for it. Nowhere near sleep, she rolled over in her slightly squeaky bed and switched on the lamp before sitting up, knees drawn to her chest, and reaching for the telephone receiver. She missed Goody, even though the silly cat would only have hopped down from the bed and stalked away, indignant at having his slumber interrupted.

"Hello?"

She could hear the screams in the background. "Can you talk to her?" Logan said without preamble.

"Yes, of course." She heard him explaining to Amanda Sue that Emily was on the telephone, and wanted to talk to her, but Amanda Sue was having none of it. Emily sighed.

For three nights in a row now, Amanda Sue had awakened demanding to see her. The first night Logan had not called. He'd simply endured, and it had taken its toll on him and Amanda Sue both the next morning. Emily had never seen him looking so tired and beaten. For her part, Amanda Sue had hung around Emily's neck and wept as if her heart was broken. She'd stayed glued to Emily's side throughout the day and demanded her father several times, which they'd accomplished via telephone. He'd come home early from work, only to call later that evening to ask her to speak to Amanda Sue. That had seemed to calm her, but yesterday had been a difficult day with Amanda Sue pitching a fit when her father had left for work and again when Emily had left for home. Now she was refusing to speak to Emily on the telephone, demanding instead that Emily come to her.

"Maybe she's sick," Logan ventured, coming back to the phone defeated.

"Have you taken her temperature?"

"I tried to, but she screamed, 'No. Mimly.' I guess that means she wants you to do it. In fact, she seems to want you to do everything."

"Just when I'm not there apparently," Emily told him. "She was the same way about you today. She wouldn't eat her lunch, just kept demanding, 'Daddy, Daddy, Daddy.'"

"I should never have taken that trip," he said, and his voice sounded muffled, as if he were rubbing a hand over his face.

"You didn't have any choice in the matter, as I recall," Emily told him briskly. "Anyway, the question is, what do we do now?"

Logan sighed, Amanda Sue sobbing in the background. "I was hoping you'd tell me. You're the expert."

She ignored that, knowing the acerbic tone was due more to exhaustion than anything else. Mentally, she went through their options. It didn't take long. They didn't have many. "I think I should call the pediatrician tomorrow and make an appointment. Tonight, I suggest a mild analgesic and a bottle of warm milk."

"I've tried that," he said with great frustration. "She threw it at me and demanded that you do it."

"All right," Emily said, resignedly making a decision she'd rather have avoided. "I'll be right over."

"Emily's coming," she heard him tell Amanda Sue as he hung up the phone.

As she pulled on her clothes, she couldn't help musing sadly that he'd offered no words of gratitude or praise this time. But then why should he? It was a job, nothing more. She was quite sure that she'd find overtime compensation included in her next paycheck, and that was the way it should be, the way she wanted it.

So why did it hurt so badly?

Eleven

The next morning, Logan and Emily took Amanda Sue to the doctor. Her examination complete, Dr. Costas sat down at the minuscule desk built into one wall and gave them her diagnosis. "Her ears, throat and nose are a little red, but that's to be expected with all this crying. Also, her gums are a little swollen. She's probably cutting teeth. Otherwise she seems in excellent condition. I'd say the problem is emotional, and that's understandable—no?—with all she's been through."

"How do you mean that exactly?" Logan asked, and Dr. Costas shrugged.

"Children grieve as we do, Mr. Fortune. She lost her mother. Strangers took over her care. She made that adjustment, and now she has her father and—I'm sure you see the logic in this—also a mother in you, Emily. I suspect that she was just truly growing secure again when you had to go out of town. Emily was there all the time, of course, but there was anxiety. Then, as soon as her father returned, Emily began disappearing again for long periods. She has to be confused. What child would not be, eh? She is afraid, Mr. Fortune, and it's quite natural. We call it separation anxiety. I think she will adjust in time, but the fewer changes the better for a while."

Logan glanced at Emily, then down at his daughter who contentedly played in Emily's lap, and his jaw hardened. He turned back to the doctor. "Would it help if Emily stayed the night with her? If she moved in for a while?"

Dr. Costas nodded. "That would be ideal, actually, but it

might take some weeks for Amanda Sue to grow secure enough to begin weaning her away with occasional absences, but if it's done gradually, I'm sure she will come to accept Emily's absence without fear. Is that possible, Emily?''

Emily knew she had to do it, even though she felt most unfairly trapped by the situation. She nodded resignedly. "Yes, I can move in temporarily.''

Dr. Costas seemed pleased, but had a final caution. "I would suggest that you avoid going out of town again anytime soon, Mr. Fortune, if at all possible.''

"Don't worry,'' he said, stroking Amanda Sue's head. "I'm not going anywhere until she understands that I'll return to her.''

"I'll write a prescription for an analgesic,'' the doctor said, doing just that, "something to reduce inflammation. But I'd rather not give her an antibiotic at this time. If she should start to run a fever, though, please call the office at once.'' She tore off the prescription and handed it to Logan, who folded it and put it in his pocket. "Now,'' she said with a smile, "can I do anything else for you?''

Logan shook his head. "No. Thank you for seeing us so quickly, though, Dr. Costas.''

"My pleasure,'' she said, getting to her feet. She shook Amanda Sue's small hand, saying, "Goodbye, Amanda Sue Fortune. Be well.'' With that, she smiled and left the room.

Emily hung the last of her meager temporary wardrobe in the guest room closet and closed the bifold door. She was unpacked. She had moved into the house with Logan Fortune and his troubled daughter. The psych ward couldn't be far away. How was she going to endure living side by side with the one man she wanted but could not have? She turned toward the door, only to find Logan standing there, arms folded, watching her.

"All settled in?''

She nodded, not trusting herself to speak. He stepped into

the room, his hands going to his hips and his gaze to the bed where they had come so near to making love. The expression with which he faced her again was shuttered.

"I, um, hope you know how much I appreciate this," he began. "You'll be suitably compensated, I promise."

That stung—unfairly, she thought. "Stop it!" she snapped. "You know very well that I'm not doing this to earn money."

He bowed his head. "Of course. You care about Amanda Sue. I didn't mean to imply that you don't. I guess I just have a hard time accepting that you don't care about me."

She had to stiffen her arms to keep from throwing them around him. Swallowing, she turned away. "That isn't so. I care about you very much, but that doesn't have to lead to sex, you know. It's the sex I consider inappropriate."

"You didn't seem to find it inappropriate the last time we were in this room together."

She whirled around, surprised that he'd say it—especially since he was right. "You took me by surprise," she murmured. "I wasn't thinking clearly."

"Who was the last man who could do that to you, Emily?" he asked quietly. "Has there been…is there someone else?"

She stared at him, dismayed beyond words. Of course there was no one else. She hadn't even had a coffee date in…nearly two years now. *Oh, God,* she thought. *Oh, God, please show me that I haven't been waiting for this, that I haven't been secretly comparing every other man to him, loving him from afar, cutting myself off from everyone else. We aren't right for one another. He'll never love me like I need him to!* She wanted to cry. How could she fight him and herself? Especially now. Here. She couldn't know that pleading and hopelessness spilled from her eyes.

"I'd better start dinner," she mumbled and, brushing past him, she hurried away, safe for another moment. Safe and alone.

* * *

"Two gentlemen to see you, sir. Mr. Matthew Fortune and a Sheriff Grayhawk."

Logan stared at Hal's combative stance and wondered two things. One, what on earth were Matt and Grayhawk doing here in his office? And two, was the efficient and muscular Hal about to add physical defense to the job description of temporary executive assistant? He almost smiled at the thought but couldn't quite muster the energy.

Amanda Sue continued to wake repeatedly throughout the night demanding both Emily and himself. He wondered how much longer he could go on like this, bumping into Emily in those damnable pajamas all night long, worrying about his precious daughter, reining in his unruly desires. It was torture, having Emily living in the house, wondering if he would ever be enough for his confused little girl and why he couldn't be enough for Emily.

How ironic was that? For years he'd fended off the would-be wives with dollar signs in their eyes and Fortune in their sights, only to fall in love with the one female who wouldn't have him on a silver platter. They would both be here soon, Emily and his Amanda Sue, to interview a nanny applicant. With his little girl having problems, now was not the best time to be interviewing for the position, but it was getting harder and harder to find applicants, and he hadn't wanted to cancel the appointment.

Hal cleared his throat, calling Logan back to the matter at hand. "Send them in, Hal, and thanks," he said mildly. Hal neither questioned nor delayed.

"This way, gentlemen. Mr. Fortune will see you now."

Logan got up and came around his desk to properly greet his cousin. "Matt," he said, smiling and extending his hand, "to what do I owe this unexpected pleasure?"

Matthew made a sheepish nod toward Grayhawk. "You know Wyatt."

"Sheriff," Logan said, offering his hand a second time. Wyatt Grayhawk shifted his cowboy hat to his left hand and gripped Logan's with his right.

"What happened to Wyatt?" he asked, grinning. "A lawman can get suspicious when his friends start calling him by his title, even if they haven't seen each other in too long."

Logan chuckled. "It has been a while. How's it going, Wyatt?"

"So-so. How about yourself?"

Logan sighed. "You wouldn't know because you don't have children," he said, "but it's damned exhausting work."

"What about the marvelous Emily?" Matt asked, eyes twinkling knowingly.

Logan disciplined himself to make a sedate reply. "The marvelous Emily is as exhausted as I am. Amanda Sue's having a difficult time right now, abandonment issues, according to the doctor."

"I'd say that's understandable," Matthew told him, reverting to his competent physician mode. "Her mother's death must have confused her terribly, but it'll work out. She obviously adores you, and vice versa."

Logan smiled. "True, but you didn't come here to talk about my amazing daughter." He leaned back against the desk and crossed his ankles. "Have a seat, boys, and tell me what this is about."

While lowering himself into one of the chairs in front of the desk, Matt cast a look over his shoulder at Hal, who remained in the open doorway.

Logan smiled at his overly protective assistant and said, "Hal, now might be a good time for you to run down and get those figures we requested from Dan Talbot in accounting." He knew perfectly well, of course, as did Hal, that Dan would phone with the figures the moment he had them, but true to form, Hal hurried away to do just as he was told. Logan turned back to his cousin. "What's up, Matt? Does this have to do with the kidnapping?"

Matthew nodded and cleared his throat, seeming uncomfortable with what he had to say. "In a way, yes. As you know, when Devin recovered the baby thought to be our precious Bryan, we discovered he wasn't ours. But since Taylor had the hereditary crown-shaped birthmark and rare blood type we knew he was a Fortune."

"Right. The whole family's talking about it, and you must admit it's a fascinating mystery," Logan said. "How did the kidnappers get this other baby instead of Bryan? And whose child is Taylor?"

"That's the problem exactly," Wyatt said, shifting forward in his chair, his hat balanced lightly between his hands.

Matt hastened to explain. "Frankly, Logan, we're baffled, and Wyatt thinks that it would help to know just exactly who Taylor belongs to."

Logan lifted a hand to pinch his chin, considering. Could Taylor somehow be his? Before Amanda Sue he would have scoffed at the idea, but no longer. It was possible. He couldn't believe that Taylor was his, but he couldn't deny the possibility, either.

"What do you want me to do?" he asked.

Matthew glanced at Grayhawk with apparent relief. "It's a simple test," he said. "I'm taking it myself and we're hoping all the other Fortune men will, too. Since we would've known if a Fortune woman had been pregnant, it makes more sense to test the men. All you have to do is get down to the lab and have some blood drawn. Wyatt will give you a card with the address and hours on it."

Wyatt fished the card out of his shirt pocket and handed it over. Logan glanced at it and placed it in his own pocket. "All right. I'll try to do it today."

"Excellent," Grayhawk said, getting to his feet. "The sooner, the better. These things can take weeks as it is. I hope the others are as cooperative."

"If it'll help get baby Bryan home," Logan said, looking at Matt, "I'm glad to do it."

Smiling Matt rose and reached out to clap Logan on the arm. "Thanks. I knew you'd understand, being a father and all."

Logan could only shake his head. "It's amazing, isn't it? How it changes everything?" He looked at the sheriff. "What about you, Wyatt? Any chance you'll be setting up a nursery anytime soon?'

Wyatt shook his dark head adamantly. "Not me. Being sheriff keeps me up plenty of nights as it is."

The others chuckled lightly, but then Matt said, "Being a doctor does that, too, but it's not the same." For the first time, Logan really heard the agony in his voice, heard it and identified with it. He put his arm around Matt's shoulders, a true comrade. He couldn't imagine losing Amanda Sue now that they'd finally found each other?

"We'll get him home," he said. "Somehow he'll come home."

Matt nodded, head bowed. "I keep telling his mom that, and I try to believe it myself. Otherwise—" He didn't say more; he didn't have to.

"I think you know this, but I'm going to say it, anyway," Logan told him. "If there's anything else I can do, you just have to let me know."

Matthew smiled. "You bet."

"Thanks, Logan," Wyatt said, clapping him on the shoulder as he moved toward the door. "We'd better move. Still have lots to do. I really appreciate your cooperation, though." He stopped in the hallway and looked over one shoulder, adding carefully, "You know, your father wouldn't have been as understanding."

That knocked Logan back momentarily. "You're absolutely right," he said thoughtfully, but then he smiled. "One thing I've definitely learned, though, is that I'm not my father."

"Funny how long it takes us to learn some things, isn't it?" Matthew said, following the sheriff at a slower pace.

"And sad sometimes what it takes to teach us," Logan added, right behind him. "I'll get down to the lab as soon as I'm free this afternoon. You'll let me know what the test turns up, won't you, who Taylor belongs to?"

"Absolutely," Matthew said. "I just pray that somehow it leads us to Bryan."

"Hold that thought," Logan told him, opening the outer door for them and watching them walk through. "Nice to see you both. So long now."

He stepped back and let the heavy glass door swing closed. Poor Matt and Claudia. To have a child, an infant, taken from you. Everyone said that having Taylor with them helped them deal with the loss, but Logan knew that no child could be replaced by another. If he lost Amanda Sue, finding out that Taylor was his wouldn't fill that hole in his heart at all, not that it wouldn't be nice to have a son, too.

A son. He shook his head, wondering at himself. He really wasn't like his father. Smiling wanly, he turned toward the office once more, and that's when he saw Emily and Amanda Sue sitting quietly at Hal's, no, *her* desk. She didn't have to tell him that she'd heard it all. The look on her face was telling enough.

Emily knew that he was taking a test to determine if he had fathered yet another unknown child, and it was just one more obstacle between them. One more reason she couldn't bring herself to love him.

Emily sat crosswise in the chair, her legs hanging over one arm, and stared with desultory concentration at the television screen, where a late-night talk show played out in goofy gags and goofier discussion. Suddenly, without warning, the picture changed, images flickering past at lightning speed. Irritation got the better of her. She sat up straight.

"Hey, I was watching that!"

Logan, who was stretched out on the couch, simultaneously turned his head and lifted his finger off the button on the remote control. "Sorry," he mumbled. Aiming the remote at the television, he punched in the appropriate numbers, bringing up the proper channel, only to display the credits rolling past the host's face. Sighing, he sat up and braced his elbows on his knees. "Sorry," he said again. "I—I wasn't thinking."

"It's okay," she said, mimicking his posture. "You probably forgot I was here."

"Huh!" He tossed the remote onto the cushion next to him. "As if I could."

It was her turn to apologize. "Sorry. I'll, um, find something to read and go back up to bed."

"No, don't," he said, screwing up his face. "It's not your fault you can't sleep." He glanced at the top of the stairs. "Looks like Amanda Sue's the only one who can—for once."

Emily nodded. It did seem as though the child would sleep through the night. Emily knew that she ought to be following suit, but the short nights seemed to have rewired her internal clock. She'd tossed for what had seemed like hours before tiptoeing down to find Logan fighting insomnia himself. They'd both gone for the only television in the house, for all the good it had done.

"Maybe some music will help," Logan said, getting up to shut off the television and turn on the CD player. "What do you like?"

He started naming performers, and when he came to a particular pop singer with an uncanny resemblance to Elvis and a haunting, romantic sound, Emily spoke up. "I didn't know you liked him."

He sent a look over his shoulder, just a hint of humor in his blue eyes. "Seems we have quite a bit in common." He popped the CD into the player and quickly began filling the changer. Music wafted into the room. Emily sat back and let it soothe her.

After a moment Logan wandered back to the sofa, sat down and began to speak. "Do you think maybe she's turned a corner?" he asked.

"Maybe. These things take time, you know."

"I shouldn't have gone to New York," he said, looking away guiltily.

"You didn't have a choice," she pointed out. "If anyone's to blame, I am. I should have done what you asked and gone with you."

He shook his head. "That was foolishness. It was too much for a child her age."

"But it might have been better than the alternative."

He pushed his hands over his face. "I don't know. What does it matter now? Somehow I just have to get through this and find a way to get on with my life."

Emily nodded. It seemed as good an opening as she was likely to get for what had been on her mind. Strictly speaking, it was none of her business, of course, but she just couldn't quell the need to know. She licked her lips. "Speaking of the future, Logan, I couldn't help overhearing your conversation with your cousin and the sheriff this afternoon."

He tilted his head, smirking somewhat. "I noticed."

"You can tell me to mind my own business, if you want."

He shook his head and folded his hands. "No, I've been waiting for it. Go ahead, get it off your chest."

She bit the inside of her cheek lightly. "Have you thought about what you'll do if that little boy is yours?"

He nodded slowly. "For one thing," he said carefully, "I'll have to get a bigger place. I've been thinking about that, anyway. Kids need play room outside, and even if we spend summers on the ranch—and I really want to do that—we'll still need room for jungle gyms and swing sets, that sort of thing." He spread an arm along the back of the couch, obviously mulling it over. "You don't think it would be best to leave Taylor with Matt and Claudia, do you? They've already lost one child, but if he's my son then he belongs with me." Logan shook his head. "He probably isn't, though. I'm not saying it isn't possible, it's just…how likely would that be? First I find a daughter and then a son?" He sat forward suddenly. "Would it be terribly selfish of me to hope just a tiny bit that he is mine?"

Emily was flabbergasted. "You mean, you'd welcome another child?"

Logan sat back again. "You have to ask that?"

"After everything you've been through with Amanda Sue, I wouldn't blame you if you were overwhelmed by the idea of another child."

He chuckled. "It's crazy, isn't it? Being a father is the most difficult thing I've ever done—and the easiest. The past few weeks have been the best of my life and the very worst, but I wouldn't change anything. Well, maybe one thing. I'd make you want me as much as I want you." The smile faded from his face even as he was speaking.

Emily felt her heart turn over. "It isn't that, Logan."

He got up abruptly and turned away. "Sorry, Em, I didn't mean...never mind." He walked over to the CD player and began going through the CDs again.

She was halfway across the room before she realized what she was doing, but she didn't stop. She kept going until she could place an understanding hand upon his shoulder. "Logan, please—"

To her shock, he jerked away. "Don't!" he snapped.

"But, Logan—" she began, stunned.

"Don't touch me," he demanded angrily, his hand going to his shoulder as if she'd injured him with her touch. "I can't bear it! Don't you understand that you're driving me crazy? You're killing me, Em! I can't sleep. I can't think. During the day I can't wait to get home, and then I can't stand to be here! Most of all, I can't stop wanting you."

She knew then that she loved him enough to do what he wanted, to give him as much of herself as necessary to ease his pain, for she didn't doubt that he was in pain or that she possessed the means to soothe him. That, after all, was Logan. Women were almost a drug to him, a means of coping, perhaps, and when had he ever had more with which to cope? She wouldn't think beyond her love for him, not now, not in this moment. *Besides,* said a little voice inside her head, *you want to be with him.* She couldn't deny it.

"Logan, I—"

"I shouldn't have said anything," he complained. "I promised myself I wouldn't."

She stepped closer and laid two fingers across his mouth. "Hush. Listen to me. I do want you."

He was shaking his head, and she knew she wasn't making her point and that she wasn't going to with words, so she kissed him, just placed her hands on either side of his face and lifted her mouth to his. He froze in place for a long moment, but then his mouth moved beneath hers, widened and negotiated for a better fit, and she granted him easy access, meeting her tongue with his, sliding her arms around his neck.

She half expected him to do the chivalrous thing, to pull back, give her time to rethink, to be sure. He did not. Instead, he found ways to kiss her even as he yanked the knot out of the belt of her bathrobe and shoved the garment off her shoulders. He kept on kissing her as he stripped her pajama shirt off over her head and pushed down her pajama bottoms, stepped on them, and lifted her free. Just that quickly she was standing naked before him. The next instant he swept her up into his arms and headed for the bedroom.

Leaving the door open, he dropped her on the bed. The bedcovers had been folded back, but he ripped them from beneath her, tossing them over the footboard. He danced back into the shadows, away from the light fanning through the door. Emily pushed up onto her forearms, listening to the sounds of fabric moving, shoes dropping, drawers opening and closing against the backdrop of dreamy music. He muttered anxious, unintelligible words, and then he was beside her, kissing her again, running his hands over her body.

"Will you hate me if I don't wait?" he asked, panting.

"No." She wasn't even sure what he meant, but it didn't matter.

He slid atop her, kissing her face, her eyes, her nose, her mouth. The hand that reached down and lifted her knee trembled. He eased between her legs. His fingers probed gently, found her moist and open to him, and suddenly she was panting, as well. He slid into her slowly, lifting himself up onto his arms, his forehead meeting hers. "Oh, Emily," he said, "my Emily."

As he filled her, she caught her breath, and her breasts seemed to swell toward him, nipples hard. She bowed her back, and he met that silent plea with the firm wall of his chest, his hands going into her hair as his mouth captured hers. The sensation of being filled by him was incredible, but it only seemed to awaken the need for more. She had to move, simply had to. He answered her by withdrawing and plunging in again. Of its own volition, her head went back and a sound somewhere between a groan of ecstasy and a howl of torture came up out of her throat. She was embarrassed—somewhere in the back of her mind. He was inflamed.

Suddenly he was stroking into her with swift, sure precision. Calling her name, he surged deep and rocked his hips with the same maddening pace. She wrapped her legs around him, her head starting to spin. She heard him gasp into her ear that it was too late, and she wanted to say that she was sorry about that, but she was soaring so high and fast that she couldn't speak. She heard someone crying out, and then dimly became aware that he was stroking into her again while she did nothing but float somewhere inside her own mind. Only when he collapsed atop her did she realize that she hadn't left him behind, after all.

With great effort and tremendous force of will, she lifted a hand and stroked it through his dark hair. He breathed gusts of fire against the curve of her neck, his heart beating like a jackhammer against her breast and keeping time with hers. After a long while, he lifted his head and shifted to one side. His hand drifted up to one breast, stroking it reverently. He kissed her temple, wrapped his arms around her.

Gradually, gently, he began to make love to her again. Only when he left her briefly and returned did she realize that he had done so in order to avail himself of a fresh condom. She was intensely grateful—and too ashamed to admit that she hadn't even thought of protection.

Shame and all else burned away in awe as he lived up to his reputation, inciting her body to the peak of desire and satisfying it utterly. She could not believe it when he began again, could not believe, even, that she could respond, until he proved much more knowledgeable than she. The words of love that he whispered and the compliments that he heaped upon her worked magic that even his hands and mouth could not replicate, and yet she dared not believe them. How could she? How could she, plain, efficient Emily who had sat beneath his nose for two long years, be his one true love? How had she suddenly become beautiful in his eyes? How could her breasts be perfect and her belly make him insane with need? She tried not to listen, but failing that, she determined not to believe. For the moment, it was enough that she loved him.

Thankfully Amanda Sue never woke that night, not that it mattered, for they never slept.

Twelve

Amanda Sue dug a determined finger between their mouths and pried them apart. Logan laughed indulgently and spoke to the child on his hip. "Don't you want Daddy to kiss Emily?"

Amanda Sue shook her head. "No! No tiss Mimly."

Logan pushed out his bottom lip, pretending to pout. When the lip began to tremble, Amanda Sue threw back her head and laughed, then pointed a finger at Emily and ordered, "Tiss! Tiss Mimly!"

This time it was Logan who shook his head, his grin as wide as his face. "I'd better not," he said, cutting a heated look at Emily. "If I kiss her again I may not leave for work at all."

Emily couldn't help smiling, even if it was all a farce on her part. She'd known with a dead certainty from the moment she'd left the bed this morning how this would have to end for her, but he was happy, if only for this moment, and that was enough to smile about. So she gave him the smile, as she had given him her body and her heart and the next weeks. Besides, she had best smile while she could, for the time was coming when smiles would be in very short supply and pain all too abundant.

"I'll call you," he whispered, nuzzling her temple, "and if I can, I'll be home early."

She kissed his cheek and pulled Amanda Sue into her arms. He ruffled his daughter's hair. "See you later, sweetheart. I love you." He kissed Emily on the top of her head, a nice, safe, chaste farewell. "I love you, too."

She knew he wanted to hear the words in return, but she couldn't say them, not because they weren't true, but because they were. "See you," she said lightly, lifting Amanda Sue's hand in a wave. "'Bye-bye, Daddy."

"Seeouuu!" Amanda Sue cried as he moved down the entry hall.

"This afternoon!" he called, going through the door.

Emily felt the tenseness in Amanda Sue, understood the niggling of doubt that shadowed her brilliant eyes. She looked at Emily and pointed at the door at the end of the hall. "Daddy," she said in a small, questioning voice. Emily smiled and kissed her.

Talking, she carried Amanda Sue to the couch. "Your daddy loves you. He'll be home this afternoon. He doesn't like to be away from you, but he's an important man and a lot of people depend on him to do his job. He'll always come home to you, Amanda Sue, because you are the one true love of his life. Even when I'm not here, he will take care of you, always. I know it."

The child seemed to be listening, but Emily could only guess how much she understood. Emily hugged her and turned her thoughts toward the day ahead. She would not dwell on tomorrow or last night, only now, this day. Maybe she could survive what she had to do that way.

Logan watched Emily moving around the room, picking up this toy, straightening that cushion. They were little things that occupied her, little homey things that made him feel warm and content and gave him an odd pleasure that seemed to wrap around his heart. He loved to just look at her, to measure the grace with which she walked and bent and grasped. She used her hands with such delicacy, and yet their strength was evident. The way she turned her head, lifted her chin, quirked her mouth, smoothed her hair, pushed her glasses up on her nose and swung her foot when reading: it all fascinated him and made him think that he was the only one to ever see, appreciate and revel in all that was Emily.

Because of her, he was absurdly happy. Amanda Sue had brought depth and meaning to his life, qualities he hadn't even known he was missing, and somehow his little girl had become absolutely essential to his well-being. But it was Em who made him sing in the shower. Em who made him believe that anything was possible, that life could be good even at its worst.

He wanted to go to bed. Nothing was as perfect as holding Emily in his arms in the dark of night, but it was only seven. Amanda Sue wasn't even down yet. She lay on the floor next to Goody, trying to purr with sublime concentration. In just a moment he would have to get up from the couch and take her upstairs for her bath. He hoped she slept through the night. It was an iffy thing just now; some nights were good, some nights were not.

No one in this house was getting as much sleep as needed, but at least when he did sleep it was deeply, almost profoundly—and it wasn't just because of the sex. Truth be told, he'd noticed Emily sometimes held herself back in the bedroom. But he knew that each time they made love was a step toward deepening trust and intimacy, drawing them closer and closer together.

Yet Emily was holding back emotionally too. He knew it, even as she stopped straightening the room and smiled at him in that almost secretive way that told him she, too, was thinking of bed. Yes, she was holding part of herself back from him, but he couldn't fault her. His reputation worked against him, and he had no one to blame but himself. Given time, however, he believed that she would come to trust and accept his feelings.

On occasion he found himself worrying that her trust and acceptance would not be enough, but he talked himself out of that quite easily. Emily simply would not sleep with a man for whom she had no genuine feeling. Fun and games in bed with no strings attached was simply not part of her makeup. No, his Emily was one of those women who he'd spent his life avoiding, the type who needed commitment, and he found to his bemusement that he couldn't be happier about that fact.

He'd learned as much about himself lately as he had Em. For one thing, he simply could not stop saying that he loved her. Both the feeling and the words came so easily that they were like breathing. Trying not to tell her how he felt was like trying to hold his breath. At times these past days he'd silently vowed not to say those words again until she could say them to him, but that pledge rarely endured longer than several minutes. Better that he should say it until she believed him.

Suddenly the compulsion to be near her, to touch her reasserted itself strongly. He got up and stalked across the room. Coming up behind her as she bent to swipe a tiny sock off the seat of the armchair, he wrapped an arm around her waist and pulled her back against him, his imagination conjuring any number of ways to make her dissolve into mindless rapture. Noting that his daughter's head had come up with interest, he contented himself with the jolt to his groin that came from Emily suddenly straightening against him.

He nuzzled her ear, whispering, "Have I told you how happy you make me?"

She laid her head back against his shoulder. "I wish it could always be like this."

"Why can't it?"

She turned her head and kissed him quickly but firmly on the mouth, saying, "Because your daughter needs her bath."

That was mere half-truth, and he knew it, but he didn't press her. Instead he slid a hand downward, splaying it across the gentle mound of her belly. "When we find a nanny," he said, "we'll have more time together, just the two of us."

For a moment she said nothing, then, "I'm glad you brought that up. I've been meaning to speak to you about it."

He smiled against her ear. "Spending more time together?"

She turned in his arms. "Finding a nanny."

"Ah." He locked his hands together against the small of her back and rocked his pelvis into a perfect fit with hers. "Unfortunately we have no new applicants at the moment, but we can go back to the agencies, if you want."

"That might be best," she said, running her hands up his arms but not quite meeting his gaze. "I have too much invested in my career to stay out of play indefinitely."

"I understand," he said, "but you know you don't have anything to worry about. We'll find a place for Hal when you're ready to come back—or we can find another place for you. I think you're due a promotion."

She shook her head, pushing away. "No. No, that wouldn't be right."

"You've earned it," he said, reaching out for her again. "You earned it a long time ago, but I was too selfish to let you go. I still am."

She smiled as he pulled her to him. "We can talk about this later."

If something about that smile spoke more of sadness than joy, he ignored it, concentrating instead on the kiss she granted him, deepening it until her hands were knotted in the fabric of his shirt and the quickening rise and fall of her breasts against his chest told him that she was as needful of more as he. Only then did he rein in this desire that she alone could sate but never tame. "Any chance we can turn in early?" he asked raspily.

Emily turned a look down at Amanda Sue, who was lying on her back, one ankle crossed jauntily over the opposite knee, watching them avidly. "You're asking the wrong person," she said with a meaningful chuckle.

"Don't ever let her think she's the boss," he warned with deadpan sincerity. "It's bad enough that she is."

Emily laughed as he pulled away to swoop down on his daughter, exclaiming, "Bath time, 'Manda mine." Amanda

Sue practically hurled herself into his arms. Of course, getting his darling daughter *into* her bath was never as difficult as getting her *out* of it again. Ah, well, the sooner wet, the sooner the battle won.

Actually, for once, she didn't put up much of a fight. Either that, or he was getting better about quelling her little shows of temper. Whatever, he had her clean and in a dry diaper and a footed sleeper with only a few squirms, squeals, kicks, screams and a halfhearted selection of phony sobs, grunts and pleas from her vast repertoire of theatrics. Emily showed up to provide counterpoint, smoothing barely ruffled feathers with suitably sympathetic gestures. Once settled, Amanda Sue dropped off with a minimum of fuss, and he summarily hauled Emily straight to the bedroom, where she thrilled him with a slow striptease.

Hours later, he was roused from the edge of sleep by the sounds of mewling cries coming from the monitor on the bedside table. Realizing that Emily was deeply asleep, he quickly reached over and turned down the monitor before slipping out of bed and into his jeans. Carefully zipping up, he padded barefoot out of the room. Amanda Sue was just truly waking when he reached her. It was almost as if she dreamed her distress. She reached for him with a little sob, and he gathered her into his arms, hugging and kissing her.

"I'm here, angel. Daddy's here."

"Mimly?" she asked, sleepily rubbing her face against his chest.

He smiled and whispered words of comfort. Within moments she sighed contentedly. Mindful of what Emily had repeatedly said about giving reassurance but letting Amanda Sue learn to get herself back to sleep, he tucked his little daughter into her crib, stroked her curly head and whispered a good-night. Stepping back into the shadows, he waited a few minutes until he was certain that she had dropped off again. Then he turned and quickly retraced his steps.

When he slipped back into bed beside Emily, she roused

enough to ask if Amanda Sue had awakened. "Yes," he told her softly, "but I took care of it."

Emily rolled onto her back, pushing hair out of her face. "She didn't ask for me?"

"Actually she did," he said, smoothing that hair with one hand while he balanced his upper body weight on the other elbow. "But I told her that you were asleep in my bed where you belong, and that seemed enough. She went right back to sleep."

Emily looked at him as if she didn't believe him or as if she might scold him, but then she smiled. "As long as she's okay."

"Amanda Sue's fine," he promised.

She closed her eyes and rolled onto her side. He cuddled up next to her, fitting his body to hers and sliding his arms around her. Sleepily, she tangled her legs with his and threaded her fingers through his where they lay against her abdomen, getting comfortable. A moment later she sighed peacefully and suddenly he was so overcome by those simple gestures of acceptance and completion that he felt close to tears.

"I love you, Emily," he whispered. Then he closed his eyes and silently begged, *Please let yourself love me, too. Just give us a chance. Give me a chance to finally get it right.*

Logan got up from his desk and hugged his sister, smiling. He couldn't seem to stop smiling anymore. Every night with Emily was more amazing than the one before, and he felt like the luckiest of men.

Eden pulled back and looked up at him knowingly. "Who is this absurdly happy man?"

He laughed and brushed back the sides of his jacket to slide his hands into his pockets. "Well, I'll tell you one thing, he's not our father."

Eyebrows aloft, Eden sat down in one of the chairs facing his desk and crossed her long, slender legs, tucking a small pocketbook into the seat beside her. "I never realized you felt that way."

He shrugged and walked around his desk to retake his chair. "It's not something you talk about casually."

She nodded and templed her fingers, elbows braced against the arms of the chair. "I've always feared being attracted to men like him, with good reason, but it never occurred to me that you or Holden might worry about being like him. I always thought he was the ideal for other men."

Logan shook his head. "I never wanted to be like him and always feared, perhaps even believed, that I was."

"And now?"

He smiled, linking his hands over his middle in a gesture of satisfaction. "Amanda Sue and Emily have changed everything," he said.

"Amanda Sue *and* Emily?"

He went on smiling.

Eden sighed and tilted her head. "I thought something had changed. I saw Emily and Amanda Sue yesterday, you know, and I sensed it."

He nodded. "She doesn't completely trust me yet."

"Emily, you mean," Eden prompted.

"She's holding back," he said. "She makes love with me." He closed his eyes overwhelmed with joy. "Oh, how she makes love with me! But she's keeping her distance still. She insists on occasionally going out in the evening alone or with her friend Ciara Wilde. She's kept her apartment, says she has to have a little time for herself. I think that's understandable after spending all day every day with Amanda Sue, who is a delight but difficult, all the same."

"Are you going to marry her?" Eden asked bluntly.

It was a question he had tried not to ask himself, but now that it was out there in the open, he was surprised to find that he knew the answer, had known it for a long time. "Yes."

"Have you asked her yet?"

"Not yet."

"Why not?"

He took a deep breath but couldn't bring himself to do more than skirt the issue. "I will, eventually."

"Why not now, Logan?"

"I want her to get comfortable with the idea," he said lightly. *I want to know that she loves me first,* he thought, and his happiness dimmed somewhat. He pushed the thought away, telling himself how lucky he was already to have found Amanda Sue and her. Eden, he noticed, seemed about to say something else, but then she decided not to, subsiding with a lame smile. He let it pass, knowing without admitting to it that he wouldn't like what she'd considered, that it would dim the light of his happiness again if he was stupid enough to pry it out of her.

Abruptly, Eden uncrossed her legs and cleared her throat. "Are you still looking for a nanny?"

"Yes, actually we are. Why?"

"I may have a prospect you'll like."

He grabbed an ink pen and pulled a notepad forward. "What's her name?"

"Carol Jefferson. She put up an advertisement on the bulletin board in Dr. Costas's office, so I asked about her when I had Sawyer in for his booster shot. Dr. Costas recommends her highly."

He lifted his eyebrows. "Sounds promising. Got a phone number?" She pulled a slip of paper from her purse and read off the number to him. "I'll call and set up an appointment today," he said.

"Let me know how it works out," Eden murmured.

"I will. Thanks, sis."

They talked awhile longer, about Ryan and the kidnapping of Matt's and Claudia's baby Bryan and the testing to find baby Taylor's parent. Finally Eden rose to take her leave.

"Just one thing," she said, pausing in his doorway. "Don't wait too long, with Emily, I mean. Women like her need commitment, Logan. Women like us, I should say."

He nodded and smiled, knowing that she'd just shown

him a part of herself that she usually kept carefully hidden
so he'd put stock in what she'd said. He was grateful for
that, very much so, but he couldn't help thinking that Eden
didn't have all the facts. Emily was the one holding back.
Emily needed time to understand that she loved him. It
would do no good to ask her to marry him until then, because Emily Applegate would only marry for love. How
ironic that the one woman he would ever consider marrying
had to be convinced. How many others had tried to trap him,
knowing he didn't love them and that they didn't love him?
It would never be the money or the prestige with Emily. She
just needed some time to fully trust him and understand that
he was the only man for her. Then he would ask her, and
she would say yes, and they could move forward together.

He smiled to himself, wondering how long they should
wait to begin thinking about another child. He wanted that
deeply, and was pleased with himself because of it. Logan
Fortune, family man. And happy about it! So very happy
about it. Happy enough to wait, to be patient, as long as it
took.

"I like her," Logan whispered, sliding his arm around
Emily's waist.

"Me, too."

Carol Jefferson had come to the office to interview for
the nanny position. She and Amanda Sue got along wonderfully and both Logan and Emily were pleased by her
credentials.

He raised his voice. "Ms. Jefferson, I have one more
question, if you don't mind."

The woman had been playing on the floor with Amanda
Sue. At Logan's question, she sat up straight and shifted
around on the floor to face him, legs folded. Not content to
lose her attention, Amanda Sue promptly climbed into the
woman's lap. The nanny shifted and rocked to accommodate
her with the same ease she'd use to pull on a sweater or tie
her shoes. She wasn't at all what Emily had expected,

frankly. Dressed casually in loose, knit pants and a print cotton smock worn over a gray turtleneck sweater, she was not the most professional-looking applicant they had interviewed. Her thin, dark blond hair was pulled back into a skinny ponytail at the nape of her neck and held with a green rubber band. Her plain face was round and flat, her front tooth chipped noticeably, but the sparkle in her otherwise colorless eyes was positively jolly. Her manner was utterly relaxed and casually friendly. Emily suspected that she was younger than she looked, but appearance didn't seem to matter to the woman in the least.

"I don't like to be called Ms. Jefferson," she told Logan mildly. "Just call me Carol." Her voice seemed to contain a measure of laughter in it, whatever the words.

Logan smiled, a natural response. Carol Jefferson was a woman to whom one wanted to be nice. "All right, Carol. You were in your last position ten years. According to what we've seen, that's an uncommonly long tenure," Logan stated carefully. "I guess I'd like to know why you stayed so long."

Carol shrugged. "They kept on having babies, you know, after the twins. Besides, I love them. They're like my family. Half the time we were off someplace in the world. I've been all over, wherever the Major was stationed, except in the wars."

"So why leave them now?" Logan asked, finally getting to the point.

"Not leaving them," she said. "They're leaving me. I grew up right here in San Antonio, and this is where they picked me up. I'm just ready to stay home now. 'Sides, they don't need me anymore. The baby's starting school this year, and the missus says there won't be another."

"It must have been difficult to let you go after all those years," Emily said.

"Oh, they haven't let me go," she said. "The missus says she don't know what she'll do without me. But California is where they mean to settle, and the truth is, I just can't see myself living out there." She shivered dramatically. "All those earthquakes. Why, the whole place is like to fall off into the ocean one day. And my old mama is here, you know. She lives with my brother and his family, so she's taken care of, but I'm figuring maybe we don't have too many years left together, so I'm for home now. Besides, I'm ready for another little one." She looked down at Amanda Sue, smiling placidly. "She sure is sweet and a real strong mind, too. Won't never be boring with her around, I bet."

Logan chuckled. "You've got that right."

The nanny hugged Amanda Sue close, and Amanda Sue allowed it with considerable aplomb. "I'm thinking she's just what I'm looking for," Carol said firmly.

Emily looked at Logan, and he cleared his throat. "Emily and I agree that she ought to stay home with Amanda Sue a while longer. We've explained the adjustments she's had to make. I assume you have no objections to that."

"Jeepers, no," Carol Jefferson said. "My last missus, she always stayed home. We got on fine."

Logan looked at Emily. She shrugged. "I can't think of anything else."

He looked at Carol. "Anything you want to ask us?"

Carol's expression turned canny. "Any chance you'll be having more babies along the way?"

Emily nearly fell off the arm of the chair. "Uh—"

Logan clamped a hand over her knee, saying, "It's a possibility."

"Good," Carol said blithely. "I'd like the job."

"When can you start?" Logan asked, and it was done.

She got up, lifting Amanda Sue with her. "I'll get the Major to help me move my things over tonight. My folks would feel better if they could see where and who I'm going to." Carol carried Amanda Sue over to them and placed her in her father's lap. "Well, I guess I'll see ya'll after dinner."

Emily smiled. Logan nodded.

"Okay, then." Carol bent down and put her nose to Amanda Sue's. She poked a finger gently into the baby's belly. "Glad to have met you, Miss Amanda Sue." Amanda Sue sprawled back against her father's chest and grinned as if delighted. Carol winked and walked toward the door. "We're gonna do good together," she said confidently, and then she waved and walked down the hall.

Logan leaned his chair back, throwing Emily against his shoulder and making Amanda Sue look up in surprise. Logan dropped a kiss on his daughter's forehead, then turned his face up to Emily, kissing her with deliberate thoroughness. Breaking the kiss, he said with deep satisfaction, "We finally found a nanny."

Emily smiled, her happiness in finding Carol a mere veneer over the soul-deep personal sadness growing within her. Carol was going to work out wonderfully, which meant that her time with Logan and Amanda Sue was growing short. She could stay and endure a long, slow torture as Logan grew tired of her and disenchanted with monogamy, or she could make a clean break before she began to hope that what he felt was real. She feared the pathetic, clinging creature she might become if she let hope take root in such rocky soil. No, it was better to go sooner rather than later.

It was a strained, hectic scene in the Fortune household that evening. Carol's "folks" came along en masse to deliver their former nanny to her new home. The ten-year-old twins, both boys, solemnly flanked her as she introduced them. Their older brother, all of thirteen, kept patting the shoulder of his six-year-old little sister, whose trembling lip threatened tears at any moment, while the eight-year-old stomped around frowning, anger flashing in her belligerent eyes. The "missus" sniffed and dabbed, supported by her husband with his military bearing and commanding manner, which did little to hide the distress roiling just beneath the surface of his stern expression. Carol calmly directed the placement of her boxes and bags, even as she comforted her former charges with pats and hugs and whispers.

Logan did his best to put them all at ease, announcing

that Carol was free to make any decorating changes to her room that she desired and talking about the larger home he intended to buy soon and the summers to be spent on the ranch. He rattled on about how many applicants he and Emily had screened and how he couldn't trust his Amanda Sue to just anyone. He had introduced Emily only by her first name, and it was obvious they all thought that she was his wife, despite the fact that she had introduced herself to Carol as Emily Applegate. She could only wonder what Carol would make of the fact that she and Logan were sharing a bedroom together. Perhaps she thought Emily had simply chosen to retain her maiden name for professional purposes. Or perhaps even Carol realized that she was likely to be in residence much longer than Emily herself.

Emily tried not to be embarrassed about the situation. It was no one else's business but hers and Logan's, after all. Somehow she couldn't quite manage the necessary detachment, though. She did not have Logan's experience with this kind of thing, nor did she intend to. Sharing her body and a bedroom with a man who did not fully own her heart was unthinkable to Emily. She fully expected this to be her one and only experience. Deep down, she knew she wouldn't, couldn't, love again. She wondered wildly if Carol Jefferson could understand that, but how could she when Emily didn't understand it herself?

The farewell was as tearful and tugging as expected. The children huddled around Carol and wept noisily or surreptitiously wiped at their noses with their sleeves. Then their mother threw her arms around Carol and bawled gratitude and affection all over her. Even the Major unbent enough to hug the nanny. It was Carol who remained calm and placid, sweet and encouraging through it all. She herded them gently down the hall and out the door, promising to keep in touch and come for visits. Then she cheerfully returned to the living room to announce that she was going to her room to unpack and "boo-hoo" for a bit before giving Amanda Sue her bath and getting her ready for bed.

Logan watched her climb the stairs with his hands on his hips. When she disappeared from view, Logan turned to Emily, spread his arms wide and said, "I think we won the nanny lottery." Then he whooped and threw his arms around her, swirling her high off the floor, a trick Amanda Sue thought superb and demanded he repeat on her. They swung around and around until, dizzy, they collapsed on the couch, laughing. Snagging Emily's hand, he pulled her down with them and looped an arm around her neck.

"Ah, what could be better," he asked rhetorically, "than having three wonderful women in my life? I love you both, and something tells me that Carol is going to make her own place in all our hearts." He pulled Emily close and whispered, "Especially if she gives me just a little more time to spend with you."

A little more time. She couldn't help thinking, even as she returned his kisses, how sadly true that was. Just a little more time was all they had left.

Thirteen

Emily pushed hair out of her eyes and wandered into the living room, dressed only in her pajamas. Instinct told her that it was far later than normal. It had been so long since she'd awakened to anything but the buzz of the alarm clock or the sound of Amanda Sue's cries that she couldn't quite figure out what had roused her. Amanda Sue was sitting on the sofa with Carol and Goody. Carol was folding laundry.

"Mimly!" Amanda Sue shouted, plopping over to slide off the couch.

"Hello, sweetheart." Emily went down on her knees and opened her arms. Amanda Sue hurled herself into them exuberantly, babbling.

"I kwite. Shhh-shhh. Mimly sweep Daddy werg Curl pol cwos."

Emily sat down on her bottom on the floor and painstakingly translated Amanda Sue-speak into English while dispensing kisses. "Let's see. You were quiet so I could sleep—you angel child—and Daddy's gone to work. Is that right?"

Amanda Sue put her finger to her puckered lips and shh-shhed, then nodded. "Yeah, Daddy werk. Wuv oo." She kissed Emily with a loud smacking sound.

Emily laughed. "Did Daddy tell you to give me kisses?"

Amanda Sue nodded, vastly pleased with herself.

"What a sweet daddy," Emily said. "Now what's this about Carol?"

"Curl po-fwol cwoes."

"Carol is folding clothes, is she? That's very nice of her."

Carol chuckled from her seat on the sofa. "I just did the little tyke's laundry with some things of my own. Mr. Logan said it was all right."

"Certainly," Emily said. "Did Logan also tell you to let me sleep?"

"He did," Carol confirmed. "He had to show the little one that you were, indeed, home, but once she saw you, she was very, very good about staying quiet. Once she even told the cat it was purring too loud."

"What a good girl," Emily said, giving Amanda Sue another hug. "Daddy will be so proud."

"Yeah," Amanda Sue said, nodding authoritatively. Emily could only laugh.

"He said to call when you were awake," Carol informed her. "There's coffee in the pot and hotcakes in the oven, if you want to eat first."

Emily got up, taking Amanda Sue with her, though it was a struggle. "You're getting big," she said to Amanda Sue, noting how difficult it was to lift her weight to a full stand. To Carol she said, "You must have made breakfast. Logan couldn't put together hotcakes if his life depended on it."

Carol chuckled. "He was prepared to settle for crackers and peanut butter, but I like to cook, so it was no imposition."

"Carol, you're too good," Emily said, carrying Amanda Sue toward the kitchen. "I can't remember the last time I could sleep until I was ready to wake up, but we're not going to make a habit of this. I'll be going back to work soon, so there's no sense in getting out of the habit of rising at a reasonable hour."

"That's something you should take up with Mr. Logan," Carol said with a knowing smile. "I get the feeling that he likes indulging you."

Emily just smiled, thinking that she liked to indulge him, too, so much so that she was practically living with him, not to mention sleeping with him. She wondered what Carol thought of this situation, but she didn't dare ask. Carol might actually tell her!

She used the cordless phone to call Logan while eating Carol's excellent hotcakes. All in all, it was a pretty disjointed talk. Not only did Amanda Sue demand that Emily share both her food and the phone but Logan was giving orders to Hal on his end of the conversation, as well. Emily thanked him for the opportunity to sleep late and even managed to insist that he not do such a thing again. He whispered something about loving to watch her sleep but made no promises. She decided that she would have to take the matter up with him later.

Meanwhile, she couldn't help noticing how well he seemed to be getting along with Hal. The two communicated business matters in the same kind of spoken shorthand that she and Logan had once shared, but they also cracked jokes with the easy camaraderie of two friends of the same gender, something she and Logan could never do. Oh, they had teased; she'd become quick and creative with acerbic, slightly barbed put-downs and comments, but she realized now that they'd always been loaded with an unwanted awareness of him as a member of the opposite sex. She almost grieved for what could never be again, the tightrope walk between professionalism and familiarity that had been her relationship with Logan before Amanda Sue.

Well, it didn't matter now. She'd fallen off the rope. Fallen? Heck, she'd dived off headfirst, even knowing that she had no net to catch her. One day soon she'd hit the ground, and if the only thing that shattered was her heart, she'd count herself lucky. Going back to work at the Fortune company wasn't an option anyway. It would be impossible to spend her days with him and not her nights. However it ended, she had spent her last day in that office in any official capacity, but she wouldn't worry about that now. She could always find another job. When the time came.

After her late breakfast, she hurried to get dressed, managing it just moments before the phone rang. Emily went to answer it, but before she reached the phone, Carol called, "It's for you, Ms. Emily, someone named Cathy Wazorski."

"Thanks, Carol." Emily smiled thinking how Cathy's real name was so ordinary compared to her movie star name, Ciara Wilde.

Emily answered the phone, happy to hear from her childhood friend, even though Cathy sounded tired and troubled. Emily knew that the movie star had grave misgivings about her upcoming wedding with action film star Brendan Swift and was dissatisfied with the track her career had taken. To hear Cathy tell it, her film career consisted of a string of cheesy thrillers, wherein the main thrills were numbered by the articles of clothing she was willing to discard in a given scene. It was Emily's opinion that Cathy was both too good and too smart for the role she'd been assigned by Hollywood, but she also thought that Cathy sold herself rather short.

After a quick chat, Emily parlayed a luncheon date two weeks in advance at a restaurant in Cathy's hotel where she, Eden and Cathy could sit down together and have a good old-fashioned hen party. Emily had been meaning to update her wardrobe and this outing was the perfect excuse for at least one new outfit.

When she mentioned to Logan that evening that she might do some shopping in a few days, he offered to take off work and go with her. "You can't do that!" Emily protested.

"I can so," he countered. "After all, I'm the boss."

She shook her head. "It wouldn't be right to pull you away from work for something like this."

"Aw, come on, Em," he said plaintively. "I like shopping, really I do. And I love you. I want to go."

Carol chuckled. "A man who likes shopping. I wouldn't let that get out if I were you, Ms. Emily. There are women out there who would kill for a man like that."

Emily had to laugh, especially when Logan put on his pitiful face, prompting an uncomprehending Amanda Sue to abandon Goody to give him a hug. Logan shamelessly enlisted her aid.

"Amanda Sue, tell Emily to let Daddy take her shopping."

Amanda Sue shook a finger at Emily and babbled an edict. "Mimly wet Daddy soppin'."

"Oh, all right," Emily grumbled, feigning great reluctance.

"Yeah!" Logan jumped up and took a victory jog around the room, Amanda Sue on his shoulders. "Yeah! The crowd roars approval as Daddy wins another one. Great play, Amanda Sue! We're number one! We're number one!"

"We erber one!" Amanda Sue sang. "We erber one!"

Emily laughed and applauded, telling herself that she would treasure these moments forever. And why shouldn't she have a day with Logan, just the two of them? That wasn't too much to ask, was it? She had the rest of her life to regret her behavior and miss what was only temporarily hers now. Better to enjoy the fall while she could; the landing was going to be a killer.

He bought silk and lace, things she would never wear for anyone but him. She bought practical shoes and half a dozen separates that could be mixed and matched. He spent thirty minutes choosing a perfume for her; she spent ten picking a reversible belt. The rest of the time they argued about what he wanted to buy for her and what she would allow. Then, on sheer impulse, they took in a movie and found themselves sharing a darkened theater with a trio of elderly women and a college-age couple who obviously had no more private place to go. They were more entertaining to watch than the movie. Their huffing and puffing raised the temperature in the whole room. Embarrassed and downright envious, Emily couldn't quite keep her gaze off them, and the way Logan began fidgeting in his chair told her that he was having the same problem. Finally he grabbed her hand and headed for the exit.

"This is just too much."

"What about the movie?" Emily hissed.

"We'll catch it on video," he said. "I have something else much more important, not to mention entertaining and positively wicked, in mind."

"What on earth are you talking about?"

"Wait and see, darlin'. Wait and see."

He hauled her out to the mall parking lot, locked their purchases in the trunk of the car and got behind the wheel. "Where are we going?" she asked.

"To the pharmacy," he replied, adding enigmatically, "first."

Emily could only laugh. Obviously he wasn't going to say more. She sat back and prepared to be surprised. He left her sitting in the car while he ran into the pharmacy, returning only moments later without seeming to have purchased a thing. She asked again where they were going, but he only smiled and waggled an eyebrow leeringly. Without further ado he drove out onto the freeway. It soon became evident that they were headed downtown and then to the river and finally, to one of the best hotels on the Riverwalk.

Pulling up into the valet area, Logan flipped a small box of condoms out of his coat pocket and into her lap, saying, "You might want to put those in your purse."

"Logan!" she exclaimed, frantically stashing the package as the parking valet came toward the car. "You can't mean to—"

"Oh, but I do," he confirmed, leaning over to kiss her quickly on the mouth before opening his door and hopping out. The valet opened her door, leaving her little recourse but to get out and allow Logan to lead her inside, not that she really wanted to balk. Already her blood was singing in her veins, anticipating the "wicked entertainment" to come.

Logan registered them as Mr. and Mrs., paying with a credit card. Emily could only wonder how many times he'd done that very same thing with other women, but she pushed the thought from her mind as he took her arm and steered her toward the elevator. The lobby was not terribly busy in the middle of the afternoon, so they had the elevator to themselves. As soon as the doors closed, Logan pulled her into a deep, hot kiss. Then, just as abruptly, he turned her around, reached up beneath her thigh-length wool coat and unzipped the matching column dress.

"Logan!" She screeched and tried to twist away, but he pushed aside her coat and slid his arms around her waist inside her dress, pulling her back against him to nip at her earlobe. Suddenly the elevator slowed. Logan yanked his hands out of her dress and shoved her back into the corner. Emily yanked at her coat as the doors opened and a portly gentleman in a tweed jacket and sweater vest got on board with barely a nod in their direction. He pushed the number for the floor above and faced the door, hands folded behind his back. Logan winked at Emily, whose cheeks burned pink, and folded his arms, puckering his lips in a silent whistle of feigned innocence. Emily rolled her eyes. The portly man got off the elevator, and the instant the doors closed Logan grabbed her.

Turning her by the shoulders, he reached up under the coat again and unerringly found the catch of her bra, releasing it with a flick. She gasped and crossed her arms against her chest, not that the bra was likely to fall off while she had the dress on.

"Okay, now your underthings," he said.

"*What?*"

Kneeling, he ignored her and reached up under the hem of her dress to grasp the bottom of her half-slip and pull it down. Gasping, laughing, scolding, she stepped out of it and watched as he opened his navy wool sport coat and tucked the slip into a chest pocket, leaving at least half of it dangling down inside his jacket. When he reached up under her skirt again, she had the presence of mind to dance away, only to come up against the corner of the elevator.

"You do it, then," he said, "and be quick!"

Exasperated, intrigued, and knowing full well that if she

didn't do it, he'd do it for her, she quickly turned her back to the door, hiked her skirt a few inches and snagged the top of her panty hose, shimmying them down even as she kicked off her shoes. He took over once they reached her knees, leaving her to pull down her panties. By the time the elevator door opened on their floor, he was tucking the panties into his pants' pocket as he rose to his feet, the stockings hidden in his jacket. Laughing nervously, she fumbled for her second shoe, got her toe into it and stomped it on even as he took her arm and ushered her out into the hallway. She shrugged her dress farther up on her shoulders beneath her coat, clutched her handbag to her side, and tried to behave normally as they turned the corner and moved swiftly down the hall. Her heart was thumping so hard that she felt certain the beats were visible beneath the fabric of her dress.

A maid pushed her cart out of a room ahead and rolled it toward them, smiling and nodding. They smiled and nodded in return. As soon as they passed her, Logan began unbuttoning his nubby, cocoa-brown silk shirt with his free hand. Emily stifled a giggle. He sent her a conspiratorial wink and moved his hand to the buckle of his belt. By the time they reached the room, he was held together by a single snap on the waistband of his slacks. He produced the computerized key card from a pocket and slid it into the lock slot. The little light blinked, and he opened the door. Practically shoving her inside with a hand on the middle of her back, he closed the door, flipped the lock to Do Not Disturb and whirled to face her.

Grinning lecherously, he began pulling her intimate garments from his pockets as he stalked her across the room. Laughing, she kicked her shoes off as she backed away.

"I want you now, right this minute, as naked as the day you were born."

Bumping up against the elegant rosewood table situated in front of the picture window that opened to overlook the Riverwalk twenty stories below, she dropped her purse, whipped off her coat and tossed it at the richly upholstered armchair in the corner. "You are incorrigible."

Logan tossed her slip on the dresser and then his jacket on top of that. "True."

Emily shrugged her dress off her shoulders and let it pool at her waist. "Insatiable."

Tossing her panties on the bedside table and her stockings over the lamp shade, he stepped out of his shoes and stripped off his socks. "True again."

Emily swept the straps off her shoulders and tossed the bra away. "Insane."

"Every time you get near me," he confirmed, and his shirt followed his jacket.

"Did I mention irresistible?" Emily whispered, letting the dress fall to the floor.

"That's you," he said roughly, looking his fill before shucking his slacks and briefs in one swift movement.

They both stepped forward at the same time. One long drugging kiss and she was ready for the big bed standing opposite the luxurious bath. But Logan had other ideas.

"I promised you wicked," he said, lifting her onto the table. "Let me show you how heavenly wicked can be."

A long time later Emily found the presence of mind to sigh and admit, "I had no idea."

Two weeks later Emily blushed to be back in the hotel where she'd so recently spent an afternoon indulging in wildly creative, hotly romantic sex. Even if she was only on her way to the rooftop restaurant, she couldn't help wondering if someone might recognize her as the woman with whom Logan Fortune had registered little more than a week earlier. Worse, what if Cathy had seen her and was just waiting until today to tease her face-to-face, in front of Eden, no less? Emily had completely forgotten that day that Cathy was staying here. She'd forgotten her name that day and everything else but the intensely satisfying, hopelessly addictive, unbelievably inventive ways in which Logan had made love to her. Even now a suddenly remembered sensation whispered over her nerve endings, shutting down her thought processes and transporting her there to that room again. She closed her eyes, reliving the moment.

Eden poked her in the ribs with an elbow. "Emily! You haven't heard a word I've said."

Emily started, the haze of remembered lovemaking subsiding. "I'm sorry. I just... This is my very favorite hotel, you know."

"So you keep telling me, and it is very nice, but—"

Thankfully, the elevator slid to a stop just then and the doors opened smoothly. "Oh, there's Cathy—I mean, Ciara," Emily said, waving at the elegant blonde seated next to a glass wall that overlooked a tropical garden complete with waterfall.

Obviously the maître d' had been told to expect them, for he stepped forward with menus in hand. "Ladies, Miss Wilde is expecting you."

"Thank you," Eden said, following him through the airy chrome, glass and marble room. Very Art Deco with a definite Southwest bent—all the cacti and longhorn skulls were polished steel and brushed aluminum—it was 1930s opulence meets the coyote. Cathy, in her Veronica Lake guise, was very much part of the element, even while wearing skinny jeans and a cashmere sweater with a faux fur collar. She rose as Emily and Eden approached, towering over them in three-inch heels to throw her arms around her dear friend and shake hands with Eden while Emily made the introductions.

"Cathy, this is my friend, Eden Fortune. Eden, I'd like you to meet...well—"

"Ciara Wilde. No one calls me Cathy anymore, except Em."

Emily laughed. "And no one calls me Em except you and...ah, a few other people." She cleared her throat, wondering if either Cathy or Eden would put together "other people" and Logan.

"Let's sit down," the tall, voluptuous blonde said. "I've ordered a bottle of wine, if that's all right with you two." Up close, Emily noted, faint bluish smudges were visible beneath Cathy's astonishingly vibrant eyes.

"Fine with me," Eden said, "but only one glass. I'm driving."

"What about you, Em?" Cathy asked as the steward approached.

"Yes, thank you."

Their glasses were filled, and Eden offered a toast. "To new friends and smart single women."

"Here, here."

They clinked glasses and sipped. Afterward, Eden added, "Although, I doubt we'll be able to make that toast for much longer. I understand that the two of you are on the downward slope to matrimony."

Emily was shocked. "Where on earth did you get that idea? I'm not marrying anyone."

"But I thought—" Eden shut her mouth again with an audible click.

Cathy looked at the dime-sized diamond on her left hand. "I'm not so sure I will be, either."

Eden sat back in her chair with a plop. "Well, I really put my foot in that one, didn't I?"

Cathy looked at Emily. "You didn't tell her?"

"Of course not. You spoke to me in confidence."

Cathy reached across the table and squeezed Emily's hand. "I'm sorry, Em. I should've known I could count on you. In this business, though, you learn not to trust anyone."

"Must be tough," Eden said, "living in the fishbowl."

Cathy leaned forward, speaking softly. "Honestly? It's pure hell. The fishbowl has sharks. Don't get me wrong, I'm grateful, but I'm also burned-out, worn to a frazzle. I'm just too tired and confused to trust my own judgment at the moment. It's all I can do to stay in the swim, and I'm not sure I even want to anymore."

Eden sighed sympathetically. "I'd never have guessed.

You make this Hollywood thing look so fun and glamorous. When I see you on the news or in a magazine, you don't seem to have a care in the world.''

Cathy grinned. "That's why they call it acting, sweety."

"Well, darn," Eden teased, "there goes my very last illusion."

They all laughed, and the waiter appeared to urge them to study their menus. They did so for some time, finally chose and ordered. By the time the food came they were chatting about their respective lives with the ease of old friends. Cathy talked primarily about the movie she was working on. Eden made mention of her family, beginning with her son and touching on the current developments, including the kidnapping, her uncle's ugly divorce and a number of recent marriages. Emily talked about Amanda Sue and Carol, careful to keep mentions of Logan to a minimum.

The food was excellent, but the company was better and the conversation particularly engaging, more so as time wore on. Assured of confidentiality, Cathy told some truly hilarious stories about her experiences in Hollywood and dropped some juicy bits of gossip about well-known personalities. Emily and Eden traded stories about Amanda Sue and Sawyer. Emily was able to tell a few tales on Cathy from their childhood and vice versa. Eden ratted on her siblings, focusing on Logan more than Holden, and confessed some pretty unpalatable information about her late father, giving Emily a better understanding of Logan's attitude and behavior. By meal's end, they were laughing uproariously at something Eden's housekeeper had done and said.

"Oh, gosh!" Cathy gasped. "I wish we could do this every day. My sanity might hold then."

"What you need is a good, long rest," Emily said flatly.

Cathy nodded and pushed a thick blond wave out of her eye. "I know. I want to vegetate until I regain my energy, then I need to give some deep thought to my future. I just can't keep going the way I am. The problem is that I have to find someplace away from the press, someplace where I can be alone, and that's not easy. Believe me, I've tried.''

"Sounds like you need a deserted island," Emily said.

"Or a secluded cabin in the mountains," Cathy added.

Eden gasped and sat up straight. "Oh, my goodness, that's it!''

Emily and Cathy looked at one another in puzzlement before turning their gazes on Eden again. "What are you talking about?'' Emily asked. "Don't tell me the Fortunes own a tropical island somewhere.''

"No, but we do own a cabin in the mountains.''

Cathy's eyes grew round. "Oh, please don't say it's a house in Vail or Steam Boat or—''

"No, no, it's nothing like that. It's just a cabin in the mountains northeast of El Paso. My grandparents bought it years and years ago. It hardly ever gets used anymore because it's *not* in one of the trendy spots. We used to go up a lot when we were all kids at home, but some years it doesn't get used at all now. I have a key, if you're interested.''

"You're sure it's secluded?'' Cathy asked hopefully.

"Maybe too much so," Eden said. "Nearest neighbors are miles away. No TV, no microwave, but the plumbing works, and it has a wonderful fireplace and a hot tub.''

"It sounds heavenly," Cathy said with a sigh. "Whatever the rent is, I'll gladly—''

"No way!'' Eden exclaimed. "Why should you pay rent when it's sitting there empty? You can use the cabin anytime you want.''

Cathy chewed her lip. "What about your brothers?''

"Oh, they won't care," Eden said dismissively. "They'll probably get a kick out of it.''

"That's the thing, though," Cathy said with a slow wince. "I'd have to ask you to keep this strictly between us.''

Eden shrugged. "Okay. I don't have a problem with that.''

"But would your brothers and uncle have a problem with it?" Cathy pressed.

"I can't imagine that any of them would mind," Eden said, "and what they don't know won't hurt them, right? Besides, I'm reasonably sure that none of the family will be using the place this season, not with all that's going on."

Cathy seemed to be holding her breath. Suddenly, tears welled up in her eyes. She grabbed her napkin and dabbed at them, laughing nervously. "You can't understand what this means to me, to have someplace safe and private to go to. Maybe I can get through the rest of this picture now. Maybe I can think about the future without feeling hysteria well up inside of me."

Emily reached across the table to take her hand. Eden, likewise, reached for the other. "I didn't realize it was that bad," Emily said gently. "I knew you were struggling, but you were always the fighter, Cath."

Cathy gripped her hand hard. "I know, and I haven't given up. I'm not beaten, kiddo, not by a long shot, but I was beginning to think I'd have to make the hard decisions in public, and I just don't know if I could cope with that right now. This way, I can at least see a safe haven on the horizon." Cathy put her head back and sighed, visibly relaxing. "I can't begin to thank you, either of you."

Eden let go of her hand and gave it a little pat, saying, "Don't mention it."

"We won't if you don't," Emily quipped, and they all laughed.

Cathy wiped her eyes again, her smile a little brighter, her beauty a little more radiant. "You've helped me more than you know. I'm pretty sure what I'm going to do now, at least for the immediate future."

Eden snatched up her water glass this time and held it aloft. "To good friends and smart single women!"

"Long may we live!" Cathy added, raising her own glass.

Emily lifted her own glass. If anyone noticed the sadness behind the smile this time, it wasn't mentioned. Maybe they were smart, but if that was the case, then why did single feel so lonely?

She already knew that she wasn't as smart as she'd once believed. A really smart woman wouldn't have behaved as she had, sleeping with a man she couldn't have, a man destined to break her heart. Like Cathy, it was time for Emily to think of the future. She only wished that her own future looked a little less bleak.

Fourteen

It was time. She'd waited too long as it was, and her only excuse was that she didn't want Amanda Sue to feel abandoned again. But she couldn't go on as she was. Every day with Logan and Amanda Sue, every night with him, she gave a little more of herself, loved a little deeper, wanted a little more from him. The real danger was in the wanting, she knew. She'd already realized that she couldn't do anything about the loving. She loved Logan Fortune and his amazingly intelligent daughter as she would never again love anyone else in the same way. They were part of her, and it was killing her to think of going, but how much worse would it be if she waited until they left her? Maybe the miracle would happen, and she wouldn't have to go. Eden, after all, had intimated that she expected Logan to marry Emily.

She took a deep breath and sent a glance sideways at Logan, who was taking a rare moment to actually read a newspaper.

"You haven't really asked me about my lunch with Eden and Cathy."

"Hmm?"

"My lunch with Eden and Cathy."

He collapsed the newspaper into his lap. "Oh, right. How did that go?"

She shrugged. "It was fun, lots of talk and joking around. I think Eden and Cathy really like each other."

"That's good," he said lightly. "What'd you think of the restaurant?" He waggled his eyebrows suggestively. "Did

the, um, service measure up to what you got the last time
you were there?''

Torn between embarrassment and laughter, she chose the
latter, bursting out with it. ''Really, Logan, you have to do
something about that low self-esteem of yours.''

He just grinned at her, and she knew he was remembering
much of what washed over her in that moment. She cleared
her throat. ''We were talking about my lunch with Cathy
and Eden.''

''Mmm-hmm, and you were saying?''

She was appalled at how easily her tone adjusted to non-
chalance. She hated anything that smacked of manipulation,
and yet here she was, fishing for—what? A marriage proposal? The words slid out almost unaided. ''Cathy is thinking about breaking her engagement with Brendan Swift.''

Logan sat back in some surprise. ''Whoa. Brendan Swift
is one of the top box-office draws in the country. Has he
been cheating on her?''

''Not that I know of.''

''What's the problem, then?''

''I'm not sure really.''

He shook his head derisively. ''She must feel something
for him if she accepted his proposal. Is she anti-marriage?
What?''

''I think it's more a life-style thing. I mean, he's the ultimate Hollywood insider, you know, and Cathy's tired of
the whole Hollywood scene. She's really thinking of giving
it all up.''

Logan shrugged meaningfully. ''Couldn't she give up acting and still support him in his work? I mean, if she really
loved him...''

Emily sighed, wondering why he was so concerned about
this. ''You're right, of course. If she really loved him, it
wouldn't matter, would it? So I guess she just doesn't love
him like she should.''

''Poor guy.'' Logan shook his head contemplatively.

Emily had to laugh. ''Logan, he's a billionaire! He's a

movie star! I'm betting the line of women willing to comfort him is already forming."

"What difference does that make, if the guy's in love with *her?*" Logan argued.

Emily bit her lip. Dare she hope that he felt the same way about her? "You're right again. It doesn't make any difference. When you love someone, really love them, nothing else matters, does it?"

"That's the way I see it," he muttered, lifting his paper again. "Poor sap probably just assumed she was crazy about him, and look what it got him."

"I'm sure she didn't mean to hurt him."

"Well, that's likely cold comfort to him, don't you think?" he said sharply, turning down one corner of the paper to glare at her.

"I guess."

"And women wonder why men aren't chasing them down to propose marriage," he muttered.

Emily closed her eyes. She had her answer. Logan Fortune had no intention of proposing marriage to her, none. Whatever Eden had meant, it obviously had nothing to do with the facts of hers and Logan's situation. Yes, it was time to make the break. She just had to keep reminding herself that as difficult as it was to do now, it would be much more devastating later. She got up off the couch and went into the bedroom. If the end was upon them, she meant to make the most of what time was left.

Logan looked up from his desk and smiled with sheer pleasure. It had been a long time since the professional Emily had walked through his office door. He took one look at the conservative suit, the prim white blouse and the reading glasses and congratulated himself on knowing so well the delicious woman who lay beneath it all. Her hair was twisted up into a sophisticated roll, and he thought how it shimmered and shined when spread out against his pillow, how it flowed around him when she leaned over to put her mouth to his. His body hardened in response, the result so instantaneous that he deemed it unwise to rise just then. Instead, he leaned back in his chair and let his smile be his welcome.

"Well, well. And to what do I owe this pleasure?"

She surprised him further by carefully closing the door before approaching his desk. He waited with bated breath for her to skirt the desk and approach him, perhaps sinking down onto his lap. When it became apparent that she wasn't going to do that, he cleared his throat and disciplined his thoughts.

"I assume that you don't have Amanda Sue with you."

Finally she spoke. "No, Amanda Sue is with Carol. She hardly seemed to notice when I kissed her goodbye. Carol made her homemade play dough."

Logan chuckled. "That Carol's a gem, isn't she?"

Emily nodded. "Yes, she is. You're very lucky to have found her. Amanda Sue seems to feel very secure with her, and that's why I'm doing this now." She opened the purse hanging at her side from the shoulder strap and extracted a white envelope, which she dropped in the center of his desk mat.

He couldn't imagine what was going on, but he was willing to play along with anything Emily might have in mind. Smiling coyly, he leaned forward and picked up the envelope, saying, "This is all very mysterious." She bowed her head, standing almost at attention while he opened the envelope and extracted the single sheet inside.

Forcing his attention away from her and onto the sheet of paper, he unfolded it and started to read. He couldn't believe it. He spread the letter flat on his desk and read it again. Resigning? She was resigning? His mind rebelled at the thought. Looking up at her, he said simply, "I don't understand."

She took a deep breath. "It's very simple really. I can't come back to this office. It wouldn't be fair to Hal."

"I've already told you—"

She shook her head, saying, "I can't take a promotion, either, Logan."

"Why not?"

"You know what people would say," she told him. "And they'd be right. I've been sleeping with the boss. Any promotion, any job here, would be suspect."

He sat back with a gusty sigh of resignation. "Okay. I don't agree, but if this is how you want it, I'll go along. So what exactly are your plans? I take it you'll be going to work for someone we know, and I can live with that, I just wish you'd talked it over with me first." He was envisioning a two-income family, him and her both hurrying off to work of a morning, juggling schedules, trusting Carol to care for Amanda Sue when they couldn't be there.

She licked her lips. "I don't think you've quite gotten the message," she said, her voice trembling. "I tried to make you see how it would be from the beginning. I tried to make you understand. Now, I have no choice but to…t-take myself out of the picture."

That cozy, if confused, little scene he'd been conjuring evaporated like so much mist. "Out of the picture," he echoed, knowing but unable to accept what she really meant. Out of his life.

"I've moved all my things out of the town house," she said evenly, "and I've taken a job with—"

He didn't know he was going to stand up until he did, his hands planted flat on the surface of his desk. "You're leaving me. Us?"

She gulped and backed up a step. "I—I can't just abandon Amanda Sue. I don't believe you want that, either. So, I thought, if it was all right with you, I could see her on my lunch hour two or three or times a week."

He could only stare at her for a long, agonizing moment. Him. She was leaving him. He should have known. Why hadn't he known? She'd fought him every step of the way. Not once had she ever said that she loved him. He wondered if he was going to be sick. Dimly he became aware that his eyes were closed and that she was speaking somewhere in the distance. He tried to focus on her voice.

"Please understand. I don't have any choice. I have to do this."

Sure that her next words would be that she didn't love him, he waved her away with a sweep of his arm. "Go," he gasped. "Just go."

Sometime later he realized that his legs were trembling, and that if he didn't sit he was going to fall. He sat with a plop, as lifeless and powerless as tissue paper. He took breath, and pain rushed in instead of air.

Left him. Gone. She didn't love him, had never loved him. He remembered times when the shoe had been on the other foot, times when women had vowed undying devotion, how they had cried when he'd explained that physical attraction did not necessarily lead to love. He'd always been honest about that. He'd always let them know from the very beginning that love wasn't part of it for him, and yet so often they'd seemed to expect it to find him between the sheets of their beds. Eventually he'd learned to steer clear of those whose control of their emotions he could not trust.

Perhaps it served him right. If anyone could understand that physical attraction didn't necessarily equal love, he could. And yet he'd been caught in his own trap. He loved Emily. He had always loved Emily, far longer than he'd even known. But she didn't love him. She'd given him the most amazingly satisfying sex of his life—but not her love. Poetic justice? No doubt.

The question now was, how did he survive it? How did he survive losing Emily?

It was a genuine coup, proof that she could do anything she set her mind to. This gambit had made her career. Emily sat back in the big leather chair and looked around her plush new office. She had reached high, and she had grasped the brass ring. Head of real estate management for one of the largest banks in the area. It boggled the mind. So why wasn't she jubilant? Where was the joy? She glanced at her watch. Two more hours until she could see Amanda Sue. Would Carol have a message for her from Logan?

Shaking her head, Emily reached for a file folder and pulled it toward her. She had a lot of reading to do before she could even begin to take on her duties. Half an hour later she reached for another folder, but even as she opened it, tears filled her eyes. It was so hard to stay away, to be apart. Why hadn't she stuck to her guns? Why had she allowed herself to fall into his bed, to share his life? Worse, how was she going to survive without him now? No job, no career, no lap full of file folders could make up for the barren emotional desert her life had become. She didn't even have her blasted cat anymore.

Logan folded his hands behind his head and smiled at his precocious daughter, who sat astride his chest, attempting to balance a wooden block on his nose. It didn't take her long to realize that the nose was not an ideal building site. Heaving a sound of pure disgust, she switched to the spot between his eyes, succeeded in placing one wooden cube and added another. When the tower grew to three blocks, she swept out her hand and jubilantly knocked it down, laughing as he squeezed his eyes shut and turned his head to avoid the falling blocks. Laughing with her now, he sat up, using his hands to catch her as she tumbled backward. Executing a neat flip, Amanda Sue came up on one knee, jubilant about this new trick.

He allowed her to push him down again and throw herself across his chest. Tickling and tussling, he wrestled with her until, exhausted, she sat down on the floor, leaned back against his side and crossed one ankle over the opposite knee. Judging it safe now, Goody ambled over and plopped down next to her, purring loudly, while his striped tail flicked rhythmically in Logan's face.

Couldn't she have taken her damned cat with her? he grumbled mentally, but then he sighed, seeing Amanda Sue dig her fingers into the cat's fur. Why couldn't she have loved him? It had seemed so perfect, the two of them and Amanda Sue. He should have known it was an illusion, a mirage. At least he hadn't humiliated himself by asking her to marry him. Cold comfort when he missed her so.

As if reading his thoughts, Amanda Sue put her head back against his chest and said, "Oan Mimly ome."

Logan swallowed a sudden lump in his throat. "I know, angel. I want Emily to come home, too, but Emily has to work." He sat up again and pulled Amanda Sue into his lap, searching for words to explain. "You know how Daddy goes to work every day and comes home at night to be with Amanda Sue. Emily used to stay here to take care of you while I'm gone, but now Carol does that."

Amanda Sue pointed to the top of the stairs with a finger damp from her mouth and said, "Carl woom."

"Yes, Carol's in her room now, writing letters, but when Daddy isn't here, Carol takes care of you. So Emily has decided to go back to work." He knew he was making a hash of it, but he didn't know how else to explain. He licked his lips and stumbled on. "The thing is, see, Emily doesn't work at the place that I do anymore, and she…she can't be here so much anymore, but you see her sometimes during the day, don't you?" He knew that Emily had been there that very day during her lunch hour. Carol, apparently, had made her a sandwich.

Amanda Sue turned over and stood in his lap so that she was eye level with him. Placing a hand on his cheek, she said pleadingly, "Oan Mimly."

He hugged her close, feeling as if he were drowning in his own misery. "I know, sweetie. I want Emily, too."

Shoving away from him, she went to the chairside table where the cordless phone rested. Pointing at it, she insisted, "Caw Mimly."

For a moment, Logan felt perilously close to tears. How could he explain to his innocent little daughter that he did not dare call Emily? He couldn't bear to speak to her now.

He just couldn't. Choosing the coward's way out, he leaped to his feet, declaring brightly. "Bathtime! Aren't you ready for your bath?"

Emily put aside for the moment, Amanda Sue nodded eagerly and lifted her arms to be taken up. Logan swung her onto his hip and headed for the stairs, knowing that he was sentencing himself to another agonizingly long night. It was early for her bath, and once bathtime was over, bedtime came, which meant that Logan would find himself alone even earlier than usual. He'd sleep on the couch again, unable to face that big, empty bed—not that he'd get much rest, either way. Broken hearts and unfulfilled desires didn't seem to take breathers.

"At least I have you, 'Manda mine," he whispered as he climbed the stairs with his daughter in his arms. "Thank God for that." He didn't even want to think about his life now without her. He wasn't sure he'd have the strength to survive this pain without his daughter. He wasn't even sure he'd want to.

Emily steeled herself. For the first time in weeks she would actually see him. Her heart was pounding like a big brass band, her hands knotted beneath the conference table. When the heavy, oak-paneled door opened, her breath seemed to solidify in her lungs, neither coming in nor going out. Her boss and co-workers got to their feet as Logan and the efficient Hal entered the room, but Emily could not bring herself to make the effort; she was doing all she could do to keep herself intact. Hands were shaking all around her, greetings were murmured. The sound of his voice slid over her nerve endings like balm on a scrape, but she knew that the sting would be quick in coming and severe.

She felt it the instant he realized she was there. His hand came momentarily into her view, but she made no move to take it, and it disappeared with a jerk. So she sat, both dreading and longing for the moment when Logan spoke to her.

He didn't. Instead, he simply turned away and walked to

an empty chair farther down the table. Jerkily, he opened his briefcase and began extracting papers, Hal at his elbow. Emily lifted her hands to the tabletop and sat forward, forearms braced against the smooth, glassy surface. A cup of coffee appeared at her elbow, dispensed by a silent secretary in beige wool crepe. Her boss was saying something pompous about market returns and overbuilt suburbs. The goal, she knew, was winning a hike of half a percentage point in the interest rate on a development loan. She personally expected Logan to walk out. She'd told her boss that he could go anywhere for financing on this project; he didn't need them, but for some reason her current employer felt now was the time to try for the hike.

Logan listened to the spiel, his gaze carefully averted, then suddenly he slid his papers back into his briefcase and snapped it shut. Abruptly, he turned his head and skewered Emily with his gaze. "Was this your idea? Kick him while he's down? Hit him where it hurts?"

She shook her head, appalled that he could think that. "No."

He jerked his gaze back to her sputtering employer. "Go to hell," he said flatly, and he headed for the door. "I'll get the money somewhere else."

Shocked, Mr. Warwick leaped to his feet. "Mr. Fortune, surely we can talk about this!"

Logan spun around and jabbed a finger at Emily. "With her in the room? I don't think so!"

"I'll go," Emily said quietly, getting to her feet. She kept her face straight only by dint of will.

"Yeah, you do that!" Logan snapped. "You're good at going. You've had recent practice."

Mr. Warwick, to his credit, stepped up to take the blame. "It's my fault, Fortune. She told me you wouldn't appreciate her being here."

Logan didn't even look at him. He stared straight at Emily and ordered, "Get out of here, all of you." Despite the fact that it wasn't his conference room and he wasn't the boss here, the bank personnel obeyed, all except Emily, who wasn't stupid enough to think he wanted to be alone in this big room. "You, too, Hal," Logan growled when the assistant hesitated. Hal walked out swiftly, closing the door behind him.

Emily folded her arms and braced her shoulders against the wall. Part of her rejoiced at the very idea of being alone with him again; part of her girded for war. Logan brought his hands to his waist and demanded, "Was that hike in interest rate your idea?"

"No."

"But did you advise him to go for it?"

"No."

He snorted as if he didn't believe her, but then he said, "What did you advise him about it?"

She opened her mouth to answer, then closed it again. Lifting her chin she said, "I don't think it would be ethical to discuss that with you."

He jumped all over that as if it were just the opening for which he'd been waiting. "Oh, and you're good at ethics, aren't you? Business ethics! Personal ethics, now that's something else again."

Anger flared in her. "I resent that!"

"You resent it? How do you think I feel?" She winced because he was shouting. He moderated his voice, but what it lacked in volume it made up for in venom. "Just how ethical is it to sleep with someone for weeks on end, letting him think you love him, and then just walk away without a backward glance?"

She gasped. "I never said—"

"So you sleep with just anybody who sparks the urge?"

"You know I don't!"

"Maybe you never said it," he went on scathingly, "but you never said you *didn't* love me, either."

That she couldn't argue with, and it irritated her. "I suppose you never let another woman think—never even said it—to anyone but me!"

He leaned forward, placing his big hands flat on the shiny tabletop. "That's right," he said flatly. "Only you." He straightened again abruptly. "And what did it get me? I tried to give you time, and you left us without so much as word of warning."

She was trying to decipher the significance of those two surprising words, *Only you.* Shaking her head to clear it, she managed to say, "I—I thought a clean break was best."

"For you maybe," he retorted. "It certainly wasn't best for me or my daughter."

"Stop behaving like I've abandoned Amanda Sue," she said angrily. "I was there to see her just yesterday."

"Yes, but you weren't there the other night when she cried for you, were you? When she begged to call you on the telephone? You aren't there when she pleads for Emily to come home!"

Home. The very word evoked memories so sweet that tears filled her eyes. Home. Oh, if only…. She pushed away the wish, telling herself that she mustn't lose her way now. Closing her eyes, she searched for words and found them.

"I'll always be here for Amanda Sue," she managed softly. "She can call me anytime. She—"

"But you won't be coming home," he said bitterly. "And that's the problem."

Exasperated, Emily told him what she'd been telling herself so sensibly. "Logan, that's your home, not mine. It was never my home, and I never meant it to be. You know I refused to give up my apartment from the very beginning."

"Do you think Amanda Sue understands that?" he demanded hotly.

Of course she didn't, and the unfairness of it all hit Emily with dark, heavy sadness. And she blamed him. If he hadn't been so damned irresistible, if he hadn't pursued her, wanted her! Deep down, she knew that she was as much to blame, but in that moment she wanted to believe that he had caused all this anger and pain and loss on his own. She had tried to be sensible! She had tried to be good! He just hadn't let her, and he knew it.

"This isn't about Amanda Sue," she said flatly, strongly. "This is about you! You're the one who's supposed to walk out, aren't you? And you're mad because I beat you to it! Your women don't walk out on you, do they, Logan? Oh, no. They just watch while you walk away. Well, how does it feel, Mr. Fortune? This time you're the one watching—and *I* am walking away!"

With that she turned sharply and strode out of the room, slinging the door wide as she reached it. Ignoring the shocked, eager faces gathered in the hallway, she stalked past them, not even slowing until she reached her own office. There, finally, she slammed the door, twice, much to the chagrin of her personal secretary. Then she plopped down in her big executive chair, turned her face to the window and cried, the tears rolling silently down her cheeks.

At some point, she found that the tears had stopped and reflection had returned. Words, thoughts replayed in her head, his words, his thoughts.

You let me think you loved me. But you won't be coming home. I told you that I love you. And what did it get me? You won't be coming home. Home. I've loved only you.... Only you.

Was it possible? Did he love her? Had she walked out on her only hope of permanence, happiness? She shook her head. It couldn't be. She was not the sort of woman Logan Fortune could love. Was she?

Only you.

He knew her so well, better than she'd realized. He knew she wouldn't, couldn't share her body with a man whom she didn't love. He even knew that she hadn't told him how she felt as a sort of protection.

I tried to give you time.

But time couldn't change the facts. He always left. She'd watched him. During the past two years he'd wafted in and out of the lives and beds of any number of women, like a leaf flitting from branch to branch on its way to the ground.

But every leaf eventually did reach the ground, didn't it? Yes, of course, but that didn't mean it stayed there. Unless...something, someone, kept it there. She shook her head. He didn't love her, not really. He only thought he did because of the situation. He would have left her, eventually, just as soon as the situation changed—except suddenly she wasn't quite sure how that change might have occurred. Amanda Sue was here to stay, certainly. Another child might possibly be added to the equation, but that only enhanced the situation, didn't it? Logan had talked about a bigger house, someplace with a backyard and real privacy. None of that was reason for her to go. Another woman, maybe?

Certainly. Now that she wasn't there.

Emily put her hands to her head, her mind reeling. Surely she hadn't tossed her one chance at real love into the trash can out of simple fear. Had she? For the first time she doubted the wisdom of the course she'd set herself. For the first time, she wondered if she wasn't twice the fool.

Wordlessly, Logan tossed the keys to Hal and walked around the front end of the car to the passenger side. Had he ever felt so drained, so empty?

"Want to talk about it?" Hal asked, unlocking the car.

"No." Logan yanked the door open and plopped down inside. His tone left no room for argument, not that Hal was likely to argue. It was one of the things he liked best about Hal; the boy knew when to put his two cents worth in and when to keep his mouth shut, just like...

Emily. He closed his eyes, hands going to his temples. His head hurt. His heart hurt. Emily.

How does it feel, watching me walk away?

He wanted to tell her that it felt like hell. He wanted to beg her to come back, to love him. He wanted to say that he'd been punished enough, that he'd reaped all the agony he'd inadvertently sowed, believing that honesty was enough to justify all the women he'd disappointed. He wanted to weep, and only the quiet presence of Hal beside him kept him from it, that and one other thing.

She still had never said that she didn't love him, and somewhere, deep inside, he had to believe that she did. Without that, he just couldn't rationalize the way she'd come to his bed. He couldn't believe that she would have sex with a man she didn't love. It was important to him to believe that, though it never had been before. It was important because it was Emily. But if she loved him, why had she left him?

Your women don't walk out on you, do they, Logan? Oh, no, they just watch while you walk away. You're just mad because I beat you to it.... I beat you to it.

Suddenly he understood that she believed he would have left her. Somehow he hadn't convinced her that he loved her. For the first time Logan Fortune found himself at a loss with a woman. How could he counter his reputation? How could he possibly make her see how much he had changed? If Emily couldn't see, no one could! And yet, his family was constantly remarking about it. Why was it that Emily couldn't see it? And was there anything at all that he could do about it?

"I tried to give you time," he whispered, wondering if he might not have been wiser to rush her to the altar. If she hadn't given in and allowed him to make love to her, might he have married her to accomplish it? He rather thought that he might have, and he was frankly surprised by the notion. But then, why hadn't he just married her and been done with it? Why had he waited? Was it her fear or his that had ruined it all?

He didn't know anymore, and he didn't care. He only knew, with heartbreaking certainty, that he wanted Emily. Only Emily.

Fifteen

"Ms. Emily?"

Even if she hadn't recognized Carol's voice, the screams in the background would have told her who was calling. Emily gripped the telephone receiver, signaling to her secretary that she could leave the room. Something had happened to Amanda Sue. Emily felt it in the pit of her stomach.

"What's wrong?"

"We're at Dr. Costas's office right now. Amanda's been ill, and Mr. Logan is trapped in Chicago by bad weather. He put you down as the person to contact in his absence, so we need you to meet us at the hospital just as soon as—"

"Oh, my God!" Emily bent forward, bracing her free hand on the desktop. Amanda Sue was ill! *Please God, don't let it be serious.* "What's wrong with her?"

"We're not sure, but her fever's dangerously high, and she's not responding to the typical treatments, so the doctor thinks it would be best to put her in the hospital for tests and such. But we need you to sign her in. And I really think Amanda Sue needs you there."

"Which hospital?"

"Mercy's Gate."

"I'll meet you there in ten minutes."

"Thank you." Carol sounded relieved and exhausted.

Emily wondered how long Amanda Sue had been ill and why someone hadn't called her before, but those questions could wait. The priority now was getting to the hospital. She grabbed her handbag from the bottom drawer of her desk and snagged her coat from the coat tree in the corner on her way to the door. She issued brief instructions to her secretary and sprinted to the parking lot. In less than eight minutes she was running across the street against the light to the small but select private hospital near Logan's home.

A quick survey of the lobby and a pointed question at the admitting desk revealed that Carol and Amanda Sue had not yet arrived. Dr. Costas had called with instructions, but the papers were not yet ready for a signature, so Emily raced back outside to await the baby's arrival. Three or four minutes of frantic pacing later, she spied Carol getting out of a cab with Amanda Sue and her safety seat. She met them on the edge of the sidewalk, taking Amanda Sue and freeing Carol to deal with the safety seat and diaper bag.

When Amanda Sue laid her head on Emily's shoulder, Emily was shocked by the heat radiating through her heavy clothing and the blanket in which she was wrapped against the chill weather. "They should be ready for us by now," she told Carol, turning toward the hospital entrance again. Unfortunately, she underestimated the speed at which even the best hospitals seemed to operate. Almost an hour passed before they had Amanda Sue settled into a crib in a private room. Sick and cranky, she didn't want Emily out of her sight, not for tests, not for treatment.

Watching the lab tech draw blood was pure torture for Emily, especially as Amanda Sue fought him every step of the way. Getting the child to lie still long enough for a chest X ray was a feat of extraordinary patience and skill—and darn hard work. They were still trying to get a urine sample and hoping to avoid a catheter in the process. Amanda Sue had some experience, thanks to Carol, at using the potty, but she was balking at using the bedpan. Thinking that Carol might be able to persuade her, Emily glanced in the nanny's direction, only to find the poor woman literally asleep on her feet where she stood against the wall, arms folded, eyes closed, head bowed. Emily realized then that she'd probably been awake all night long with a sick, crying child. Leaving

Amanda Sue momentarily to the care of the nurse, Emily approached Carol and called her name softly.

Carol's eyes popped open instantly. "Sorry. Long night."

"I figured that much. How long has she been ill, anyway?"

"She started being fussy a couple days ago. I put it down to her dad having to go out of town. When she started running a fever, though, I took her to the doctor. Apparently she's teething and that promoted an ear infection, so the doctor prescribed an antibiotic, but Amanda Sue has gotten steadily worse, so I don't know what to think now."

"And Logan's in Chicago?"

Carol nodded. "He was only supposed to be gone overnight, but the weather turned nasty and the airport canceled flights."

"O'Hare's infamous for delaying flights," Emily commented. "Does he know that Amanda Sue's in the hospital?"

"We called him from the doctor's office. He's been camped out at the airport for a day and a half now, but he's got his cell phone."

"Right. Well, I'm sure he'll be here just as soon as he can."

Carol nodded. "Yes, he's devoted to that little girl." She fixed Emily with a level gaze. "He sure does miss you, though. They both do."

Emily bit her lip. "I've missed them, too," she said softly. "And I'm not going anywhere as long as Amanda Sue needs me, so why don't you go back to the town house and get some sleep? This is the last of the tests for the time being, so the worst is probably behind us. If anything comes up, I'll call."

Carol smiled wisely. "I don't suppose it will serve any purpose for both of us to be worn-out. I'll telephone for a cab."

Emily nodded and returned to the crib where the nurse was still trying to cajole a confused and irritable Amanda

Sue into using a bedpan. Her optimism about the worst of the day being behind them, however, was misplaced. Amanda Sue simply could not use the bedpan, and even the use of a catheter did not provide enough urine for the necessary tests. When it became obvious that the baby's temperature was not going down and was probably causing dehydration that prevented urination, the doctor ordered an ice bath. They didn't use actual ice, but the cool water must have felt like ice against Amanda Sue's hot skin. She certainly screamed as if she were being scalded, and the only way Emily knew to help was to strip off and get into the cold spray bath with her.

Emily was blue by the time Amanda Sue's fever was sufficiently lowered. Together they dried off and dressed. Emily could only hope that the experience had not turned their little water baby into a complete landlubber. An injection of medication helped to further lower Amanda Sue's temperature. After rocking with Emily and Sugar Bear in a chair provided by the hospital, Amanda Sue was hungry and readily drank everything they brought to her from juice to broth. She was also calmer and happier, but when they had to reinsert the catheter to obtain the urine sample, the poor little dear let them know in no uncertain terms that she considered it the height of insult and aggravation.

All in all, by the time the doctor put in an appearance early in the evening, both Amanda Sue and Emily were exhausted. The news, however, was fair.

"Now, all the test results aren't in," Dr. Costas warned. "But we've eliminated the big concerns. She shows no signs of pneumonia or contagion. In fact, what we've found so far leads me to believe that Amanda Sue has had a reaction to the antibiotic I prescribed for her a few days ago to combat this ongoing infection."

"Shouldn't she have a rash, then?" Emily asked uncertainly.

"Not necessarily, and frankly I'm more concerned about other implications of such sensitivity. She still has an ear infection, and we have to find some way to combat that. Ideally, that would be another antibiotic, one she can tolerate. Anyway, I'll know more in the morning. In the meantime, I've prescribed ear drops, decongestant, analgesics and fluids, but I don't want her using a straw or a nipple, no sucking to clog the ear canals further. Otherwise, try to get some rest, both of you.''

"Thanks, Dr. Costas,'' Emily said, and the diminutive physician swept out of the room on a smile and a wave.

Relief warred with exhaustion and the need to help Amanda Sue feel better, but Emily knew that she had to try to call Logan. He would want to know what was wrong with his daughter. She called his cell phone number repeatedly but continually got the system message that he was unavailable. Finally she called Carol and delegated the task, passing on the news in the process. By the time Amanda Sue had eaten her dinner, been wrestled into submission for the application of ear drops and had her vitals taken for the third time, Emily was emotionally and physically drained, but the baby was so clingy that she did not dare try to put her down for a nap. Instead, they curled up together in the rocking chair and turned on the television, choosing a program designed for toddlers. They were sitting there like zombies when the nurse came in with more medication for Amanda Sue.

This time the medicine made Amanda Sue sleepy, and Emily was finally able to kick off her shoes and stretch out on the bed provided for that purpose. Her last thoughts as she succumbed to the pull of sleep was for Logan. She hoped Carol had reached him and that he now knew Amanda Sue was going to be okay. She couldn't help wondering, too, what he would say and do when he saw her again. Would he be angry as before, or did they have a chance of getting together for good, of being a real family?

Logan fought the urge to run and call attention to himself. His long, duster-style coat billowed out behind him as he strode through the impersonal corridors, trying to find his way with only the aid of small signs posted on the occasional corner. After persuading the emergency room nurse to give him Amanda Sue's room number and slipping past the security guard, he wasn't about to provide anyone with a reason to toss him out now. The hospital was proving to be a warren of corridors, squares inside of squares bisected by other squares, but eventually he found a promising sign and followed the arrow in the direction indicated. Thankfully, the nurse's station was temporarily abandoned. He strode past without a pause. When he came to what he assumed to be the correct room, he had a decision to make. Did he knock and disturb whoever was inside or did he just slip in and take a look? He opted for slipping in quietly. What he found warmed him immensely.

Emily reclined with her back to the door on a bed next to the crib where Amanda Sue slept. He went to his daughter first, judging her condition by the gentle rise and fall of her chest and the paleness of her skin. His hands gripped the cold metal rails of the crib as he prayed again for the health and quick recovery of his precious little girl. At least, he told himself, she was resting peacefully.

Turning away, he bent over Emily. Shadows of weariness bruised the delicate skin beneath her eyes, and her clothing was rumpled and creased. Obviously she had come straight from the office, without taking time to change into more suitable attire. He hated to wake her, but at the same time he desperately needed to hear the sound of her voice and learn news of his daughter. He placed a hand on her shoulder and gently shook it. She came awake slowly, first murmuring, then rolling onto her back before opening her eyes. He lifted a finger to his lips, requesting silence, but she merely rubbed her eyes and looked up at him again.

"Logan?" she whispered, struggling up onto her elbows. He signaled for quiet again, pointed to the door, then picked up the shoes she'd left on the floor beside the bed. Sitting up, she slipped the shoes onto her feet and slid off the bed, while checking to see that Amanda Sue still slept. Together they moved out into the corridor.

"How did you get here?" she asked softly. "The last newscast I saw said O'Hare was still socked in."

He made a gesture of dismissal even as he answered her. "That doesn't matter. What about Amanda Sue? How is she? What does the doctor say?"

Emily told him exactly what Dr. Costas had told her. He sagged against the wall in relief and bowed his head. When he opened his eyes, they were filled with tears. "She is going to be all right, then? They'll find an antibiotic to fight the infection?"

"I'm sure they will," Emily assured him, gripping his hand. "The nurse says they have lots of new drugs to choose from. It's just a matter of finding the one she responds to best."

Logan nodded wearily, lifting her hand to his cheek. "Thank God. Thank God. And thank you for being here. What would I do without her? Or you?"

To his surprise, she turned her hand to cup his cheek. "I want to be here," she said softly, "for both of you."

He searched her eyes for a long moment, praying that she meant that in the way he hoped. "I'm going to hold you to that," he told her finally. She nodded and leaned into him, sliding her arms around his waist.

He'd done a lot of thinking these past few days, and he'd come to the reluctant conclusion that if he'd asked her to marry him early on rather than reverting to habit and settling for seduction, they might have been together all along. One thing was certain, he'd been in love with Emily Applegate for a long time, but he'd been unwilling to admit it, even to himself. How could he expect her to believe his love was real without the ultimate commitment from him? He was determined to remedy that, and for the moment at least, she seemed willing to let him try. Pressing his cheek to the top of her head, he wrapped her in a fierce hug.

"We have to talk, Em," he told her meaningfully.

"I know."

Before he could say anything else, a nurse bustled up.

"The planes are flying out of Chicago again, I see," she commented with a wry smile.

"I wouldn't know about that," Logan told her. "I rented a car and drove south until I found an open airport, then I hit Atlanta, Memphis and Dallas before I finally got a flight to San Antonio."

"You must be exhausted," Emily exclaimed, sounding endearingly concerned.

He nodded. "No more so than you, I expect."

"I hate to say it," the nurse interjected, pushing open the door, "but I have to wake this little lady now, so prepare yourselves for a bit more stress."

Emily sighed, but Logan couldn't help feeling glad for the opportunity to hug his daughter. Capturing Emily's hand, he kept her close as they followed the nurse into the room. Going to the crib, the nurse reached up and snapped on the overhead light. Amanda Sue screwed up her eyes but then lifted an arm to shield them and snoozed on. The nurse took out a stethoscope, warmed it against her palm and lifted Amanda Sue's gown to press it to her chest. Gradually, Amanda Sue roused and looked around her. Pushing at the nurse, she cried for Emily.

"I'm here, angel," Emily said in a soothing tone, stepping close to the crib. "And look who else."

Logan stepped to Emily's side and smiled at his little girl. Amanda Sue blinked against the light, then her eyes flew wide and she hurled herself upward, crying, "Daddy!"

Logan caught her and lifted her against him. "Hello, 'Manda mine. Oh, I've missed you so much! I'm so sorry I wasn't here when you got sick. Give me hugs."

Amanda Sue wrapped her arms around his neck and nearly crushed it in her exuberance. She immediately twisted around then and pointed toward the door. "Oan go home."

Logan chuckled, delighted to find that she was still his

strong, willful little girl. "We can't go home just yet, sweetheart. You have to get better first."

"Which means, I have to take your temperature," the
nurse said, coming around the crib to try to insert the tip of
the digital thermometer into Amanda Sue's ear.

The fight was on then, and Logan wound up sitting in the
rocker with Amanda Sue in his lap, her arms trapped in a
hug while Emily inserted the thermometer and the nurse
stood across the room demonstrating empty hands. Eventually, they got through the vitals check and managed to pour
Amanda Sue's medicine down her. After the nurse left them,
Logan spent several happy minutes with his daughter, talking to her, kissing her, and holding her close until the medication began to work again and her eyelids drooped over
her beautiful eyes. When at last she slept again, he laid her
in her crib, covered her gently and stood watching her. When
Emily moved to his side, he wrapped an arm around her and
held her close. This was what he wanted. Amanda Sue and
Emily. Emily and Amanda Sue. Always.

"I'd better go." Emily whispered. "I know you want to
stay here, and you need to get some sleep."

"So do you," he said, "and I don't like the idea of you
driving alone so very late when you're this tired. Don't go.
I won't rest if you do."

"But there's only the one bed," she pointed out.

"I know, and it's only a single, but I don't mind if you
don't. I'm so tired I'll drop right off—especially if I have
you close to me." He coaxed her with a pleading look and
a brush of his knuckles against her cheek. "I've missed you
more than I can even tell you. Just let me hold you. Please."

She nodded almost shyly, whispering, "I'd like that."

For a moment he wished it could be more, much more,
but here and now was not the place or time for more, and
he was determined that if and when he made love with her
again the time, the place and the circumstances would be
perfect. He turned off the light and finally shrugged out of
his coat, draping it over the rocker. Silently, he and Emily

sat on opposite sides of the bed and removed their shoes. Then very carefully he lay down on his side and opened his arms. Emily sank down next to him, her back to his chest, and he looped his arms around her. After a moment she snuggled closer, and so did he. Closing his eyes, he began a prayer of thanks.

Emily stretched, happily aware of Logan's big, warm body next to her. She hadn't slept so soundly in a very long time. Somehow, she had to find a way to go back to him, a way to overcome her doubts and fears, because living without him just was not an option any longer. Perhaps it never had been.

"Well, good morning."

The sound of a woman's voice, slightly amused, definitely questioning, had Emily's eyes popping open. A well-dressed redhead with an expensive handbag hanging from one arm stood next to Amanda Sue's crib. Emily sat up, rousing Logan.

"Hello." Her gaze went to Amanda Sue, who sat in her crib calmly trying to fit her teddy bear's head into a plastic cup. Emily slipped off the bed, torn between embarrassment and mild alarm. Who was this woman? And should she be standing so close to Amanda Sue?

Logan groaned and sat up sluggishly, saying, "Hello, Mother."

Emily's gaze flew to Mary Ellen Fortune. She saw the resemblance now, but she wouldn't have guessed at first glance that this woman could have grown children as old as Logan and Eden, not to mention Holden who was even older. Conscious of her own rumpled clothing and falling hair, Emily inwardly grimaced.

"You must be Emily," Mary Ellen said, reaching across the crib to offer her hand. Emily gave it a quick shake and tried to smooth her skirt.

"Yes. How did you know?"

Mary Ellen smiled wryly. "Let's just say mother's intuition.'' With that she turned to Logan. "I see you made it in. The nurse tells me our Amanda Sue is going to be just fine. Thanks for calling, by the way. Frankly, when my phone rings in the middle of the night I tend to assume it's my wayward brother Jace. Then—would you believe it?— he called me this morning just as I was leaving the house.''

Logan nodded groggily and got to his feet. "How is Uncle Jace?''

Mary Ellen made a face. "Who knows? He sounded tired to me. Apparently this has been a difficult assignment.''

"Aren't they all?'' Logan quipped, smiling at his daughter. "Good morning, sunshine.'' He walked around the bed and stood next to Emily, a hand on her shoulder. "How'd you sleep?'' he asked softly.

She attempted a smile, heat working its way toward her face. "Fine.''

"Me, too.'' He kissed her on the temple and turned to his mother. "Did Jace say where he is?''

She waved a hand. "Afghanistan? Turkey? He didn't really say. In fact, all he did say is that he's coming home— for good this time—and he really sounded like he meant it.''

"I wouldn't make book on it,'' Logan said. To Emily he explained, "Jace is a reporter with a taste for danger. You probably saw his face on TV during the Gulf War. Jace Lockhart?''

She considered. "Name sounds familiar.''

"But enough about Jace,'' Mary Ellen said. "What does the doctor say about my granddaughter?''

Logan explained the prognosis while Emily excused herself to freshen up in the bathroom. Not that she could do much with the tiny hairbrush and the few cosmetics that she carried in her purse. Fortunately sample bottles of mouthwash and liquid soap were provided by the hospital and stored in the bathroom medicine cabinet. After cleaning up, Emily had to be content with brushing out her hair and applying a little lipstick.

When she went out, Logan quickly took her place. Mary

Ellen was changing a diaper. Other than seeming subdued, Amanda Sue appeared well. She pointed at Emily and announced to her grandmother, "Mimly."

Mary Ellen barely glanced up. "We're very grateful to Emily, aren't we?" she said to her granddaughter. "She's taken very good care of you."

Emily smiled at the backhanded compliment and approached the bed to stroke Amanda Sue's hair. "I'm glad I could be here."

Mary Ellen finished the diapering job and lifted Amanda Sue into her arms. "So am I," she told Emily forthrightly. "I know that Logan trusts no one more than you when it comes to his daughter."

"Well, Carol is certainly capable—" Emily began, but Mary Ellen cut her off.

"Carol is a dream, I'm sure, but my granddaughter—and my son—need more than Carol or any other nanny can give them."

Emily didn't know what to say to that. The implication seemed to be that Emily could, and should be, willing to be more than a caregiver to Amanda Sue and Logan alike. But it wasn't that simple, and how could she possibly explain the situation to Logan's mother? Cravenly, she was ready to bolt for the door when Logan reappeared.

"Mom, would you mind staying with Amanda Sue for a few minutes? I'd like to buy Emily a cup of coffee."

Mary Ellen was delighted to occupy her granddaughter for a time. Logan gave Amanda Sue a kiss, assured her that Daddy and Emily would be right back, and steered Emily out the door without ever bothering to ask what she thought about his arrangements. Fortunately, she was only too willing to escape Mary Ellen Fortune's sharp gaze.

"We can get coffee at the canteen just up the hall," she pointed out as Logan steered her in the opposite direction.

"I don't want coffee, I want privacy," he said tersely. "I have something to say to you."

Emily bit her lip, almost afraid to hear it, but she sensed

that it would do no good to balk. She let him steer her through the maze of hallways, first one way and then another, until she began to wonder if he knew where he was going. Finally, he stopped at a small chapel.

"This might do." He opened the door and practically shoved her inside. She looked around. They were, indeed, alone.

He led her to a short bench and indicated that she should sit down. She did so, and he sat next to her, taking her hand in his.

"First of all," he began, "I understand why you left."

She opened her mouth, intending to explain again what she'd been thinking and feeling, but he raised a hand to stop her.

"Let me finish, please."

"All right."

He seemed to search for the words. "Emily, I'm not proud of my record with women. I've been a fun-and-games kind of guy, and I always tried to be honest about it up front, but I realize now that I was fooling myself about that being enough. The truth is, I was afraid to try for more, afraid I'd be like my father."

"Eden's told me a good deal about him," Emily said. "I think I understand that part of it better now."

He nodded and rubbed the back of her hand with his thumb. "So do I. But I still let my...uncertainty cause me to make mistakes, and I apologize for that."

She shook her head. "You don't owe me any apologies."

"Yes, I do. I owe both of us an apology, because I didn't do what I needed to do to make you believe that I love you with all my heart."

Emily gasped, tears starting behind her eyes. "Oh, Logan."

"Wait," he said, "let me finish this." She nodded, wiping away tears with her free hand, and he went on. "As usual, I focused on the sex—which was wonderful and I've missed it terribly, by the way—but it's just a part of what I feel for you. It's not even what I most want from you."

"No?" she whispered tearfully, a terrible hope building inside of her.

"No. And it's not someone to care for Amanda Sue, either," he went on. "I have that. But my daughter has opened my eyes. Because of her, I've come to realize that fun and games is not enough for me." He slid off the bench onto his knee, and Emily's heart climbed into her throat. "Emily," he said, "I cannot live the rest of my life without you. Please say you'll marry me."

For a moment, Emily couldn't believe her ears, and then she laughed—and cried—and laughed again. "Logan, I love you!" she exclaimed, throwing her arms around his neck.

He pulled her off the bench and down onto her knees next to him, kissing her tenderly. "Is that a yes?" he asked afterward, his voice trembling with laughter and uncertainty.

She could only nod as tears began in earnest now. "If you're sure. If you're really sure."

"Sweet heaven, Em, I've never been more sure of anything in my life," he vowed. "I think I've been in love with you for a long time, but I never pushed for any kind of relationship outside of the office because I knew that you deserved better than I was willing to give. Then Amanda Sue came into my life, and everything shifted. I realized that I could be a good father and that I needed much more from you than an executive assistant. I thought that once I got you in my bed that would be enough, and in some ways it was. I was so happy with you, Em. I knew I was in love, and I wanted you to know it, too. In my heart, it was as if we were married already, and I let that be enough. I told myself that I was waiting for you to love me, too, but I knew that you'd never have *made* love with me if you weren't *in* love with me. I avoided the commitment, Emily, and I'm so sorry for that. I *want* that commitment. I want you tied to me for the rest of my life, and I'm warning you now, I will never let you go again."

"Don't," she said, too choked up to say all that was in her heart. "Not ever. No matter what."

He kissed her forehead. "I promise I'll be a good husband. I know I can be a good husband, especially if you help me. You've helped me be a good father."

Emily laughed. "Be half as good a husband as you are a father, and I'll always be as deliriously happy as I am right now."

"That brings up something else we should talk about," he said, rising and helping her to rise, as well. He slid onto the bench and urged her down next to him. "Taylor."

She cocked her head. "What about him?"

"If Taylor's mine, I want him," he said gently. She waited, and he went on. "Are you okay with that?"

"Why wouldn't I be? Logan, you know that I adore Amanda Sue. I'll feel the same way about any other child we're lucky enough to have."

"Then you don't mind the idea of more children?" he asked carefully.

"Of course not! I'm counting on it, in fact."

"But your career—"

"We'll work it out," she said. "We'll share child-rearing responsibilities, and we always have Carol."

He slumped with obvious relief, but then he straightened again and leaped to his feet. "We need to start house shopping."

Emily laughed in sheer delight.

"No, I mean it. For Carol's sake if nothing else. She could use a private sitting room, and we want to keep her happy. We need her!"

"Carol isn't going anywhere," Emily chortled. She got up and leaned into him, wrapping her arms around his neck. "And neither am I, because I love you, Logan Fortune, and I want more than anything in the world to be your wife and the mother of your children—all your children."

He framed her face with his hands and bowed his head. This kiss was a vow, a promise, a pledge. When the door creaked open and a man entered the little chapel, they both turned their heads. Obviously embarrassed, he bowed his pink, bald head and muttered, ''Uh, excuse me.''

''Oh, it's all right!'' Logan told him brightly. Locking his hands together in the small of Emily's back, he proudly announced, ''We're getting married!''

The stranger glanced around the chapel as though expecting flowers and a minister. Then, shaking his head and murmuring doubtful congratulations, he backed out the door.

Confused, Logan looked at a beaming Emily. ''Well, we are,'' he said, ''and soon.''

''Yes, darling,'' she told him, lifting her mouth to his once more, ''but not, I think, in the hospital chapel.''

He didn't argue. He didn't argue at all, and Emily considered it a very good sign. Logan Fortune—corporate giant, playboy and daddy—was turning out to be excellent husband material. Funny what love could do. Love and a willful little toddler with her daddy's heart twisted around her little finger.

Then again, perhaps they were one and the same.

* * * * *

Here's a preview of next month's

*Can a runaway celebrity bride
resist the tempting bachelor
who shows up at her secluded hideaway in
SNOWBOUND CINDERELLA
by
Ruth Langan*

"**Y**ou move a muscle and you're dead." The woman's voice sounded a little too breathy. But whether from fear or anger, Jace Lockhart couldn't determine. He froze as he felt the muzzle of the rifle jammed against his ribs. In the same instant, a blinding beam from a flashlight flooded his eyes.

His voice was low with fury. "Who the hell are you?"

"I'll ask the questions, buster. And you'd better have some very good answers, or you'll answer to this rifle."

She took a step closer, and as his eyes adjusted to the light, he realized she was a wild-eyed, gorgeous blonde, wearing nothing more than sexy underwear. "Now who are you, and what are you doing here in the middle of nowhere?"

His words were tight, angry. "My name is Jace Lockhart. My sister Mary Ellen Fortune owns this cabin."

His answer was greeted with stunned silence.

He took no more than a moment to figure the odds before he swung his duffel bag, knocking the rifle from the woman's hands. As it clattered to the floor he tossed aside his carryall and in one quick motion wrapped his arms around her, pinning her arms to her sides. The flashlight dropped from her fingers and the light flickered for a moment, then the cabin was plunged into darkness.

His voice was a rasp of fury against her temple. "Now I'll ask the questions. And I'd better like your answers. Who the hell are you?"

"My name is…Ciara."

The way she hesitated, he figured she was probably making this up as she went along. "Okay, Ciara, or whatever your name is. What are you doing in my family's cabin?"

"I'm…" Her voice nearly faltered and she had to swallow several times before she found the courage to speak. "I'm a friend of Eden Fortune."

"Eden?"

"Yes. She told me the cabin would be empty. Isolated and…private. She never said a word about you."

His tone grew thoughtful. "She wouldn't have known. Until now, I've been out of the country. And I swore my sister to secrecy about my return."

Jace felt heat building inside, and blamed it on the rifle. Having the business end of a gun pointed at the heart tended to make a man sweat. Still, it didn't help to have a half-naked woman pressing against him. It had been the better part of a year since he'd held a woman, but his body, it seemed, hadn't forgotten the proper responses.

He released her and in one fluid movement bent to retrieve the rifle and flashlight. When he switched on the beam of light he saw the way her eyes widened, and could read the fear in them.

"Don't worry. I'm not going to shoot you. Unless you decide to come at me with another weapon. Then you'll just have to accept the consequences."

"I don't want any trouble." She lifted a hand to shield her eyes. "I thought…I thought you were here because you'd found out that I was hidi…that I was here." She cursed herself for her lapse. But he seemed too angry to notice.

"Then you can relax. The only reason I'm here is to be alone." He slowly circled the room with the light until he located a lamp on a nearby end table. He stepped over his luggage and switched it on, flooding the cabin with lamplight.

Now he could see the rugged, oversize furniture grouped around a magnificent stone fireplace that soared all the way to the high-beamed ceiling.

"That's better." He turned in time to see the young woman glance down at herself with dismay. When she looked up, he was boldly staring. He didn't bother to look away.

She had a fantastic body. Displayed in the most provocative manner possible. He looked her down, then up, from those long, long legs, to the lavender lace thong. His throat went dry and he forced his gaze upward. Her waist was so small he was certain his hands could easily span it. The bra was nothing more than two tiny bits of lavender lace, revealing more than they covered. And what they revealed was a body that would make any man's pulse go haywire. Then there was the face. Fantastic enough to grace magazine covers. Full pouty lips, at the moment turned down into a frown. High cheekbones that a model would kill for. A small, perfect nose, and arched brows over eyes that were more green than blue. Her hair was a riot of soft blond waves that fell to her shoulders.

For one wild moment he wondered whether he was imagining this whole thing. This woman was too beautiful to be real. And this whole situation had the feeling of some wild fantasy gone awry. Maybe he really was losing it, and his imagination had taken over his senses.

To her credit she didn't flinch or try to cover herself. With her hands on her hips she returned the stare. "Seen enough?" The words were said between clenched teeth. Had she been a cat, he thought, she'd have been hissing and spitting.

"You didn't leave much for the imagination." He nearly grinned before he caught himself. "But you might want to put on some clothes before you catch a chill."

She turned away and stormed into the bedroom. Over her shoulder she called, "While I'm doing that, you can return your luggage to your car. Since I was here first, you'll just have to leave and find yourself a lodge somewhere nearby."

He walked to the window and stared morosely at the snowdrifts that were already up to the porch. "Sorry I can't oblige you. I'm afraid we're stuck with each other. At least for tonight.''

She came running, tying the sash of her robe as she did. Her frown was more pronounced. "What do you mean?"

"See for yourself." He pointed. "Looks like we're in the middle of a spring blizzard. Nobody's going anywhere."

Silhouette

SPECIAL EDITION

Stories of love and life, these powerful
novels are tales that you can identify with—
romances with "something special" added
in!

Fall in love with the stories of authors such
as **Nora Roberts, Diana Palmer, Ginna Gray**
and many more of your special favorites—as
well as wonderful new voices!

Special Edition brings you
entertainment for the heart!

SILHOUETTE®
Desire®

Do you want...

Dangerously handsome heroes

Evocative, everlasting love stories

Sizzling and tantalizing sensuality

Incredibly sexy miniseries like **MAN OF THE MONTH**

Red-hot romance

Enticing entertainment that can't be beat!

You'll find all of this, and much *more* each and every month in **SILHOUETTE DESIRE**. Don't miss these unforgettable love stories by some of romance's hottest authors. Silhouette Desire—where your fantasies will always come true....

DES-GEN

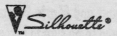

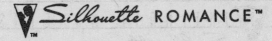

**What's a single dad to do when he needs a
wife by next Thursday?**

**Who's a confirmed bachelor to call when he
finds a baby on his doorstep?**

**How does a plain Jane in love with her gor-
geous boss get him to notice her?**

From classic love stories to romantic comedies to emotional
heart tuggers, **Silhouette Romance** offers six irresistible
novels every month by some of your favorite authors!
Such as…beloved bestsellers **Diana Palmer,**
Annette Broadrick, Suzanne Carey,
Elizabeth August and **Marie Ferrarella,** to name
just a few—and some sure to become favorites!

Fabulous Fathers…Bundles of Joy…Miniseries…
Months of blushing brides and convenient weddings…
Holiday celebrations… You'll find all this and much more
in **Silhouette Romance**—always emotional, always
enjoyable, always about love!

SR-GEN